Killer Jam

Center Point
Large Print

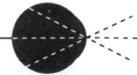

**This Large Print Book carries the
Seal of Approval of N.A.V.H.**

Killer Jam

A Dewberry Farm Mystery

Karen MacInerney

CENTER POINT LARGE PRINT
THORNDIKE, MAINE

This Center Point Large Print edition is published
in the year 2017 by arrangement with
Amazon Publishing, www.apub.com.

The text of this Large Print edition is unabridged.
In other aspects, this book may vary
from the original edition.
Printed in the United States of America
on permanent paper.
Set in 16-point Times New Roman type.

ISBN: 978-1-68324-315-1

Library of Congress Cataloging-in-Publication Data

Names: MacInerney, Karen, 1970– author.
Title: Killer jam : a Dewberry Farm mystery / Karen MacInerney.
Description: Center Point Large Print edition. | Thorndike, Maine :
Center Point Large Print, 2017.
Identifiers: LCCN 2016056406 | ISBN 9781683243151
    (hardcover : alk. paper)
Subjects: LCSH: Large type books. | GSAFD: Mystery fiction.
Classification: LCC PS3613.A27254 K55 2017 | DDC 813/.6—dc23
LC record available at https://lccn.loc.gov/2016056406

For Maryann and Clovis Heimsath

Chapter 1

I've always heard it's no use crying over spilled milk. But after three days of attempting to milk Blossom the cow (formerly HeifeFour-or #82), only to have her deliver a well-timed kick that deposited the entire contents of my bucket on the stall floor, it was hard not to feel a few tears of frustration forming in the corners of my eyes.

Stifling a sigh, I surveyed the giant puddle on the floor of the milking stall and reached for the hose. I'd tried surrounding the bucket with blocks, holding it in place with my feet—even tying the handle to the side of the stall with a length of twine. But for the sixth straight time, I had just squeezed the last drops from the teats when Blossom swung her right rear hoof in a kind of bovine hook kick, walloping the top of the bucket and sending gallons of the creamy white fluid spilling across both the concrete floor and my boots. I reprimanded her, but she simply tossed her head and grabbed another mouthful of the feed I affectionately called "cow chow."

She looked so unassuming. So velvety-nosed and kind, with big, long-lashed eyes. At least she had on the day I'd selected her from the line of cows for sale at the Double-Bar Ranch. Despite all the reading I'd done on selecting a heifer, when she pressed her soft nose up against my cheek, I knew she belonged at Dewberry Farm. Thankfully, the rancher I'd purchased her from had seemed more than happy to let her go, extolling her good nature and excellent production.

He'd somehow failed to mention her phobia of filled buckets.

Now, as I watched the tawny heifer gamboling into the pasture beside my farmhouse, kicking her heels up in what I imagined was a cow's version of the middle finger, I took a deep breath and tried to be philosophical about the whole thing. She still had those big brown eyes, and it made me happy to think of her in my pasture rather than the cramped conditions at Double-Bar Ranch. And she'd only kicked the milk bucket, not me.

Despite the farm's growing pains, as I turned toward the farmhouse, I couldn't help but smile. After fifteen years of life in Houston, I now lived in a century-old yellow farmhouse—the one I'd dreamed of owning my whole life—with ten acres of rolling pasture and field, a peach orchard, a patch of dewberries, and a quaint, bustling town just up the road. The mayor had even installed a Wi-Fi transmitter on the water tower, which meant I could someday put up a website for the farm. So what if Blossom was more trouble than I'd expected, I told myself. I'd only been a dairy farmer for seventy-two hours; how could I expect to know everything?

In fact, it had only been six months since my college roommate, Natalie Barnes, had convinced me to buy the farm that had once belonged to my grandparents. Natalie had cashed in her chips a few years back and bought an inn in Maine, and I'd never seen her happier. With my friend's encouragement, I'd gone after the dream of reliving those childhood summers, which I'd spent fishing in the creek and learning to put up jam at my grandmother's elbow.

It had been a long time since those magical days in Grandma Vogel's steamy, deliciously scented kitchen. I'd spent several years as a reporter for the *Houston Chronicle*, fantasizing about a simpler life as I wrote about big-city crime and corruption. As an antidote to the heartache I'd seen in my job, I'd grown tomatoes in a sunny patch of the backyard, made batches of soap on the kitchen stove, and even kept a couple of chickens until the neighbors complained.

Ever since those long summer days, I'd always fantasized about living in Buttercup, but it wasn't until two events happened almost simultaneously that my dream moved from fantasy to reality. First, the paper I worked for, which like most newspapers was suffering from the onset of the digital age, laid off half the staff, offering me a buyout that, combined with my savings and the equity on my small house, would give me a nice nest egg. And second, as I browsed the web one day, I discovered that my grandmother's farm—which she'd sold fifteen years ago, after my grandfather passed—was up for sale.

Ignoring my financial advisor's advice—and fending off questions from friends who questioned my sanity—I raided the library for every homesteading book I could find, cobbled together a plan I hoped would keep me from starving, took the buyout from the paper, and put an offer in on Dewberry Farm. Within a month, I went from being Lucy Resnick, reporter, to Lucy Resnick, unemployed homesteader of my grandparents' derelict farm. Now, after months of backbreaking work, I surveyed the rows of fresh green lettuce and broccoli plants sprouting up in the fields behind the house with a deep sense of satisfaction. I might not be rich, and I might not know how to milk a cow, but I was living the life I'd always wanted.

I focused on the tasks for the day, mentally crossing cheese making off the list as I headed for the little yellow farmhouse. There might not be fresh mozzarella on the menu, but I did have two more batches of soap to make, along with shade cover to spread over the lettuce, cucumber seeds to plant, chickens to feed, and buckets of dewberries to pick and turn into jam. I also needed to stop by and pick up some beeswax from the Bees' Knees, owned by local beekeeper Nancy Shaw. The little beeswax candles I made in short mason jars were a top seller at Buttercup Market Days, and I needed to make more.

Fortunately, it was a gorgeous late spring day, with late bluebonnets carpeting the roadsides and larkspur blanketing the meadow beside the house, the tall flowers' ruffled lavender and pink spikes bringing a smile to my face. They'd make beautiful bouquets for the market this coming weekend—and for the pitcher in the middle of my kitchen table. Although the yellow Victorian-style farmhouse had been neglected and left vacant for the past decade or more, many of my grandmother's furnishings remained. She hadn't been able to take them with her to the retirement home, and for some reason, nobody else had claimed or moved them out, so many things I remembered from my childhood were still there.

The house had good bones, and with a bit of paint and elbow grease, I had quickly made it a comfortable home. The white tiled countertop sparkled again, and my grandmother's pie safe with its punched tin panels was filled with jars of jam for the market. I smoothed my hand over the enormous pine table my grandmother had served Sunday dinners on for years. I'd had to work to refinish it, sanding it down before adding several layers of polyurethane to the weathered surface, but I felt connected to my grandmother every time I sat down to a meal.

The outside had taken a bit more effort.

Although the graceful oaks still sheltered the house, looking much like they had when I had visited as a child, the line of roses that lined the picket fence had suffered from neglect, and the irises were lost in a thicket of Johnson grass. The land itself had been in worse shape; the dewberries the farm had been named for had crept up into where the garden used to be, hiding in a sea of mesquite saplings and giant purple thistles. I had had to pay someone to plow a few acres for planting, and had lost some of the extra poundage I'd picked up at my desk job rooting out the rest. Although it was a continual battle against weeds, the greens I had put in that spring were looking lush and healthy—and the dewberries had been corralled to the banks of Dewberry Creek, which ran along the back side of the property. The peach trees in the small orchard had been cloaked in gorgeous pink blossoms and now were laden with tiny fruits. In a few short months, I'd be trying out the honey-peach preserves recipe I'd found in my grandmother's handwritten cookbook, which was my most treasured possession. Sometimes, when I flipped through its yellowed pages, I almost felt as if my grandmother were standing next to me.

Now, I stifled a sigh of frustration as I watched the heifer browse the pasture. With time, I was hoping to get a cheese concern going; right now, I only had Blossom, but hopefully she'd calve a heifer, and with luck, I'd have two or three milkers soon. Money was on the tight side, and I might have to consider driving to farmers' markets in Austin to make ends meet—or maybe finding some kind of part-time job—but now that I'd found my way to Buttercup, I didn't want to leave.

I readjusted my ponytail—now that I didn't need to dress for work, I usually pulled my long brown hair back in the mornings—and mentally reviewed my to-do list. Picking dewberries was next, a delightful change from the more mundane tasks of my city days. I needed a few more batches of jam for Buttercup's Founders' Day Festival and Jam-Off, which was coming up in a few days. I'd pick before it got too hot; it had been a few days since I'd been down by the creek, and I hoped to harvest another several quarts.

Chuck, the small apricot rescue poodle who had been my constant companion for the past five years, joined me as I grabbed a pair of gardening gloves and the galvanized silver bucket I kept by the back door, then headed past the garden in the back and down to the creek, where the sweet smell of sycamores filled the air. I didn't let Chuck near Blossom—I was afraid she would do the same thing to him that she did to the milk bucket—but he accompanied me almost everywhere else on the farm, prancing through the tall grass, guarding me from wayward squirrels and crickets, and— unfortunately—picking up hundreds of burrs. I'd had to shave him within a week of arriving at the farm, and I was still getting used to having a bald poodle. This morning, he romped through the tall grass, occasionally stopping to sniff a particularly compelling tuft of grass. His pink skin showed through his clipped fur, and I found myself wondering if there was such a thing as doggie sunscreen.

The creek was running well this spring—we'd had plenty of rain, which was always welcome in Texas, and a giant bullfrog plopped into the water as I approached the mass of brambles with their dark, sweet berries. They were similar to the blackberries I bought in the store, but a bit longer, with a sweet-tart tang that I loved. I popped the first few in my mouth.

I went to work filling the bucket, using a stick to push the brambles aside, and had filled it about halfway when I heard the grumble of a motor coming up the long driveway. Chuck, who had been trying to figure out how to get to the fish that were darting in the deeper part of the creek, turned and growled. I shushed him as we headed back toward the farmhouse, the bucket swinging at my side.

A lanky man in jeans and a button-down shirt was unfolding himself from the front seat of the truck as I opened the back gate. Chuck surged ahead of me, barking and growling, then slinking to my ankle when I shushed him with a sharp word.

"Can I help you?" I asked the man. He was in his midforties, with work-worn boots and the roughened skin of a man who'd spent most of his life outdoors.

"You Lucy Resnick?" he asked.

"I am," I said, putting down the bucket. Chuck growled again and put himself between us.

"Butch Simmons, Lone Star Exploration," the man said, squinting at me.

"Nice to meet you," I said, extending a hand. Chuck yipped, and I apologized.

"Good doggie," the man said, reaching down to let the poodle sniff him. Usually, that was all the little dog needed to become comfortable, but something about the man upset him. He growled, backing away.

"I don't know what's gotten into him," I said, scooping him up in my arms. "Can I help you with something?" I asked again, holding the squirming poodle tight.

"Mind if I take a few pictures? We're surveying the property before we start the exploration process."

"Exploration process?" I asked.

"Didn't anyone tell you?"

"Tell me what?"

He turned his head and spit out a wad of snuff. I wrinkled my nose, revolted by the glob of brown goo on the caliche driveway. "We're drillin' for oil."

15

Chapter 2

"Drilling for oil?" I said. Chuck squirmed in my arms. "Here?"

"Yes, ma'am," he said.

I hugged Chuck tight to my chest. "You can't do that! I bought this property!"

"I understand that, ma'am, but you only bought the surface rights."

"What do you mean?"

"You own the dirt on top, not what's underneath. The owner of the mineral rights thinks there might be something here, so they've hired me to check it out."

Despite the warm morning, I suddenly felt icy cold. "What if I refuse?"

"I'm afraid that would be against the law."

Chuck gave a mighty squirm and leaped from my arms, hackles bristling, and began barking furiously. I grabbed his collar out of instinct as the man pulled out a camera and began taking pictures of my house.

"What are you doing?" I asked.

"Taking pictures of what it looks like now so we can restore it when the drilling's over," he said.

My stomach did a slow flip-flop. "Restore it? What are you planning to do, exactly?"

"Don't know yet." He spat out another wad of

slimy snuff, and I recoiled. "Don't you worry about it. We'll put everything to rights."

A horrible image of an oil well smack dab in the middle of my broccoli patch materialized in my mind's eye. I shook my head as if that could dislodge it. "Nobody's doing anything without my permission," I said. "Who owns these so-called mineral rights, anyway?"

"Nettie Kocurek," he said, lifting the camera and snapping another shot. Nettie Kocurek was the woman who had sold me the property several months ago.

"It doesn't make sense. Why drill now?" I asked. "She owned the place for fifteen years."

"You'll have to ask her that," he said, taking a photo of the pasture, where Blossom was munching on grass.

"Believe me, I will," I said. "But in the meantime, I'm going to have to ask you to leave."

He took one more picture, then turned off the camera. "I'm done for now anyway. We'll have a thumper truck later this week, likely."

"A thumper truck?"

He nodded. "Get a read on what's underneath. Shouldn't take more than a day or two." He tipped an imaginary hat before turning back to the truck. "Thanks for your time, ma'am."

Chuck didn't stop growling until the truck had turned out of our driveway and headed back toward town, leaving a cloud of dust in its wake.

"He says he's sending a thumper truck out this week," I said, rinsing several pints of dewberries in a colander as my friend, Quinn Sloane, wrestled a mound of bread dough onto a floured marble board. Despite the interruption, I'd picked about twenty pints that morning and taken them to the Blue Onion. Quinn had snagged a few pints to add to her fruit salads—she often bought my extra produce for the cafe, which had gone a long way toward helping me make ends meet—and I was processing the rest. I could have made jam at home, but after the visit that morning, I needed company. I had spent many afternoons in Quinn's kitchen, enjoying the breeze that wafted through the red-checked curtains and the delicious smells emanating from her oven.

"A thumper truck?" Quinn dropped the dough with a thwack. "What the heck's a thumper truck?"

"I tried Googling it, but the wireless is down," I said, pouring the berries into a large pot. The signal, which came from a transmitter located at the top of Buttercup's water tower, was notoriously spotty. "Apparently it has to do with oil exploration."

"Not fracking, though," she said.

"Fracking?"

"That was a big deal in town a few months back. Some company called Frac-Tex came into town trying to lease everybody's mineral rights to get to the natural gas." She reached for a canister of flour. "They were negotiating with half a dozen farmers to agree to terms before the mayor found out and got involved. Thing is, fracking on one property can really mess with the water for everyone else—and water's a big deal in this part of the world."

I knew water was precious here; although it had been a wet spring, Texas had been teetering on the edge of a drought the last few years. "I read about fracking a few months ago. It uses a lot of water, doesn't it?"

She nodded. "And the chemicals they pump down mess with everybody's wells. It can kill grass, cattle . . . pretty scary stuff. That's why the town passed a resolution prohibiting leasing to companies for fracking."

"But not putting in oil wells?"

She shook her head. "Unfortunately not," Quinn said, the flour on the tip of her nose belying the serious look in her brown eyes. Topping out at just over five feet, she wore a white apron over jeans and a T-shirt; this afternoon, her curly red hair was only slightly tamed by a pink plastic headband and gave her a few extra inches. "I'm not surprised to hear she's going after your land, though; that woman is mean as a snake."

"Mrs. Kocurek? You've got to be kidding me," I said as I measured out sugar and turned the burner on. I'd sterilized the jars in the dishwasher at home and busied myself laying them out on the counter as the berries began to cook. The yield for twenty pints of berries should be about ten pints of jam, so I'd prepared eleven, just in case my count was wrong. I'd leave one for Quinn and one for Bessie Mae Jurecka, who lived down by the railroad tracks in a small cottage that used to be a way station for railroad workers. According to Quinn, she'd been born "not quite right." Now, in her early sixties, she spent her days in a rocking chair on the old depot platform, waving at the engineers and keeping a tally of them on the steno notepads supplied by Edna Orzak of the Red and White Grocery. When Bessie Mae had lost her parents ten years ago, the town took up where they left off, helping keep her lights on and the small dorm-style fridge Alfie Kramer had given her filled with goodies. The Blue Onion was on Bessie Mae's regular rounds; Quinn always passed on the tidbits I brought from the farm along with her day-old baked goods.

"Don't let Nettie Kocurek's southern charm fool you," Quinn said, a note of warning in her voice.

"She looks like she couldn't hurt a fly." When I met her at the closing, Mrs. Kocurek had been the incarnation of a sweet little southern lady; her white hair had been teased into a spun-sugar confection around her powdered face, and she was as soft-spoken and gracious as any woman I'd met. I couldn't imagine her having a mean bone in her body.

"Trust me," Quinn said. "You haven't tangled with her yet."

"What does she do if she doesn't like you?" I asked as I filled a canning pot with water and put it on the back of the range. "Poison your tea?" I found it hard to imagine her doing anything worse than a "Bless your heart" accompanied by a pitying look.

"She had a luncheon here with the Moravian Daughters of Buttercup six months ago, and then decided she'd gotten food poisoning from the chicken salad . . . even though the rest of the ladies ate the same thing and felt fine." Quinn buttered loaf pans as she spoke.

"That doesn't sound too awful," I said.

My friend gave me a look. "She called the paper and insisted they run an article on it, and called the health department and had them do a surprise inspection. She then told everyone she knew to boycott the restaurant."

"Maybe she's a hypochondriac," I said.

"Maybe," Quinn said, "but it happened the week after the paper asked me what I thought about raising funds to put a statue of her granddaddy in the middle of town square."

"What did you tell the paper?"

"I said I thought the money would be better spent on the library."

"Ah." I gave the berries and sugar a stir. This was not welcoming news—not at all. "Still. Surely there's some mistake with the mineral rights," I said, trying to push down the uneasiness that was welling inside me. "I'll go talk with her today."

"She's not the person you need to talk to," Quinn said. "I'd call a lawyer if I were you."

"Lawyers are expensive," I said, looking at the row of jars. If the jam set, it would net me maybe fifty dollars. Twenty minutes worth of legal fees. I'd have to make a lot of jam to pay for an ongoing legal battle.

She looked up at me. "Cheaper than having an oil well in your backyard."

I pulled two vanilla beans from the jar I'd brought from the farmhouse, trying to ignore the uneasiness that was lodging in my stomach. "What I don't understand is, if it is Mrs. Kocurek who ordered the drilling—which I still haven't confirmed—why do it now?" I asked, slicing one of the beans in half. "That property's been sitting there unused for fifteen years."

"She sells the property before destroying the property value this way," Quinn said, sprinkling more flour on the dough. "Probably why she decided to sell in the first place. You know, she and your grandfather were an item when they were in high school."

"You're kidding me," I said. I couldn't imagine Grandpa with anyone other than Grandma Vogel.

"Nope. They were homecoming king and queen, but your grandpa dumped her soon after the big game." She looked up at me. "For your grand-mother."

"Ouch!"

"Which may be the real reason she's now drilling on your land," Quinn suggested.

"You really think she'd hold a grudge over . . . what, sixty years?" I scraped the seeds from the second bean and dropped both beans and their seeds into the pot.

"Can't think why she wouldn't," my friend said, leaning into the dough as she spoke. "She ended up marrying the biggest jerk in town, but I think she always carried a torch for your grandfather."

I thought of my grandfather, with his engaging smile, his slow drawl, and the lump in his cheek from the tobacco he always chewed. I'd never thought of him as a heartbreaker before. "What made her husband such a jerk?" I asked.

"Apparently he ran around on her for twenty years before he died of a cardiac arrest." She cocked a dark eyebrow at me. "There were rumors that he was in someone else's bed at the time."

I sucked in my breath. "Oof."

She nodded. "Nettie Kocurek got the ranch when he bought the farm, so to speak, and she's a smart businesswoman. Turned it into something of an empire; she's known as a hard bargainer. She was head of the chamber of commerce for ten years." Quinn was a font of local information; she had grown up in Buttercup, but moved away after high school and studied English at the University of Houston before marrying Jed Stadtler, her ex. Working in restaurants to put herself through school had taught her to cook—and to run a restaurant—so when she left her husband, she started the Blue Onion Tea Shop and Cafe.

"Why did she let the farm go derelict for so long?" I asked.

"Good question," she said. "I'll tell you one thing, though. If she knew you were Elsa Vogel's grand-daughter, she never would have sold it to you."

"You think?"

"I'm sure of it," she said, starting to divide the dough into equal parts and placing them in pans. Most of the loaves would be used for the sand-wiches in the cafe, I knew, but she also sold a few at the front—and occasionally slipped an extra to me. "What are you selling at the Founders' Day Festival, by the way?" she asked.

"I'm going to cut and wrap a few batches of soap tonight, and I'm hoping to pick up some beeswax from the Bees' Knees to make some more candles." Nancy Shaw supplied me with honey and beeswax at wholesale prices and had promised to help me set up hives of my own in the next year. "I've got plenty of lettuce, broccoli, and radishes, and I'm hoping to put together some larkspur bouquets, too," I said.

"Sounds like things are humming along," she said.

"The plan seems to be working," I said. I'd spent months putting together a business plan, consulting with several other small farmers and listening to their advice, and the hard work had paid off so far. "But this oil drilling is the last thing I need; I'm just barely making it by as it is. How can I farm around an oil well?"

"It'll all work out," Quinn said, giving me an encouraging smile that showed her chipped front tooth. I'd thought it was an endearing flaw until I learned the history behind it; it was a souvenir of the time her ex-husband, Jed, slammed her into a wall. "You've got to fight Nettie Kocurek, of course," she continued, pushing a stray strand of hair out of her eyes with the back of her hand, "but it takes time to get a farm up and running. You'll get there."

"I hope so," I said.

She gave me an encouraging smile, her nose and cheek dusted with flour. "You're going to pull through. Mandy Vargas was asking about you the other day; I'll bet the paper would be interested if you're looking for a part-time job."

"That might not be a bad idea," I said. Not only would it provide some welcome income as I got the farm business going, but it would be a good opportunity to get to know the town better.

Although I'd moved to Buttercup to live

independently, I was finding that it was the connection to the other folks in town that made life here so special. When I'd taken up residence at my grandmother's farm, there had been a parade of home-cured ham, bacon, tomatoes from neighbors' gardens . . . the first week, even the mayor turned up in jeans and cowboy boots to welcome me to town and drop off one of her famous chocolate silk pies. Buttercup, I was learning, was a friendly place. With the exception of Nettie Kocurek, anyway.

Quinn was sliding the first loaf into the oven when the phone rang. As always, she eyed it warily before picking it up.

"Blue Onion Cafe, can I help you?"

I could hear the voice from across the kitchen and winced. It was her ex-husband, Jed. Since the divorce, Quinn had been taking karate twice a week; she was now a brown belt, and I knew she hadn't taken it up just for the exercise.

She put down the phone a few minutes later, looking rattled.

"What's wrong?"

"Nothing," she said, wiping her hands on her apron, her face pale under its dusting of flour. I knew she was lying, but I also knew better than to pry. She'd tell me when she was ready.

I was carrying a dozen jewel-like pints of Killer Bourbon-Vanilla Dewberry Jam and a loaf of

Quinn's fresh bread when I stepped out of the Blue Onion into the tree-lined town square an hour later. A banner advertising the upcoming Founders' Day hung across the front of the white-painted town hall, and a soft breeze ruffled the leaves of the sycamore trees whose branches shaded the sidewalk. I was looking forward to the event, a town celebration that I'd heard would involve Bubba Allen's legendary barbecue brisket and the town "Jam-Off." I was planning to submit a jar of my jam to the competition. With luck, I would be able to add "award-winning" to my handmade labels.

There was a commotion near the town hall; I squinted into the afternoon sun to see what looked like a bronze statue with a nose the size and shape of a bratwurst on the back of an ancient Chevy pickup truck. Next to it was Nettie Kocurek's enormous white Cadillac, whose front wheels were parked, as usual, on the sidewalk. A group of a half dozen men stood in a semicircle around Mrs. Kocurek and Mayor Niederberger, who appeared to be in the midst of a disagreement.

As I crossed the grassy lawn, I could hear Nettie Kocurek's soft, drawling voice. She wore a flowered dress with a lace collar, a sturdy pair of beige SAS shoes, and a floppy white hat with cabbage roses drooping over the brim. Mrs. Kocurek looked every inch a soft-spoken church lady, but now that Quinn had filled me in on her history, I noticed a firmness in her high-pitched voice that unnerved me. Perhaps, I reflected, I had misjudged Nettie Kocurek. "I think it should be right in the middle of the square, in front of the town hall, don't you?" she said. "Otherwise it's just not symmetrical."

The mayor hitched her thumbs in her belt loops and rocked back and forth on her snakeskin boots. Her belt buckle flashed in the afternoon sun. "Nettie, when I told the historical committee they could go ahead with the statue, the deal was that it would go in front of the library."

Nettie smiled sweetly. Behind her, looking almost as uncomfortable as the mayor, was her middle-aged daughter, Flora. Where Nettie had the figure of a woman with a long and undying devotion to the local bakery's kolaches, her daughter, whose face was pinched and pale, appeared to be constructed of coat hangers. As Nettie put her hands on her hips, Flora seemed to shrink a little. "But he was the founder of the town!" Nettie protested. "That's why the historical committee paid for the statue."

"Actually, the founder was Hermann Mueller," Mayor Niederberger pointed out. She unhooked her thumbs from her belt loops and raised and lowered her own hat, which was a straw Stetson. She looked unusually agitated.

Nettie waved the mayor's assertion away with a bony hand. "He doesn't count; he was German.

This is a Moravian community, and my great-grandfather, Krystof Baca, was the first Czech here. That's what that professor up in Austin put in his book."

Mayor Niederberger settled her Stetson back on her head and widened her stance. "Nettie, I'm sorry, but you can't put the statue in the middle of the square."

Nettie put her hands on her hips. "Now, Rose, I remember when you were knee-high to a grasshopper. Always were stubborn. Why don't we just put it here for now, and then we can go back to the ranch and talk about it over a nice slice of icebox lemon pie?"

"Nettie, it just won't work. I know it's a wonderful statue," Mayor Niederberger said, steel in her pale blue eyes, "but the middle of the square won't work. This is where the polka bands play for the Founders' Day Festival. This is where the barbecue tent goes for Lick Skillet Day. This is where the judging tent goes for the Moravian Festival, for heaven's sake!"

"Pepaw would love that!" Nettie said, clasping her hands together. "He'd still be part of the town!"

The mayor's voice was firm. "Nettie, the answer is no."

Chapter 3

For a moment, Nettie Kocurek's mouth looked as if she had just sucked a lemon, but in a flash, the sugar was back. "Let's bring this up at the next council meeting. That's tomorrow, isn't it?"

"Nettie . . ."

"I'm sure they'll see reason," Nettie said. "Boys, in the meantime, why don't we just leave the truck here. That way we won't have to drive it all the way back from the library tomorrow."

Leaving Mayor Niederberger openmouthed, she hobbled past the sausage-nosed statue to her Cadillac, her gangly daughter in her wake.

"Mrs. Kocurek?" I said, putting on my best smile and stepping forward before she reached her car. The timing was less than terrific, but I couldn't let the opportunity slip by. "Do you have a moment?"

"What can I do for you?" she asked, turning to look at me with an appraising eye.

"I'm sorry to bother you, but I think there's been a little mix-up. There was a geologist out at Dewberry Farm today talking about drilling for oil."

"Oh, yes," she said, nodding. "My accountant told me it would be the wise thing to do. I'm a pensioner, you know."

A pensioner who had just gotten a giant wad of cash for an abandoned piece of property, I thought.

"Yes," I said, trying not to let the strain show in my voice, "but I plan to make my living from the farm. I can't farm around an oil well, can I?"

She smiled, exposing a line of yellowed teeth behind her thin, pink-painted lips. "Oh, that geologist fellow promised me they'd put everything back to rights once they were done. I'm sure everything will be just fine."

"But . . ."

"Now, honey, I hate to run off, but if I'm late for supper, Bunny is like to kill me. Nice chattin' with you," she said. "Flora, open that door for me, will you?"

Her daughter hurried to do her mother's bidding, then rounded the car to the passenger's seat. Before she ducked into the car, she shot me a look over the top of the Cadillac. To my surprise, it had every bit as much appraisal in it as her mother's.

As I watched, Nettie Kocurek pulled off the sidewalk with a double-thunk and squealed out of the square, leaving a cloud of gray exhaust in her wake.

"I hear Nettie Kocurek is puttin' the screws to Dewberry Farm," Nancy Shaw said as we walked the pathway to her honey house. Nancy, Buttercup's local beekeeper, was a tall, slim woman in her sixties. Today, she wore faded jeans and a tank top that showed off her tan, muscular shoulders. Her husband, Martin, was a painter who sold his oils of bucolic Buttercup to daytrippers and interior decorators in Houston and Austin. Lavender bushes lined the flagstone path behind the bungalow-style house, releasing their sweet scent as we passed, and bees buzzed through the air on their way to find flowers. Several hives were lined up at the back of the property, under the dappled shade of a row of cottonwood trees.

"News travels fast," I said.

"That it does," Nancy said, her weathered face breaking into a smile. Nancy and Martin had moved to Buttercup from Wimberley twenty years ago. Between Martin's work as an architect and hers as a beekeeper, they'd made a good life for themselves. "What are you going to do about her?"

"I'm talking to an attorney on Wednesday," I said.

"Expensive," she said as she opened the door to the cool, honey-scented barn where she kept her equipment and stored honey and wax. "She's givin' us a bit of trouble, too," she added, glancing toward the barbed-wire fence I knew was the boundary between her property and the Kocureks' pasture.

"How so?" I asked.

"She's been sprayin' something on the fields, and the bees are gettin' into it. Lost a good part of four hives in the past month; thank goodness the others were out pollinating at Hensky's orchards."

"Oh no!" I said. "Did you talk to her?"

"Of course," Nancy said. "Said it was her land and she'd do what she had to do to take care of it."

I followed her into the dark, sweet-smelling building, which was lit with skylights. A steel honey extractor and several metal tables stood at the end of the room, and rows of honey jars and slabs of golden wax lined the clean wooden shelves along the back wall. A few empty frames were stacked in a corner, waiting to be slipped into the hives.

"Your grandmother had her number," Nancy said. "Nettie Kocurek wouldn't mess with her. Just about killed her to have to sell Dewberry Farm to her, though."

"I'm surprised Nettie left her alone," I said.

"Never knew why," Nancy said. "Lord knows she messes with everyone else. Now," she said, looking at the stacks of beeswax bars. "How many do you need?"

"Probably about twenty pounds," I said.

We loaded four of the fragrant five-pound bars into the cloth bag I'd brought with me, and I wrote out a check. "Here's a gallon of honey for you, too. On the house."

"Are you sure?" I asked.

"Just bring me a big ol' jar of your grandma's peach-honey jam, when the season comes," she said. "Haven't had it in almost two decades, and I miss it."

"I'd love to," I said, grateful for her generosity, and made a mental note to bring some jars of jam over to the Bees' Knees.

"How's business going out at Dewberry Farm?" she asked. "Good to see it occupied again—and by a Vogel, no less!"

"It's bumping along," I said. "I'm just worried about what will happen if there's an oil well in my backyard."

"If there's anything we can do to help, let us know," she said, shaking her head and looking over the fence toward the Kocureks' sprawling compound of brick, 1960s ranch-style houses. "Sometimes I think the whole town needs to unite and get rid of ol' Nettie!"

Founders' Day dawned cool and crisp. After a cup of coffee and a slice of Quinn's homemade bread with jam on the front porch, I herded Blossom into the milking parlor and gave her a bucketful of cow chow, then set to work filling my newly reinforced milking pail, which I had placed in a crate weighed down with a concrete block and screwed into the floor. She'd done her best to foil me, delivering a series of well-placed kicks, but my pail had held, and I now had three milkings' worth in my fridge. It looked like mozzarella would soon be on the menu.

When the pail was full—despite a few well-aimed kicks—I patted Blossom affectionately on the backside and sent her back out to pasture. The look she shot me from her long-lashed eyes gave me the distinct impression that she knew I'd won the battle but that she hadn't given up on the war. Feeling slightly smug, I crossed to the little yellow farmhouse with the pail in my hand, pausing for a moment to take in the view. The larkspur was a purple and pink carpet next to the house, my grandmother's roses were putting out a few pale pink blooms near the newly repaired picket fence, and a mockingbird sang from a branch on the sycamore behind the house. With the quaint painted farmhouse, the red barn, the roses blooming, and the wash of purples and pinks from the larkspur and the blue of bluebonnets in the distance, the scene looked like it could be a painting. Granted, I still needed to paint the fence and I'd only just begun to reclaim the gardens around the house, but if you squinted your eyes, it could almost be a painting. An impressionist one, anyway.

The screen door thunked behind me as I walked into the farmhouse with the pail of milk. Morning sun streamed through the windows, making the oak floors glow, and a breeze from the open window ruffled the white muslin curtains. I poured some of the warm milk into a glass and the rest into the sterilized jugs I'd prepared to help the milk cool faster, only spilling a little bit on the white tiled counter. Chuck strolled into the kitchen and stretched, looking at me with hope in his brown eyes.

"Hey there, big fella'." I petted his shaved head and slipped him a piece of bacon leftover from yesterday morning. It disappeared in a nano-second, as always.

"Sorry, sweetie, but that's all for today. But you can have a carrot!" I opened the fridge and offered him an orange medallion left over from dinner the night before. He took one sniff and turned his nose up at it.

"Like it or lump it," I said. "That's all you're getting. Doctor's orders."

I'd taken Chuck to the vet just last week for some ant bites he'd acquired on one of his fence-post sniffing expeditions. "Interesting looking farm dog," Dr. Brandt had said with a twinkle in his eye when he met Chuck.

"Oh, he's excellent at herding sausages," I said. "Not one ever gets away."

"I can tell," he said, eyeing Chuck's sizeable girth. I used to attribute it to the fur, but now that he was shaved almost bald, I was a bit taken aback by how much of Chuck there really was.

Dr. Brandt was what my grandmother would have called a tall drink of water. He was certainly tall, with dark blue eyes and gentle hands that made me shiver when I accidentally touched them —like, say, when I was holding Chuck down for a blood test.

I felt slightly guilty for hoping that Chuck would require more hands-on procedures in the near future, despite the fact that I couldn't afford them.

"You might want to cut back on the sausages," he suggested, much to Chuck's dismay. "And more exercise would help, too."

"He won't go further than the fence," I said. "Digs in his heels."

"He'll be easier to drag after a few weeks on low-fat kibble," Dr. Brandt said, depositing a bag of Light 'n' Lean dog food on the table next to the poodle. Chuck sniffed it and turned away with a look of disdain in his brown eyes.

"Can I give him any treats?" I asked.

"Cooked carrots," the vet suggested.

"Treats," I reiterated.

He laughed. "Try the carrots. You might be surprised."

I'd tried the carrots, but I hadn't been surprised. Chuck staunchly refused to touch them, and usually followed me around with a wistful look in his eyes until I left the kitchen. This morning, as usual, I tossed the carrot in the chicken bucket and headed out to water the vegetable garden with Chuck at my heels.

The chunky poodle sniffed along the edge of the

fence and watered one of Grandma Vogel's roses as I turned on the sprinkler for the veggies. As the jewel-like spray cascaded down on the tender leaves, I found myself wondering who had won the statue debate.

Unfortunately, however, the thought of Nettie Kocurek and her sausage nose reminded me of the threat that hung over the farm, and a memory of the rangy geologist and the looming threat of the thumper truck skidded across my thoughts like a dark cloud. The reading I'd done told me that thumper trucks essentially created small underground earthquakes, leaving scars on the landscape and potentially damaging both septic systems and wells. And if they found anything . . . I shuddered at the thought of a well in the middle of Blossom's pasture.

When the sprinklers were running, I cut and bundled two dozen larkspur bunches, putting the pink and purple bouquets into a tub filled with water. Then I gathered the eggs from the chickens and headed back inside to finish getting ready for Founders' Day.

I had put handwritten labels and a raffia bow on each small beeswax jar candle and was wrapping a bar of lavender soap when I noticed Grandma Vogel's cookbook open on the counter. Goose bumps rose on my arms as I walked over to the counter. I knew I had put it back in the bookshelf next to my bed the night before. Every time I leafed through the yellowed pages, it almost felt as if my grandmother were talking to me. Sometimes, I wondered if she really was talking to me: more than once, I'd come home to find the book open to a recipe I hadn't been planning to make, and the book had a habit of turning up in odd places.

As I walked over to the cookbook, the phone rang.

I answered on the third ring. "Hello?"

"May I speak with Lucy Resnick?" said an unfamiliar voice.

"Speaking," I said.

"I'm Mindy, with Lone Star Exploration. This is a courtesy call to inform you that we'll be sending a seismic exploration truck out to your property Monday morning."

I felt as if she had punched me right through the phone. "You can't do that," I said, feeling my chest tighten. "It's my land."

"Actually, the mineral rights were retained by the previous owner, so it is legal. I apologize for the inconvenience, but I can assure you we will restore any damage to the property."

"What about my well? And my septic system?" I glanced out the window at the rows of bright green lettuce. "And my garden?"

"As I said, we will repair any damage."

"That won't help me recoup the cost of what I've planted," I said, gripping the phone. And I could only imagine how the chickens would feel about an enormous, thumping truck on the property. Not to mention Blossom. "Can't you postpone a week?" I asked, thinking of the appointment with the attorney I'd scheduled for Wednesday.

"I'm sorry, ma'am, but it's already been scheduled."

"But . . ."

"If you have any questions, you can call us at this number," she said, reeling off an 800 number.

"One week," I pleaded. "That's all I need."

"I'm sorry, ma'am. If you have questions, call the number. Have a nice day."

And then she was gone.

I was still stewing when I drove my old Toyota truck into town an hour later, jouncing over the potholes. The bouquets of larkspur filled the tub in the back, along with the soaps, the candles, and the jam I had made yesterday. As I crossed the railroad tracks, I waved at Bessie Mae, who was sitting at her post by the depot in a red corduroy skirt and a white wool sweater, looking perfectly content despite the eighty-degree weather. Bessie Mae waved back, as always, her face breaking into a sweet, gap-toothed smile.

The town square looked festive already, with brightly colored tents and flags flapping in the wind: red and white for the Moravian population, and red, black, and yellow for the Germans. Even Krystof Baca, whose statue was situated, as Nettie had requested, in the center of the lawn, was decorated with a red-and-white lei. My heart sank at the sight of it. If Mayor Niederberger couldn't win against Nettie, what hope did I have?

The tantalizing smells of barbecue and yeasty kolaches wafted through the truck's windows as I pulled up on the edge of the square, near the Blue Onion.

"Hey, Lucy!" Quinn said as she arranged a tray of her famous maple twists on a table covered in red-and-white gingham.

"You're way ahead of me," I said, admiring her blue-and-white striped tent and the cloth-covered table. "Those look great!" I added as I lugged my own white tent from the back of the truck.

"So do those," Quinn said, coming to help me as I set up my booth. Within a few minutes, the tent was up, as was the table with my grandmother's embroidered tablecloth. I arranged a bouquet of larkspur in a large mason jar, then helped Quinn with the cooler of water bottles she was lugging from the cafe. "Looks like Nettie won the statue competition," I said, eyeing the bronze monstrosity in front of the courthouse.

"He's got a heck of a nose, doesn't he?" Quinn said. "She had it put up in the middle of the night. Mayor Niederberger was steamed over it, but there wasn't any time to take it down."

"Nettie Kocurek is a force of nature, isn't she?" I said.

"That she is," Quinn said. "And a festive one, too. Look at that!"

I followed her pointing finger to see Mrs. Kocurek, who was all decked out in a red-and-white dirndl-style dress. She was carrying a red-and-white lei, and headed in the direction of the statue. "She's submitted her Moravian prune jam again this year," Quinn said. "I doubt she'll be hard to beat."

"In that arena, maybe," I said. "I'm going to go and talk with her."

"Good luck."

I grabbed a jar of jam to enter into the Jam-Off and hustled over to Mrs. Kocurek, who was headed toward the jam tent herself.

"Mrs. Kocurek," I called out.

She turned and looked at me. Much as she might resemble a sweet Czech grandma in her traditional dress, her eyes were steely behind the caked mascara.

"What can I do for you, honey?" Her voice was syrupy sweet.

"Please don't send the thumper truck out to my house," I said. "I've put everything I have into that farm."

"I'm just exercisin' my property rights," she said. "Besides, they told me they'll put everything back the way it was when they're done."

"This is about my grandfather, isn't it?" I asked.

"Frank Vogel?" Her face was suddenly transformed; I could see the anger that had festered for decades. "That man lied to me. Cheated me." The honeyed words were gone. Her voice was harsh.

"But . . ."

"What goes around comes around," she hissed. "It's just too bad he's not around to see it."

"This isn't about money, is it?" I asked. "This is about revenge."

"You're smarter than your grandmother, at least," she said with a smile that made my stomach turn over. "Sold me the place for nothing. Desperate for money."

"I won't let you destroy the farm," I said.

"Oh really?" she said, the syrup back in her voice. "Frankly, unless you poison me with that jam of yours, I don't see how you plan to stop me."

"Aunt Nettie?"

I turned to see a uniformed man with a large paunch approach us, a concerned look on his face: Sheriff Rooster Kocurek, Nettie's nephew. "Is everything all right?"

"I do believe this young woman just threatened me," she said, the sweet little-old-lady voice back in place. "She doesn't like me exercising my property rights."

"I didn't threaten you," I objected, but I could tell by the suspicious look on the sheriff's face that it didn't matter.

"I think you should just move along now, miss," he said.

I opened my mouth to protest, but realized just in time that it would only make things worse. Gripping my jar of jam as if it were Nettie Kocurek's throat, I turned on my heel and walked toward the jam tent, head high. The only way I'd let that woman ruin my grandparents' farm was over my dead body.

Chapter 4

I had sold everything but a half dozen candles and was finishing off a delicious sliced brisket sandwich topped with onions and Bubba's smoky-sweet barbecue sauce when the announcement came that the mayor would be announcing the winner of the Jam-Off.

"Let's go," Quinn said. "Rebecca said she'd mind the store."

"You sure?" I asked the freckled teenaged girl who often gave Quinn a hand in the afternoons.

"It's just Mayor Niederberger talking about jam," she said. "Y'all go on ahead."

Quinn and I walked over to where a large square had been marked out with ribbons.

"Howdy, Miz Resnick," said Alfie Kramer, who was wearing jeans and a plaid western-style shirt. Although he was of German heritage, he viewed himself first and foremost as Texan, as did many of the cattle ranchers in the area. "How's the farmin' business?"

"Not too bad," I said. "I don't know how you deal with four hundred cattle, though. I'm having a tough time managing one!"

"I don't milk 'em," he said, grinning. "Helps."

"I'll bet."

"Heard ol' Nettie's stirrin' up trouble for you," he said.

"Who told you that?"

"Little bird," he said. "Ain't no surprise, but I'm sorry to hear it. That woman don't feel her day's work is done unless she's makin' trouble for someone. Your grandpa sure made the right choice, marryin' Elsa instead of Nettie."

I laughed. "I sure wouldn't want Nettie for a grandma. On the other hand, maybe she wouldn't be sending thumper trucks out to my farm if she was."

Alfie leaned forward and said, in a low, hoarse voice, "But then you might have the Baca nose."

I couldn't help but giggle.

"Seriously, though, young lady," he said, adjusting his hat. "If there's anything we can do to help out, just let us know. You need to borrow a tractor or need a couple of fellas to help out with some heavy work, just give me a ring; the boys and I'll be right over."

"Thanks," I said, feeling warmth inside. Alfie's wife, Molly, had invited me over to dinner the day we moved in, and she'd served up a King Ranch Chicken Casserole that was the best I'd ever tasted. Over dinner, Alfie had given me some subtle advice on the chicken coop that had probably resulted in keeping several chickens away from the raccoons and coyotes, and he'd even come over and plowed part of the back field for me. I'd brought them several buckets of dewberries over the last week or two and planned to load them up with peaches this summer (presuming I got any), but I was definitely in their debt.

"If you know a way to keep her thumper truck off my farm, that would be a help," I said.

He shook his head and his mouth pulled to the side. "Afraid I can't help you with that. Nettie never did get over your granddaddy," he said. "I'm sorry you're havin' to deal with her. There's a heap o' nice folks who kick off before their time, but she just keeps hangin' on. Seems like the mean ones always do."

"Isn't that the way of it?" I asked.

"Looks like Flora's finally steppin' out from her shadow, leastwise." He nodded toward Flora, who was dressed in a dirndl-style getup. She was holding a frosted kolache as she walked hand in hand with a man whose lederhosen strained at their buttons. As I watched, he whispered something into her ear, and she laughed; despite her graying hair and the crow's feet at the corners of her eyes, the laugh was as giddy as a teenager's.

"Is that her boyfriend?" I asked.

"Sure is. Roger Brubeck."

"Sounds German," I said.

"He is, and Nettie doesn't like it much. There's a longstanding rivalry between the Germans and the Czechs in this town. Rumor has it Flora and

Roger have been sweet on each other since high school. His wife left him about a year back, and he's started steppin' out with Flora since."

"Good for her," I said, thinking it was no wonder Flora sounded like a teenager; she was still in the throes of a teenage romance. It gave me hope that even though I was approaching the big 4-0, I might find the right person out there after all.

"Good, until Nettie writes her out of her will," he said. "Look at her over there by her grand-daddy's statue. She's givin' 'em the stink-eye even now." He nodded toward the septuagenarian, who was eyeing her offspring with the thin lips and narrowed eyes of a disapproving mother.

"You think she'd do that? Flora must be in her fifties, for goodness' sake."

"Wouldn't put it past her," Alfie said. "Was a shock when Flora announced he was taking her to the Harvest Festival. Nettie's been madder than a wet hen ever since."

"Think that's why she's drillin' on my land?"

"Oh, no," he said. "She'd a done that anyway."

As we talked, a tall, lanky young man with scraggly sideburns trotted up, wearing horn-rimmed glasses and a tie-dyed T-shirt. "Hey there, Alfie!"

"Howdy, Peter." Alfie stuck out a work-roughened hand, which Peter grasped in his much thinner, smoother one. Peter Swenson had driven in from Austin in a fry oil–powered VW about a year before I'd arrived in Buttercup and had promptly bought a herd of dairy goats and planted several rows of vegetables. Every Saturday, he drove into Austin and sold his cheese at the farmers' markets; last I heard, he was working on a contract to supply Whole Foods. The two men were as different as wheatgrass juice and Shiner Bock, but they had become friends.

"Quinn tells me you're in the dairying business now, too," Peter said, smiling at me.

"Sort of," I said with a grin. "I've just now figured out how to keep Blossom from kicking over the bucket."

"Try milking a herd of goats sometime," he said, groaning.

"No, thank you!" I said. "Although I wouldn't mind a few tips."

"Sure," he said. "And if you ever want to know about the Austin farmers' markets, let me know."

Before I could answer, a young female voice called Peter's name. I turned to see Teena Marburger, dressed in a dirndl she hadn't yet grown to fill out, trotting over to us with glowing eyes. Her family owned Marburger's Cafe and Bier Garden, where she worked as a waitress when she wasn't attending Buttercup High School. I grinned, remembering my own first high school crush. Teena's eyes were glued to Peter; Alfie and I could have been painted blue and juggling fire, and she wouldn't have noticed. "I made Daddy buy tofu bratwurst special for you," she said, her braces gleaming in the afternoon light.

"Thanks, Teena," Peter said. I noticed him take a small step back from her. "I'll be over in a little bit."

Teena suddenly swiveled and looked at me. "Somebody's trying to reach you," she said, with no expression on her face.

"Pardon me?" I said, feeling a chill up my back despite the warm afternoon.

"Look for a wolf in sheep's clothing," she said. "That's all I know."

"What?" I asked.

"Sorry, but I've got to run back to the stand or Daddy will kill me." She gave Peter another doe-eyed, hopeful smile. "See you at the stand after the awards ceremony?"

"Sure," he said, and she bounced off as if he'd just declared his undying love for her, leaving Peter looking uncomfortable and me feeling uneasy.

"What was all that about?" I asked Alfie.

"She's got it bad for Peter," Alfie said. Peter looked mortified.

"The whole town knows that," I said. "I mean what she said to me. About someone trying to reach me."

"Molly says she's got the sight," Alfie said, grimacing.

"Sight? As in . . . second sight?"

He shrugged. "I don't know. Have to ask Molly. In fact, why don't you come over for dinner sometime this week and ask her then?"

"Are you sure? I should have you over next."

"It's easier to do it at our place with the kids," he said.

"Thanks," I said, grateful for the invitation. Molly was an excellent cook, and the Kramers' house was warm and cozy and full of noise—a nice change from the calm peace of Dewberry Farm. I'd call Molly and find out what I could bring.

Just then, Mayor Niederberger picked up a megaphone. "Good afternoon, Buttercup!" she announced, smiling broadly. "I'm tickled pink that all of y'all made it out to Founders' Day!"

Hoots and hollers erupted around the square, and I settled in as the mayor gave a brief history of the settlers who came over from Moravia and Germany and supplanted the few "Anglos" in the area to found the town almost two hundred years ago. "In honor of our ancestors—and of Founders' Day—Nettie Kocurek, great-great-granddaughter of Moravian founder Krystof Baca, will be announcing the winner of the Jam-Off." There was polite applause, but Nettie Kocurek didn't materialize.

"Mrs. Kocurek?" Mayor Niederberger repeated. "Nettie?"

"I think I saw her near the jam tent," Mary Elizabeth Bedicheck, the Buttercup Garden Club president, called out.

"Go and fetch her, will you?" Mayor Niederberger said. "Sorry, folks," she said to the crowd. She'd opened her mouth to say something else when there was a bloodcurdling scream.

Chapter 5

"Everybody okay?" Mayor Niederberger asked.

Mary Elizabeth stumbled from the tent, her normally ruddy face like chalk. "She's dead!"

"Who's dead?" Mayor Niederberger asked into the microphone. The feedback made a piercing squeal, and I shuddered.

"Nettie Kocurek!" Mary Elizabeth grabbed the tent pole with a calloused hand, looking as if she needed the support. "There's blood. Everywhere!"

There was a collective intake of breath as the residents of Buttercup absorbed the shocking news, then a buzz as everyone began talking at once. A siren wailed somewhere, puncturing the burble of voices, and the scene that had seemed so festive was suddenly fraught with anxiety and fear. It was amazing how quickly things could change. Five minutes ago, we were enjoying a community celebration, and now . . . I shivered as if I'd felt death's cold breath on my neck.

I searched the crowd instinctively for Flora.

I didn't like Nettie Kocurek, but I hadn't wished her dead.

Once the vital information had been passed around—stabbed with a bratwurst skewer, and found with her feet sticking out from under one of the tables—the crowds had vanished along with Nettie Kocurek. It was almost as if people were afraid her death could be catching. With a murderer around, I realized with a shiver, it could well be.

An ambulance came and went as Quinn and I wrapped up leftover maple twists at the Blue Onion booth.

"I can't believe she's dead," Quinn breathed as they closed the yellow back doors of the ambulance.

"I can't believe someone stabbed her," I said. "At the Founders' Day festival, of all things."

"At least there are plenty of suspects," Quinn said.

I looked up from the box of pastries I was wrapping up. "Is that a good thing?"

"Probably not, now that I think of it. You think Rooster will question all of us?"

"Half of the town has already cleared out, and if he questions the other half, we'll be here for weeks."

Quinn and I watched as the ambulance pulled out of the square. "Wonder if this means the thumper truck will be delayed?" she said.

I hadn't considered that. "Do you think it might?"

She cocked an eyebrow at me. "You might want to call the exploration company and let them know the person who ordered it is no longer in a position to pay bills."

For the first time since seeing the guy from Lone Star on my property, I felt a small gleam of hope—even if the reason for it was a tragedy. "That's a good idea," I said. "Even if it's only delayed, that will at least give me time to meet with the attorney and see what my options are."

Quinn ran a hand through her mop of red curls. The humidity had made them wilder than usual today; her hair glowed like a halo around her face. "I wonder who did her in," she mused.

"Did she have many enemies?"

"Are you kidding me? She's spent the last sixty years ruffling people's feathers," Quinn said.

"She certainly ruffled mine," I said.

"I'm sure that won't have escaped her nephew's notice," Quinn said, eyeing the sheriff, who was looking both aggrieved and official. And was walking in our direction.

"Uh-oh," Quinn said as Rooster Kocurek strode over to us. He smelled like Old Spice and Skoal.

"Ms. Resnick?"

I nodded. "I'm so sorry about your aunt . . ."

"I'm going to need to ask you a few questions," he said, hitching his belt up. I watched as it slid right back down, defeated by his ample belly.

"About what?" I asked, as if I had no idea.

"About where you were this afternoon."

I swallowed. "I was here the whole time," I said. "Just like everyone else."

"Were you in the jam tent?"

"Of course," I said. "I had to drop off my jam for the judging. But not when Mrs. Kocurek died."

"You know when she died?"

"No," I said, flustered. "Of course not. But when I dropped off my jam, she wasn't there. Or at least I didn't see her."

"What time was that?" he asked, pulling a small notebook out of his pocket.

"I don't know," I said. "A couple of hours ago, I guess. Right after she and I spoke, in fact." I remembered with a sinking heart that Nettie had told the sheriff I'd threatened her.

"And you weren't in the jam tent at any other time?" Rooster Kocurek said, his brown eyes beady above his pillowy cheeks.

"I've been here most of the time," I said.

"You didn't eat, or go and browse the stalls?"

"Well, I did get a sandwich," I admitted.

"But you were here the rest of the time," he said.

"Yes."

"What about when you went to hear about the Jam-Off?" Rebecca piped up from where she was stacking trays of maple twists.

Not helpful.

"I didn't go into the tent," I said. "I was standing near the stage talking with Peter and Alfie; they'll vouch for me."

"Are you sure about that?" Rooster said, eyeing me with a satisfied look I didn't like at all. "Wouldn't take but a moment to nip into the jam tent."

"She said she didn't go into the jam tent," Quinn said firmly.

"You seem mighty concerned, Quinn." He looked at her in a way that made my skin crawl, and I suddenly remembered Quinn telling me she'd gently turned him down when he asked her to senior prom. He had not taken it well, I recalled her saying, and had spread a nasty rumor about Quinn and another boy. The Kocurek family evidently didn't take rejection well.

Quinn crossed her arms and looked at Sheriff Kocurek. "Are you saying Lucy's a suspect?" she asked.

"What do you think, Quinn?" His tone was condescending.

"I'm not the sheriff," she said, lifting her chin. "That's why I'm asking you."

"You're right about that." He hitched up his belt again and smiled at her. It wasn't a nice smile. "Well, now, Quinn. I don't know anyone else in Buttercup who threatened my aunt an hour before she turned up dead with a bratwurst skewer in her heart. Do you?"

Chuck was sound asleep on my beaten-down living room couch when the screen door slammed behind me late that afternoon. He lifted his head as I entered, then rolled on his back, presenting a round, pink tummy.

I sank into the couch beside him and rubbed his belly as he licked my hand with a preternaturally long tongue. "Hope your day was better than mine," I told him. I'd ended up taking a silver medal for my dewberry vanilla jam, finishing just behind Edna Orzak, Buttercup's perennial first-place winner, but the news had done nothing to allay the worry that had gripped me since the moment I learned Nettie Kocurek had decided to invoke her mineral rights. Not to mention the feeling of doom I got when Sheriff Kocurek fixed me with those beady eyes of his. Would he charge me with Nettie Kocurek's murder? I wondered. I couldn't see how there would be any physical evidence—after all, I hadn't even touched her that day—but I couldn't deny I had a motive.

And Sheriff Kocurek knew it.

Chuck, blissfully unaware of my mental torment, wagged harder, and I bent down and hugged him as I petted his tummy.

After a few snuggles, I coaxed him to the kitchen, where he plopped down on the rag rug in front of the refrigerator, looking at me expectantly.

"No treats," I said, and he cocked his head to the side. "It's not my call, sweetie. I'm sorry!"

He gave me a reproachful look when I opened the back door instead of the refrigerator, but waddled through it anyway. As he investigated the back fence, I picked up the phone, leaving yet another message for the property rights attorney. I hung up wondering if I should hire a criminal defense attorney as well. I dismissed the thought, at least for now. Nobody had charged me with anything.

Yet.

I picked up Grandma Vogel's cookbook, hugging it to my chest as if it were my grandmother herself. If I closed my eyes, it was almost as if she were in the kitchen with me, standing at the stove with a wooden spoon in her hand. What would she do? I wondered.

Get up and get moving, I realized. She would never just sit around and worry; she would do something productive. I set the cookbook down on the counter and flipped through it, looking for something comforting to make—and maybe sell at Market Days. I bookmarked the Moravian sugar bread, which—intriguingly—involved mashed potatoes, but decided against it for now. After all, I still had Quinn's loaf in the bread basket. I leafed through to my grandmother's spice cookies from my childhood, but they didn't feel quite right for a late spring day—she'd always baked them around the holidays, when the air was crisp. I was about to give up and weed the garden when I looked at the refrigerator and remembered I had several gallons of milk to play with . . . and the equipment I needed to try making my grandmother's cottage cheese. I flipped through until I found the recipe, which included lots of suggestions for using the final product—including filling kolaches.

She had multiple variations of the recipe, so I picked the one that used what I had on hand—milk, salt, and white vinegar.

I gathered my supplies, then poured two gallons of creamy milk into the pot and turned the stove on low. The golden cream floated to the top as I fitted the thermometer to the side of the pot, and my mouth watered at the thought of the cheese to come. As it heated, I lined a colander with a tea towel and glanced out the mullioned windows at the hummingbird feeder. The first ruby-throated hummingbirds had visited it yesterday, and as I stirred, another darted in, hovering near the red plastic flowers. Would the hummingbirds still come if there was an oil well in my side yard? The bird was about to dip its beak in when Chuck growled and then started barking.

I checked the milk's temperature and hurried to the back door. "Chuck!" I called, and scanned the pasture. There was nothing there but waving grass and a few tall thistles that I hadn't gotten around to digging up yet; I had no idea why he'd barked. "Come, Chuck," I ordered. He barked again, but after another, firmer call, he lowered his head and waddled back to the kitchen, parking himself in front of the fridge. Chuck was nothing if not an optimist.

He was still looking hopeful twenty minutes later when the milk reached the correct temperature, and I added the vinegar. My eyes on the wall clock, I stirred slowly for two minutes, watching the curds form, then withdrew the spoon and covered the pot. Thirty minutes later, I came in from weeding the cucumbers and poured the contents of the pot into the colander. When the whey had drained, I gathered the curds in a tea towel and rinsed them well, massaging the contents before putting the cheese into a bowl and seasoning it with salt.

My worries temporarily replaced by the miracle of what I'd just done—I'd made cheese! From milk I'd milked myself!—I spooned up a bit of my creation.

It was absolute heaven.

Feeling a boost of excitement—this was something I knew my market clients would love, and it had taken no more than an hour to create—I covered the cheese with plastic wrap and tucked it into the refrigerator, then turned on the water to wash my hands. I had just reached for the dish towel when the phone rang.

"Hello?" I wedged the receiver between my shoulder and my chin and dried my hands on the towel.

It was Quinn. "Lucy, is Blossom in the pasture?"

I peered out the window, looking for Blossom's familiar brown coat among the thistles. No sign of her.

"No," I said. "How did you know?"

"Because she decided to take a stroll through downtown," Quinn said.

"What?"

"In fact," my friend continued, "she just finished off the second tub of geraniums in front of the courthouse."

Chapter 6

Sure enough, when I pulled up outside the courthouse a few minutes later, Blossom was ambling across the square. She dipped her head to take a mouthful of grass as I put the truck in park, and I cringed when I saw the tubs flanking the steps. This morning, they had been filled with bright red geraniums; now, they were empty, save for a few mangled stems.

I got out of the truck and took a few steps toward Blossom, who blinked at me with her long-lashed eyes and gamboled away toward the Red and White Grocery, where the last tents were being loaded into the back of a truck. My eyes strayed to where the jam tent had been; it was hard to imagine that just a few hours ago, Nettie Kocurek had died there. Except for a few overflowing trash barrels, almost everything had been cleaned up, and the sheriff's car was long gone. Unfortunately, I was fairly sure I'd be seeing it again sometime soon.

"Lucy!" Quinn trotted over to me, her apron fluttering in the wind.

"Thanks for calling me," I said. "I can't believe she walked to town."

"Too bad she missed the Founders' Day Festival," Quinn grinned.

"I wish I had, too," I said, glancing at the courthouse and thinking of my conversation with Rooster Kocurek. I'd heard there were two jail cells up in the loft of the old building. And that one of them was haunted.

"Oh, I'm sure Rooster won't go after you," she said. She didn't sound convinced, though.

"Yeah, right," I said, turning my head to focus on Blossom, who was headed for the tomato seedlings arrayed outside the Red and White. "We need to get Blossom under control."

"Sure," she said. "But even if you do, how are you going to get her back to the farm?"

Both of us turned and looked at the truck. I had no cattle trailer, and there was no way I was driving back to the farm with Blossom in the truck bed. Even if by some miracle I got her up there, I was sure she'd be out by the time I got into the driver's seat.

"What do I do? Walk her back?" I asked.

"Dr. Brandt has a trailer, and he's only a few blocks away," Quinn said. "I'll run back to the Blue Onion and give him a call."

She hurried back to the cafe while I took another tentative few steps toward Blossom, who I now realized wore no collar, halter, or any other thing that would enable me to grab her if I could catch her. I was definitely out of my depth.

The Jersey heifer had doubled back now and was sniffing at the statue of Krystof Baca. Before

I could stop her, she wrapped her lips around the red-and-white lei Nettie Kocurek had draped around his neck and tugged it off.

It must not have been as tasty as the geraniums, though, because after a few experimental chews, she let the lei fall to the ground and began nuzzling Krystof's left kneecap.

I shooed her away from the pickle-nosed statue, and she galloped across the green, crossing the very place where the jam tent had been. The structure, including the lines of tables inside, had been taken down, and there was no crime-scene tape guarding the area. The sight made me uneasy. I knew small-town sheriff's departments weren't used to solving murder cases, but if there was any forensic evidence that might help clear my name, it didn't appear as if anyone had taken the time to gather it.

As Blossom dropped her head to crop some more grass, I found myself scanning the area. I could see by the trampled "U" of grass where the tables in the tent had been set up. I walked the area slowly, scanning the ground. There was a dark smudge on the grass along the side closest to the courthouse, and the grass in the area was flattened. Probably the EMTs and the sheriff's deputies, I decided—which meant it was a long shot that there was anything left for me to find.

A smashed plastic cup lay on the ground, and a mustard-covered bratwurst wrapper had been trampled into the grass. Something sparkled in the light, a few feet away from where Nettie must have lain; it was a shattered jam jar, the dark preserves sticky and liquid in the late afternoon heat. I poked at it with my toe, turning it over, and caught my breath when I saw a fragment of a torn handmade label. The handwriting was mine.

Why was the jam jar broken? I wondered. Had she been using it to defend herself? If so, and she'd managed to cut her assailant, it was possible the DNA was on the glass. But would the police believe me if I told them? Or would they think I planted the evidence after the fact?

Frustrated, I glanced over at Blossom, who was still trimming the town green, and peered at the ground around the broken jam jar. I knew if I did find something, there had been so many people through the area that there was no way to associate it with the murderer, but I couldn't help looking.

As I paced the area, eyes trained on the trampled ground, a scrap of red fabric caught my eye. I reached to touch it, but drew my hand back just in time; if it was evidence, I didn't want to contaminate it with my fingerprints. A pin was stuck in it, in the shape of a gold lamb; it looked like it had been torn from a garment. The metal flashed in the afternoon light as I moved it with the toe of my shoe. Had Nettie torn it when her attacker stabbed her? Had she hit him—or her—

with a jam jar and then grabbed at the murderer's clothing in a vain attempt to save herself?

"Quinn," I said when she trotted out to check on me a few minutes later, wiping her hands on her apron. "Look what I found." I showed her what I had discovered—and told her my theory.

"How did Rooster miss all this?" she asked, looking down at the little gold pin embedded in its scrap of fabric.

"I don't know," I said. "Inexperience, probably. But if I walk in there and tell him about it, with my background, he's either going to resent my sticking my nose into things or think I planted it."

"If somebody doesn't say something soon, though, it's going to get cleaned up or lost," she said.

"You know Rooster from high school," I said. "Do you think you might be able to tell him?"

She gave a wry laugh. "Rooster hates me," she said. "He's not going to want to hear it from me that he might have missed some evidence." She cocked a copper eyebrow. "Plus, I'm friends with you, so that's two strikes against me."

"What do I do, then? Leave it here?"

"I'll tell him," she said. "Somebody's got to, and it's better coming from me than you, I guess. You have Blossom under control?" she asked.

"Sure," I said, glancing over my shoulder to where she'd been cropping grass a few minutes ago. "Where'd she go?"

"Looks like she's headed for the tomato plants at the Enchanted Garden," Quinn said.

I muttered a word I'd rather not repeat and hustled over just in time to place myself between Blossom and Mary Elizabeth Bedichek's tender tomato transplants. She huffed and sauntered away, occupying herself with the strip of grass between the sidewalk and the pavement.

It was twenty minutes before Dr. Brandt arrived. Although Quinn had marched over to the sheriff's office, I hadn't seen her or Rooster Kocurek emerge. While keeping one eye on the station, I had managed to steer Blossom away from the Enchanted Garden's tomato plant display, and also from the window boxes at the Country Place Hotel, but I was having difficulty keeping her away from the bushels of peaches in front of the Red and White. Todd Schmidt, who along with several other villagers, had joined me in the square, was attempting to catch her with a lasso he had fashioned out of twine when Dr. Brandt pulled up with the trailer on the back of his green pickup. As I watched, he backed it in beside the Red and White. Even Bessie Mae had decided Blossom was more interesting than the 4:50 freight train; she stood on the perimeter, watching with an uncharacteristic gleam in her sweet but vacant blue eyes.

Dr. Brandt unfolded his long, denim-clad legs from the cab of his truck and smiled at me, a twinkle in his brown eyes. "Hear you got yourself a runner."

"I keep tryin' to lasso her, but she's quick!" Todd said, holding up his piece of twine. "Keeps trottin' off every time I get near!"

"How did she end up in the square?" Dr. Brandt asked me.

"I don't know," I said. "Quinn called me and said she was sampling the geraniums in front of the courthouse," I added, nodding toward the empty tubs, "and I came straight down. I've kept her out of Mary Elizabeth's tomato plants, and now all she wants is peaches."

"Smart cow," he said. "They look like they're going to be good this year."

I looked at the trailer, and then at Blossom, who was eyeing the fruit display avidly; evidently the geraniums hadn't been particularly filling. Dr. Brandt wasn't carrying a lasso or any other device for catching a wayward heifer. "How do we get her into the trailer?"

"Peaches, of course," he said, opening the back of the trailer and reaching for a basket. "Step away for a little bit, please, folks," he said. They did, forming something like a corridor. Blossom took a few nervous steps, and for a moment I was afraid she was going to take off and tackle the squash seedlings, but then Dr. Brandt made a soft "cush" sound and held out a peach. She calmed, her attention drawn first to the tall veterinarian, and then to the peach he held in his hand.

The square was silent except for the wind in the sycamore leaves and the sound of Dr. Brandt calling to Blossom. As if hypnotized, she stepped forward, first slowly, and then almost at a trot, as the veterinarian backed toward the trailer. At the base of the ramp, he fed her a peach, letting her take it from his open palm. She devoured it with a smacking sound and came up looking for more. He gave her one more and then stepped up onto the ramp. She balked at first, but he cushed a few more times, and before she knew it she was in the trailer with the doors closing behind her.

"Got a way with animals," Todd said, the twine lasso dangling limply from his hand.

"Meet you back at Dewberry Farm?" Dr. Brandt said as he latched the doors.

"That would be wonderful," I said. "I can't thank you enough."

"Don't mention it," he said with another one of those smiles. Despite my worry over Nettie's death —and the fact that Quinn and Rooster still hadn't emerged from the sheriff's office—I felt the heat rising to my face as I smiled back. I hated to admit it, but I was starting to have a serious crush.

"Here's your problem," Dr. Brandt said, lifting a length of loose barbed wire from the tall grass at the edge of the pasture.

"How did she do that?" I asked, leaning against a fence post.

"It looks like she loosened it by rubbing against it," he said, pointing at a tuft of brown fur mixed with a bit of sticky blood. "I'll put some ointment on her cuts; looks like she'll need it."

"I'll bet," I said. "I hope it's not too nasty."

"I'm sure it's just superficial," he said. "But if we don't fix this fence, those peaches don't have a chance. Got a staple gun? I'll put this back on the post for you."

"Be right back," I said, and hurried to the farmhouse to retrieve the gun. I confess I checked my hair and took two seconds to put on a fresh coat of lip gloss before hurrying back out, staple gun in hand.

Our fingers touched as I handed the staple gun to him, and I found myself savoring the warmth. He'd obviously had lots of experience with fences, as he fixed it in a matter of minutes, then handed the staple gun back to me. "It's temporary, but it'll do for now."

"How did you learn to fix fences?" I asked.

"My grandparents had a farm in a town just west of here," he said. "I spent summers with them, doing chores."

"You too?" I asked. Although I had to admit my chores had largely involved sampling Grandma Vogel's pies.

"That's what got me interested in veterinary

71

medicine," he said. "I loved working with the animals. I always wanted to move to this part of the world; it's a special place." He gazed out at the rolling hills, the low sun gilding the bluebonnets and dappling the leaves of the oaks that marked the fence lines.

"Me too," I said. "I just hope I'll be able to stay."

"You think Nettie's heirs will continue with the drilling?" he asked.

"How do you know about that?" I asked, surprised.

He shrugged. "It's a small town. People talk. And in my business, I don't exactly live under a rock."

"I guess not," I said. "As for the drilling; we'll see, I guess."

Blossom, who was grazing not far from us, ambled over and poked at the fence, a hopeful look in her long-lashed eyes. "Not this time," I chided her.

"Where'd you get her?" the handsome veterinarian asked, standing up and squinting at Blossom, who was now innocently cropping grass.

"Ed Zapp sold her to me, from the Double-Bar Ranch."

"I thought she looked familiar," he said. "That little spot on her left cheek, there." He pointed to a dun spot just below her eye; I'd never noticed it.

"This wouldn't happen to be the cow formerly known as number eighty-two, would it?"

"Actually, yes," I said, feeling a sense of foreboding. "Why?"

He chuckled. "You're going to have your hands full, I'm afraid."

"Uh-oh." I knew I should have brought Quinn with me when I went to pick out a heifer. "What's wrong with her?"

"She's a fine cow," he said. "Good milker."

"But . . ."

"Well, the truth is, she's something of an escape artist. The hands used to call her Harriet Houdini. Probably why Ed was happy to sell her. She mowed down half of his lettuce field last fall, and then she got into his neighbor's peach orchard and ate the bark off half the trees."

I glanced back at my small orchard with trepidation. "Wonderful," I said. So much for the idyllic farm life. Not only was I looking at having an oil well in the middle of my fields, but I had a renegade cow to make sure anything that did survive the drilling was consumed prior to harvest. Provided I didn't get tossed in jail for killing the former owner with a bratwurst skewer, making the whole thing moot.

"It's all right," he said. "Everyone will recognize her, so she won't be lost for long."

His words did little to lift my spirits, but I smiled at him anyway, thinking that at least the company was nice—not to mention the view. "What do I owe you, Dr. Brandt?" I asked. "You've been a lifesaver today."

"Just a glass of iced tea will do," he said, matching my smile with a lopsided grin of his own. He had a small dimple in his cheek and a knowing glint in his eyes that made my heart skip a beat.

"Seriously. I owe you much more than that."

"You've got plenty enough on your hands at the moment. You can bring me a peach pie sometime," he said, brushing the dust off his jeans. "And call me Tobias. The doctor thing gives me hives."

Tobias, I repeated in my head. "Only if you'll call me Lucy," I said.

"Now, how about that iced tea?" he asked, giving me a slow smile that made the heat rise to my face.

Unfortunately, at that moment, a rumble of an engine intruded. My stomach sank when I recognized the black and white of Sheriff Kocurek's car.

"Looks like trouble," Tobias said quietly.

"I think he thinks I stabbed Nettie Kocurek with a bratwurst skewer," I said.

Tobias looked at me levelly. "Well, did you?"

"No," I said. "Of course not."

"Then you should have nothing to worry about," he said in a calm voice. "The physical

74

evidence won't back it up. Besides, weren't you with Quinn all day?"

"Most of the time, anyway," I said. "Actually, maybe this is good news. We found a couple of things near the scene of the crime; when we left town, Quinn was in the station letting him know what we'd found."

"See? I'm sure you're fine."

"I hope you're right," I said, feeling my chest tighten in the beginnings of an asthma attack, which sometimes happened when stress hit. I'd been remarkably asthma-free since moving to Buttercup, but the way the week was going, something told me it might be wise to keep my inhaler on hand for a while. "I guess we should head back to the house," I said, watching the cruiser advance up the driveway, a cloud of dust like a storm in its wake.

"Let me put that ointment on Blossom and I'll be right up," he said. Then he raised an eyebrow. "Unless another time would be better?"

"No," I said quickly, thinking it would be comforting to have someone on the property besides Chuck who thought I was innocent. "I'm sure it'll be fine."

But as I walked back to the farmhouse, my breath wheezing in my chest, I knew it wasn't fine at all.

Chapter 7

It was Rooster Kocurek, of course. He parked right in front of my gate, half-flattening one of my grandmother's rosebushes.

I trotted up as he opened the cruiser's door. "What can I do for you?" I asked, my mouth dry. I could hear Chuck barking from inside the house.

"I need you to answer a few questions," he said as he heaved himself out of the car.

"Sure," I said, gesturing toward the front porch. "Can I get you a glass of iced tea? It must have been an awful day for you. I'm so sorry about your aunt." I was babbling, but couldn't seem to stop myself. "Dr. Brandt is here, too. Are you here about the geraniums?" I asked. "I promise I'll buy new ones and replant them this week."

"I'm not here on account of any flowers," he said in a slow drawl that was somehow menacing. His hair was red and thinning, and it looked like he'd spent a bit too much time in the sun without a hat; his scalp was an angry red. His eyes were equally angry, in a way that made my stomach feel watery.

"Oh, you're here about . . . your aunt, then." I swallowed. "Well, why don't you sit down on the porch, and I'll get you a glass of tea. Unless you'd like a Shiner Bock," I offered.

"I'm on duty," he said.

"Sorry. Of course. Well, why don't you pick a rocker and I'll be right back with a couple glasses of iced tea," I said, and hurried up the porch steps and into the house, trying to calm Chuck, who was still barking. And growling. And generally not helping things at all.

"Shh," I told him as I retrieved a pitcher of tea from the fridge and filled three glasses, adding a sprig of mint to each one. "I'm in trouble enough without you attacking the sheriff."

Chuck looked up at me and whined once, then abandoned the barking in favor of growling. I grabbed the glasses and headed for the front door. "Stay," I told him, then pulled open the screen door and slipped through it.

Unfortunately, Chuck slipped through after me and, before I could do anything, had firmly attached himself to the sheriff's polyester pant leg.

"Chuck!" I plunked the glasses down on the table, then grabbed him by the collar and hauled him backward. Which wasn't a good move, as it turned out, because he was still attached to Rooster's leg. There was a horrible ripping sound. When it ended, Rooster's pant leg had gained a bit of ventilation.

"Bad dog!" I pried the fabric from Chuck's mouth and instinctively handed it to Rooster. He looked at it as if I were offering him a wedge of moldy cheese. "I'm so sorry," I said, withdrawing the scrap of moist polyester. "I'll pay for replacement pants."

"Add it to the bill with the geraniums?" he said. "You sure do have difficulty controllin' your animals."

"It's been a tough day," I said.

He humphed in a way that made me think it was about to get tougher. I herded Chuck into the house and shut the door firmly. Chuck, undeterred, continued to bark and growl as I handed Rooster his tea and gestured toward a rocker.

"So," I said. "Must have been quite a shock this afternoon. How is the family taking it?"

"This here isn't a social call, Miz Resnick," he said, but he sat down in the chair anyway. It groaned slightly under his ample frame. "I'm here to get a few things straight."

"Did Quinn tell you what we . . . I mean, she found near where the jam tent was?" I asked, sitting down across from him and taking a nervous sip of my tea.

"Oh. So you were the one put her onto it?"

"Put her onto it?"

"Or up to it, more like," he said, rocking back in his chair. "Which one of you decided to put that Moravian lamb pin there? Tryin' to cast suspicion elsewhere?"

"What's a Moravian lamb?" I asked.

"You don't know what a Moravian lamb is, with

the Brethren Church just up the road from here?" He narrowed his eyes at me. "I didn't just fall off the back of a turnip truck, you know."

"I don't know why that lamb was there, or what it means—except that it looks as if it was ripped off of someone's clothing. I also don't know why there was a broken jam jar, but I suspect she may have used it to defend herself against her attacker," I said. "Isn't it possible you could have it DNA tested? Or at least see if you can get fingerprints from the lamb? Neither of us touched it."

"The scene was contaminated," Rooster said, crossing his arms over his barrel chest. "Could have your heifer's DNA on it by now."

"If you'd searched the area properly and cordoned it off, there wouldn't have been risk of contamination," I shot back, then regretted it. I'd reported on a few murder investigations in Houston, but I still wasn't an expert—and haranguing the sheriff was going to do nothing but make my situation worse.

"If you're done prattling on, I've got a few questions for you, Miz Resnick."

I took a deep breath, feeling the tightness in my lungs, and tried to calm myself down. "Okay," I said, trying to sound reasonable. "What do you want to know?"

"What were you doin' in the jam tent at twelve o'clock?"

"I don't believe I *was* in the jam tent then."

"I got a witness says otherwise," he said.

"Who?"

"That information is confidential," he told me, folding his arms over his ample midsection.

"I promise you, I was only in there once. In the morning." I mentally reviewed my day—and cringed inwardly. "Wait. I did go back, for a minute."

The sheriff gave a satisfied half smirk. "Happen to forget your skewer?"

"Of course not," I said. "I was selling jam and candles, not bratwursts. I was checking to make sure I'd remembered to label the jar."

"An hour before the announcement of the winning jam was going to be made?" he said. "Are you sure there wasn't another reason for you to slip into the tent? Maybe because you saw an opportunity?"

"Absolutely not," I said. "Your aunt and I had some issues we needed to resolve, but I did not touch a hair on her head."

"Oh, really?" he asked. He fished in his pocket for a plastic baggie. "Recognize this?"

"It's a piece of my jam jar," I said, catching my breath at the sight of the torn handwritten label stained dark with dewberry jam—and blood.

"Thought so," he said, and tucked the baggie back into his shirt pocket.

"Where did you find it?" I asked.

"It was in my aunt's hand," he said, and took a long, slurping sip of tea. Then he held the glass of amber liquid up to the light. "You didn't poison this, did you?"

"Poison?" The porch steps creaked as Tobias joined us. "Rooster," he said, smiling and extending a hand. Rooster stood and hesitated for a moment before extending his own meaty hand, looking suddenly less comfortable. "Good to see you," Tobias said. "Sorry about your aunt; she was a big part of the community."

I took a few deep breaths, feeling the tension ease slightly with the veterinarian's arrival.

"Thanks," Rooster said. "It was a real shocker."

"What brings you to Dewberry Farm?"

"Here on business," he said.

"I heard about the geraniums," Tobias said. "It's not her fault, though, really. Ed Zapp sold her number eighty-two—remember the one that kept crossing the freeway at lunch hour?"

"This isn't about the geraniums." Rooster's pink face turned a shade pinker.

"No?" Tobias raised his eyebrows. "What's going on, then?"

"Found part of the label of Ms. Resnick's jam in my poor aunt's hand," Rooster said, pulling the baggie out of his pocket.

"And you brought it here?" Tobias asked.

"Wanted her to identify it," he said.

"Hmm. Shouldn't that be on its way to a

forensic lab?" he asked. "Chain of evidence, and all that?"

I looked at Tobias, surprised. How did he know about things like "chain of evidence"?

"I know what I'm doin'," Rooster said. "We do things different out here in the country."

"The law's the law, Sheriff," Tobias said. "Besides, your aunt was found in a tent filled with jam jars. That's why it was the jam tent. Just because the jar in her hand happened to be from Ms. Resnick's farm doesn't mean Ms. Resnick was involved."

"Maybe she grabbed the closest jar and used it to defend herself," I suggested.

"Now you're making up stories. This here label was definitely on the scene, and it definitely connects you to my aunt's early demise," Rooster said, waving the baggie. "I'll bet we find her prints on it."

"I bet you will," Tobias said. "Since it's a hand-made label."

"She was in the tent," Rooster said.

"So was the rest of Buttercup."

Flummoxed, Sheriff Kocurek stood up. "I have other business to attend to," he said, putting the glass down so hard it sloshed. "You'll be wanted at the station for questioning," he told me, then marched down the porch steps to his car.

"When?" I asked.

"Tomorrow," he said. "Nine o'clock sharp. And

don't forget to bring your checkbook." He glared at the front door; Chuck was still growling from the other side of it. "You're lucky that dog's teeth didn't touch my skin, or I'd impound it."

As he slammed the door shut, a branch from the pecan tree fell, right on the hood of the car. I winced, but it rolled off without leaving a dent. Shooting me a venomous look from behind the steering wheel, he reversed the car with a jerk and gunned the engine, leaving a cloud of dust behind him.

"I don't think Dewberry Farm likes him very much," Tobias said mildly as the cruiser bumped over the cattle guard.

"I don't think I do, either," I said, and took a big sip of iced tea, thankful for the cool liquid on my tight throat. Despite Tobias's smooth talking, Rooster's visit had rattled me. First the oil drilling, now a murder in town . . . it had not been a good couple of days.

Chuck whined behind the door.

"I think it's safe to let him out now," Tobias said.

"He'd probably appreciate it," I said, getting up to open the door. Chuck wasted no time waddling over to the veterinarian and plopping down at his feet.

"Fierce dog you've got here," Tobias said, reaching down to scratch behind Chuck's ear.

"I can't believe he took a piece out of Rooster's

pants," I said. "He's never done that before."

"Must not like him much." Tobias took a sip of tea and grinned at me. "Good instinct. How are the carrots going, by the way? He doesn't look like he's slimmed down much."

"He won't touch them," I said. "And his favorite place to sit is in front of the refrigerator."

Chuck rolled over on his back while Tobias rubbed his round tummy. He was a completely different dog than he had been when Rooster Kocurek was on the porch.

"What was that you said about chain of evidence?" I asked, thinking of how quickly Rooster had departed once the veterinarian started asking questions. "How do you know about that?"

"My father was a cop," he said, and squinted after Rooster's cruiser. "I grew up with all that stuff. For a while, I thought I might want to be a police officer."

"What made you decide to be a vet instead?"

"I've always loved animals," he said, stroking Chuck's pink tummy. The shaved poodle was splayed on the porch; despite the indignities the veterinarian had foisted on him at the office the other week, the dog was putty in his hands. "My dog, a little beagle named Mustard, ran in front of a car when we were playing catch one day. He got checked pretty hard; broke a few ribs, and his leg was snapped in two."

I shuddered. "Awful," I said.

"I was twelve at the time, and I thought he wouldn't make it, but we took him to Dr. Grenowich, and he put him back together again. He didn't even have a limp."

"Is that what decided it?" I asked.

"Absolutely. I wanted to be able to help animals in that way. I spent summers helping him out after that, and by the time I graduated from high school, I knew what I wanted to do."

"That must have been great to have a sense of direction so early," I said. "I didn't figure out what I wanted until I was in my midtwenties. Took me ten years to make it happen, and I'm still figuring it out." I glanced at Blossom, who was hovering disturbingly close to the area of the fence the veterinarian had just fixed.

"Well, I'm glad you figured it out and took over the farm," Tobias said. "Nice to have a fresh face in town."

"Thank you," I said, feeling a rush of warmth at his words.

Unfortunately, his next sentence was like a bucket of cold water. "I'm worried about Rooster, though," he said. "He seems to have it in for you."

Despite the warm weather, a chill settled over me as I gazed out at the green, rolling hills, touched with blue and purple from wildflowers and gilded by the setting sun. Knowing how tenuous my place here was made it all the more beautiful. "I noticed that," I said.

"It doesn't make sense; half the town has reason to want to stick Nettie Kocurek with a skewer." He sighed. "Probably because you're new in town. He didn't go to high school with you."

I leaned forward in my chair. A warm breeze lifted the hair at the nape of my neck, and I got a whiff of Tobias's scent. Spicy, and clean. I was enjoying his company very much. "Who else had a bone to pick with Nettie Kocurek?"

"Lots of folks," he said. "You should go and talk with Myrtle Crenshaw, down at the library. She knows everything about everyone. She might be able to put you on the right track."

"I'll do that," I said. "Thanks for the tip."

He took another long swig of iced tea and stood up. "I hate to run, but I promised I'd swing by Peter's place and check on the goats. One of them is so pregnant she looks like she's going to pop."

"Thanks for coming out to help me," I said, standing up with him. "And for chasing off Rooster Kocurek."

He turned his dark eyes on me. "Be careful with him," he said. "I was thinking, you might want to get a lawyer."

"I already have to pay for one to keep the oil drillers off the farm," I said. "I'm going to have to sell a lot of jam if I'm going to do that and pay the mortgage, too."

"I'd get going on the jam, then. You just got

here," he said with a grin that made my heart skip a beat. "I don't want you to leave just yet."

Dinner was a simple one, of fresh cottage cheese spooned over Quinn's homemade bread, with sugared dewberries for dessert. The creamy cheese was delicious, and it was all I could do not to finish the entire bowl on the spot. I'd definitely be making more tomorrow, I decided—and if I could replicate the results, would have to consider adding it to my market wares. I'd need the money, with all the legal fees I appeared to be racking up.

I filled Chuck's bowl half full with Light 'n' Lean, not adding extra treats in deference to Dr. Brandt—Tobias, I reminded myself, feeling a little thrill—and headed out to give the kitchen scraps to the chickens and to milk Blossom. Thankfully, the tawny heifer had not yet figured out another escape route, and in fact was grazing not far from the barn.

Night was falling; all that was left of the sun was a light blue streak on the horizon, and Orion rode in the sky, his belt sparkling in the spreading darkness. The breeze rustled the grass as I called Blossom, who came trotting up to the milking parlor and happily headed into her stall as I fitted the reinforced bucket beneath her. It was almost as if she were apologizing for her jaunt to town, I thought—until she gave the pail a playful nudge that told me she was anything but chastened.

The rhythm of the milk hitting the pail was soothing, and my mind wandered as I milked. Except for my successful foray into the world of cheese making, Tobias had been the only good thing to happen to me the past few days, I thought to myself. I hadn't dated anyone in years, but I kept thinking of his smile, and his sense of humor. It had been very companionable with him on the front porch.

But I had bigger things to deal with right now, I thought as I squeezed another jet of warm milk into the pail. Someone had murdered Nettie with a bratwurst skewer, and the local sheriff thought I was the prime suspect.

Who had done it? I wondered. And why?

And would her death postpone the arrival of the thumper truck?

I was squeezing the last bits of milk from the udder when there was a thump from the hayloft above me.

Goose bumps rose on my arms as I turned to look; Blossom turned, too, letting out a grass-scented burst of warm air from her velvety nostrils.

"Hello?" I called, remembering too well that there was a murderer in Buttercup, and that except for the heifer, I was alone. She could be heck on milk pails, but I wouldn't want to bet on her against a skewer-wielding killer.

A cool breeze raised more goose bumps on my arms as my eyes scanned the dim barn. There was a pile of old hay in the corner, and the bin where I kept Blossom's food, along with the rusty remains of a few unidentified farm implements, but nothing I could easily pick up and use as a weapon.

It was probably just a mouse, I told myself. Or one of the neighboring farm cats.

I finished milking Blossom and let her out of the stall, keeping one eye on the hayloft. After what had happened to Nettie Kocurek, there was no way I was climbing that ladder tonight. I retrieved my pail with shaky hands and released the heifer from the barn. Maybe it was my overactive imagination, but she seemed in a particular hurry to be out of the barn and back in the pasture. She made off toward the stock tank like someone had threatened to brand her.

I was about to close the barn door when a chilly breeze swept through the barn, wafting an old, yellowed piece of newspaper down from the hayloft. I watched as it spiraled down through the air, coming to rest a few feet in front of me.

I grabbed the paper and hurried out of the barn, feeling more freaked out than I had since I'd watched my first (and last) Freddy Krueger movie. It wasn't until I closed the door of the farmhouse behind me that I realized what made the breeze so eerie.

All the windows in the hayloft were painted shut.

Chapter 8

Sleep came slowly that night; between Nettie Kocurek's death, the threat of the thumper truck, and the strange sound in the barn, I was anything but relaxed. I'd considered calling Quinn to come out and check the hayloft with me, but decided that would be silly.

Instead of calling Quinn, I locked all the doors and windows and lay in bed with one eye open, a two-by-four under the bed just in case. I'm not usually a pro-gun kind of person, but this was one of those times when I kind of wished I were. Despite the scare in the barn, though, the farm was quiet; aside from the occasional chuckle from the chickens and a stray moo from Blossom, everything was peaceful. Chuck didn't seem terribly concerned as he sprawled on his back at my feet, all four paws pointing upward. At least if Rooster—or whoever had murdered Nettie Kocurek—came to visit that night, I told myself, Chuck would likely let me know.

I must have fallen asleep eventually, because the sound of Rusty crowing jerked me awake. I opened my eyes to the pale light of dawn filtering through the lace curtains into the room I had stayed in as a child; I almost expected Grandma Vogel to appear at the door in her blue checked dress. For a second, I fancied I caught a whiff of the lavender sachets she hung in her closet, but the impression was gone as quickly as it arrived.

Groaning, I dislodged Chuck from across my feet and swung my legs over the side of the bed. Coffee was definitely in order—followed by another call to the attorney. I threw on a bathrobe and headed to the kitchen, wishing I had a morning newspaper to read while I waited for the coffee to brew; paper delivery was one thing I missed about country life. Instead, I picked up the old newspaper I'd found in the barn the night before, glancing at the headlines as the scent of coffee filled the sunlit kitchen.

The paper dated from June of 1940. The headline blared LOCAL MAN FOUND DEAD, and I wondered again at the weird breeze that had sent it floating down from the hayloft. I glanced out the window toward the barn, which was bright and cheerful in the morning sun. The thought of going up into the hayloft didn't bother me at all now that the world was bright. The thump had doubtless been a mouse, or even an owl roosting in the rafters, and as for the breeze—the back of the barn probably wasn't airtight. It was funny how things seemed spookier in the darkness.

I glanced at the paper as I drank my first cup of coffee, which I'd sweetened with sugar and topped off with the cream that had risen to the surface of one of the milk jugs. I skimmed the article on the death—the deceased was Thomas Mueller, and the sheriff was named Ed Kocurek, which was not encouraging—and wondered if they'd ever found out who did it. The yellowed pages advertised a special on potatoes at the Red and White, and seasonal kolaches at an establishment called the Little Czech Bakehouse. Who had tucked that newspaper up into the hayloft, I wondered, and why it had waited half a century to come free? And what else might be up there?

With that thought in mind, I retreated to the bedroom and tossed on a pair of shorts and a T-shirt, then headed out to milk Blossom, whom I'd spotted over by the driveway, nosing at the fence. Looking for another weak spot, no doubt. I should have known she was too good to be true.

Chuck sauntered out after me, but I waved him away when I got to the cattle guard; I didn't trust Blossom around the little poodle just yet. He gave me a perplexed look, then waddled over toward one of the rosebushes and cocked a leg. With his farm buzz cut, he was the same pale pink as the two feeble blooms on the neglected bush. Which was fine in spring but would be a problem come June, particularly in Texas. I made a mental note to ask Dr. Brandt—Tobias—about doggie sunscreen next time I talked to him. In fact, I figured I might just have to call and ask today; I'd hate for Chuck to get sunburned!

With that happy thought in mind, I turned toward the barn. Despite the bright morning, my stomach still tightened when I opened the barn doors and stepped into the dim, dusty interior. Everything looked the same as it had last night; the hay was undisturbed in the corner, and the pile of rusted equipment lay just as it had. The inside of the barn was silent, and nothing was visible in the hayloft—even when I backed out the barn door to get a better vantage point. Last night had probably been the product of an overactive imagination and a stressful day, I told myself as I climbed the ladder and poked my head cautiously into the loft.

I scanned the dusty floor. More hay. And a few mouse droppings, which were no surprise—mice were probably the source of the noise I'd heard last night, after all. The piles of ancient, dried-out hay and droppings made me feel tired. I'd have to add cleaning the hayloft to my list of things to do.

There was no stack of newspapers, though, and the windows were all closed.

I climbed the rest of the way up and walked to the back wall, looking for cracks in the wood through which a breeze might have come. There were none—and the windows were still painted shut. In fact, despite the breeze outside, the barn was still and airless.

I was about to climb down the ladder when there

was a loud clunk from below. Heart in my throat, I spun around to see Blossom nosing at the barn door, ready for her morning milking.

My heart was still hammering as I filled her bucket with food, positioned the milking pail beneath her, and wiped sanitizer on her teats. I rested my forehead against her flank as I filled the bucket, the rhythm of the milk against the side of the bucket soothing me. Maybe today would be better, I thought.

Unfortunately, I was wrong.

I reported to the sheriff's office at nine, only to find Rooster out on a call. "Big cow problem down on 71," the deputy on duty told me. I tried to pay for Rooster's pants, but the deputy had no idea what to tell me. "Opal handles all that stuff, and she's out today."

"There's no way to look it up?" I asked. I was hoping to get it taken care of so I had an excuse not to come back.

"Sorry about that, ma'am. I'll be sure to tell Rooster you stopped by."

I hurried home to make sure it wasn't Blossom and was relieved to find her nosing around the corner of the pasture by the house, trying in vain to reach my roses.

Unfortunately, the rest of the day didn't go quite as well. I'd just finished my morning chores when an enormous truck came rolling down my driveway. I hurried out to stop them, but wasn't having much luck.

"I'm sorry, ma'am, but we've got the paperwork right here." The driver raised his cap and scratched his sparsely covered scalp. His compatriot eyed me from a few yards back. From the wary look on his face, they'd done this a time or two before.

"But the woman who authorized it is dead!" I said. Or yelled, actually.

"Let me call the office," he said.

I was dying to go and call the attorney again, but there was no way I was walking away from the monstrous truck. So I tried to hush Chuck, who was growling and yipping from across the cattle guard, while the truck's operator explained the circumstances to his supervisor.

"Well?" I asked when he hung up.

"Looks like the bill's already been paid," he said. "So we're gonna go ahead."

"What?"

"I'm sorry ma'am," he said, backing away from me toward the truck. "Just following orders."

"I'm calling my attorney right now," I said, and sprinted toward the farmhouse. Hands shaking, I dialed the number and then watched out the window as I explained the situation to her receptionist, then waited to be put through.

There was a horrible rumbling sound as the engine kicked to life, and I waited for the awful thumping sound that would come, but as soon as it started, it died away. They started the truck again, and once more it died.

"Ms. Resnick?"

"Yes," I said.

"This is Janet Morgan. I'm sorry you had a hard time getting in touch with me, but I researched your case, and I'm afraid there's not much I can do about it."

"You're kidding me."

"As long as they restore the property when they're done, the mineral rights holder has the right to both search and drill for oil, I'm afraid. I'd take lots of dated pictures, if I were you."

"You mean I can't stop the thumper truck from breaking up my land?"

"No, but the mineral rights owner will have to pay for any damage to your property."

"But she just died yesterday!" I said.

"Who? The owner of the mineral rights?" the attorney asked.

"Yes."

"Well. That may change things. If the will hasn't been probated . . ."

"Of course it hasn't. It happened yesterday."

"Then it seems reasonable to put a stay on further actions until it is determined who owns that portion of the estate."

"Thank you," I said. "Now can you tell the people about to thump my land that?"

"Are they there?"

"I'll get them," I said. "Hold on." I put the phone down, well aware that I was going to pay fifty dollars just for the time necessary to retrieve the driver, and ran back outside. "My attorney's on the line," I called. "She wants to talk to you!"

The man shrugged, scratching his head again, and walked toward me.

"I still need you to talk with my lawyer," I said, leading him toward the house. He followed—very slowly, it seemed to me—and grunted when he picked up the phone. After a short conversation that probably cost me a week's proceeds, he gave the attorney the phone number of his supervisor and handed the phone back to me.

"I'll get in touch with the company today," she said. "If they try anything else, let me know."

"Do you have a cell number?" I asked.

She gave it to me, and I wrote it down on the back of a flyer. "Call me anytime," she said.

"Don't worry," I said. "I will."

The driver and I walked back out to where the truck stood. Chuck was still guarding it, growling low as if warning it not to roll any further.

"Well, looks like you guys can head out for the day," I said. "Until the estate is cleared up, no thumping."

"Truck's broke anyway," he said.

"What?" I asked. "It's in the middle of my driveway!"

"I'll try to start it, but it's deader than a doornail."

He got back up into the driver's seat and turned the key. The engine coughed a few times but didn't turn over.

"Terrific," I said. "How am I going to get in and out of the farm?"

"I don't know, ma'am," he said. "Can you give me a jump start?"

I tried, but it didn't work; the engine just wouldn't take. After the sixth try, the driver lifted his cap and smoothed down his remaining hair. "Looks like we'll have to call a tow truck."

"Is there one big enough?" I asked, eyeing the monstrous vehicle.

He shrugged. I sighed. "Well, do you want some iced tea while you're waiting? No sense standing out here in the sun."

They followed me back to the farmhouse, where I installed them in rocking chairs with glasses of tea. Then I retrieved my milk, which by now had been sitting out far too long, and checked the chickens, who had laid a lovely half dozen green and brown eggs. They were nervous nellies, and Rusty crowed repeatedly, as if telling the large interloper in the driveway that he was still in charge of his harem.

As I laid the last egg into a basket and opened the door to the chicken coop, the disturbing thought occurred to me that Rooster was right.

Of all the people I knew, I did have the most to gain from his aunt's death.

I just hoped my temporary reprieve might not be the first step on the road to prison.

The driver had informed me earlier that their supervisor had told them to hold off on any thumping until it was clear who would be responsible for the damages, which made sense. Feeling giddy with relief, I'd made the two men egg salad sandwiches from the hens' eggs and Quinn's leftover bread before melting another block of beeswax for candles. I had just poured the last mason jar candle when I heard the tow truck rumbling down the driveway, two hours and several glasses of tea later.

After adjusting the wick and replacing the pot on a cool burner, I hurried to the door.

"Thank you, ma'am, for your hospitality," the driver said, doffing his cap in an old-fashioned gesture.

"No problem," I said. "Good luck with your truck."

I stood and watched as the tow truck driver conferred with the two men. The driver climbed up into the cab one more time, evidently to test the engine once more.

The truck roared to life on the first try.

"I thought you said it was dead!" the tow truck driver said.

"It was," the man said, rubbing the top of his

balding head and looking perplexed. "Tried jumpin' it and everything."

"Well, seems to be working fine now," I said, as the driver revved the engine.

The tow truck driver grumbled a bit but backed down the long driveway anyway, followed by the thumper truck. As nice as the men were, I was glad to see the truck lumber down the driveway and out onto the road. I hoped I'd never see it again.

Chapter 9

"You must be Elsa Vogel's granddaughter." The woman behind the circulation desk peered at me through her glasses. She was probably in her late fifties, and wore her graying hair short. She had no jewelry or makeup, but her blouse was a riot of red poppies on white silk. I liked the contrast. "I'm Myrtle Crenshaw," she said. "I knew Elsa, but I don't see much resemblance between the two of you, really."

"We both like to bake and garden," I said, "but it's true; I don't much look like her." I put my purse down on the front desk of the library, which was a cozy, converted house lined with bookshelves, even if the paint scheme—pink and green—reminded me of a watermelon. Once I'd finished cleaning up after the men and picked another few quarts of dewberries for jam, I'd followed Tobias's advice and headed into town. First stop was the library, a bungalow two streets from the courthouse, shaded by tall pecan trees and bordered with a picket fence lined with impatiens in a rainbow of colors. My plan was to pay a visit to the librarian to see what I could find out about Nettie's enemies, then swing by the Blue Onion to borrow the stove and make jam.

"Heard Rooster's been after you over what happened to his aunt," Myrtle said. "Bad business."

"That's actually why I came to talk to you," I said. "Dr. Brandt suggested you might be able to help me."

"You need a book?" she asked.

"No," I said, then reconsidered. "Well, yes. If you have any books on homesteading, that would be terrific. But what I really need is some idea of who might have wanted to . . . well, you know."

Myrtle's eyes glinted as she pushed her glasses up on her nose. "Stick a bratwurst skewer into Nettie Kocurek?"

"Ah . . . yes."

"That woman was a piece of work. Sweeter than molasses pie to your face, but she did whatever she damn well pleased." The librarian covered her mouth. "Shoot. I didn't mean to cuss."

"No worries," I told her, smiling. "I understand the sentiment."

"Here's a perfect example," she said. "When she was on the library board, everybody voted against her color scheme. Guava and Avocado, if you'd believe it."

I looked behind me at the pink trim and green shelves. "Looks like Guava and Avocado won the day."

"It was six to one for Summer Sage and Dusty Peach. We asked Joe down at the Red and White for Summer Sage and Dusty Peach. The labels on the paint cans even said Summer Sage and Dusty Peach."

"Then how come it's Guava and Avocado?"

"You'd have to ask Nettie Kocurek that." Myrtle shook her head and grimaced. "I don't know how she managed it, but by the time we caught it, the whole dang place had been painted. Would have cost a fortune to redo it." She snorted. "Lucky me. Now I get a little bit of Nettie Kocurek here every time I walk in the door."

She sounded like she was still pretty hot about it, and I found myself wondering if she might have stuck a skewer into Nettie.

"So," I said. "Sounds like Nettie Kocurek had gotten under the skin of more than a few people here in Buttercup."

"You can say that again," she said.

I glanced around to make sure there was no one nearby. "Who do you think might want her dead?" I asked.

"Not to speak ill of the dead, but who wouldn't?" she asked, and leaned over the circulation desk, an old-fashioned oak store counter that had been repurposed—and, thankfully, not painted Avocado or Guava. "Whoever did her in deserves a medal, not jail time, if you ask me."

"It sounds like she was a terror."

"She was. Problem is," she said, "since you're an outsider, Rooster isn't gonna look past you.

You're easy, and with that oil business over on your farm, you've got a motive. Plus, you had a jam in the competition."

"That's why I need your help," I said, leaning forward over the antique circulation desk. "It wasn't me, but unless I can find out who did it, I'm the prime suspect."

"Oh, lots of folks had a bone to pick with her," she said. "There's Nancy Shaw, of course, over at the Bees' Knees. I know she and Nettie had it out a few times over the stuff the Kocureks are spraying on their fields."

"Nancy mentioned that when I stopped by."

"And then there's Ursula Mueller, who heads up the Daughters of the German Republic. The Kocureks and the Muellers have had a feud going on for more than half a century now," she said. Then she pursed her lips. "But I can't think why she'd wait this long to do her in."

"What was the feud over?" I asked.

"Nettie's family owned one of the two cotton gins in town; the Muellers owned the other. The Bacas—that's Nettie's maiden name—anyway, the Bacas' mill outbid the Muellers on cotton, so everybody brought their crop to the Bacas. It got so that the Muellers didn't have enough money to stay in business. You can guess who bought their land when they had to sell."

"The Bacas," I said.

"Uh-huh." She shook her head. "The Bacas

always had their fingers in other pies, so they could afford to lose money on the cotton business for a few years, but cotton was all the Muellers had. Of course, once the Mueller gin folded, the Bacas paid rock bottom prices for cotton and made a killing. They'd gotten rid of the competition, you see." She shook her head. "Lotta people still don't like them for that reason alone."

"Wow." These days, most of the fields around Buttercup were pasture, but I'd heard that fifty years ago, cotton had been king in this part of the world. "I can't imagine a cotton gin in town."

"Oh, yes. There were two, right by the railroad tracks. One's Fannie's Antiques now, and the other is Ed's Service Station. Right next to where Bessie Mae lives."

"What happened to the Muellers?"

"Ursula's head of the Daughters, of course. The family still has a small house in town and a couple of acres, but nothing like they used to."

"They're still upset about it?"

"Long memories here in Buttercup," Myrtle said. "In fact, years ago, there was at least one murder people say came out of that feud. One of the Mueller brothers wound up dead by the train tracks, shot in the chest. Police never solved it— said it must have been a hobo—but everybody in town figures one of the Bacas did him in. Rumor had it he was sweet on one of the Baca girls, and her daddy didn't like it."

"Why would they do that? They'd already run the Muellers out of business."

"There was a lot of bad blood back then," she said. "I think the Muellers weren't exactly quiet about what they thought of the Bacas—and the Kocureks, who weren't any prize package, either." She adjusted her poppy-covered blouse. "I don't know the whole story. I just know those two families get along like oil and water."

I thought about the paper that had blown down from the hayloft last night. "Was the murder back in the 1940s?" I asked.

"I think so," she said.

"I found an old newspaper in the barn that must have come out right after it happened," I said.

"It was all in the papers. A lot of excitement for Buttercup."

"Was there ever even a suspect?" I asked, curious about this half-century-old crime.

"I just don't remember," she said. "I do know it was never officially solved, though."

"Do you have the old papers on file?"

"Sadly, no. I wish I had them on microfiche here, but you know how budgeting goes; we're lucky we can afford the latest Darling Dahlia mysteries!"

"Those are terrific, aren't they?"

"The latest one just came out," she said, retrieving a hardback book from behind the counter. "Once we get you a library card, you can be the first to check it out."

"Thanks!" I said, glad for the mystery but disappointed about the lack of papers.

"If you're really interested in the murder, you might want to check out the archives at the *Zephyr*," Myrtle suggested.

"Good idea," I said. If I had time, I might drop by. "I'll bet Mandy is all in a tizzy about the latest series of events. Murder is something you just don't expect around here."

"If you do go down to the *Zephyr*, you might want to tell Mandy I heard somebody else get into it with good ol' Nettie the other day."

"Who?" I asked, my interest piqued.

"That fellow from Austin—the one with the bus that runs on fry grease? They were yowlin' like two tomcats down at the general store."

"What were they arguing about?"

"I couldn't catch all of it," she said, "but he said something about sustainable something."

"Probably has issues with the way she keeps her land," I said. "He's an organic farmer." And his land, like the Bees' Knees, was right next to one of the Kocureks' fields. "Still, that doesn't sound like it would be enough to kill someone for," I said.

"Well, somebody has it in for the Kocureks lately." Myrtle lowered her voice. "I've heard rumors someone was sabotaging their equipment.

Pouring sugar in the gas tanks at night, disabling the tractors."

"How long has this been going on?" I asked.

"A month or two," she said.

"Think it might be Nancy? Trying to keep them from spraying?"

She shrugged. "Nobody knows. But there's another thing, too."

"What?"

"Nettie wasn't too happy with one of the men her daughter was dating. Thought he was a gold digger."

"Wouldn't her daughter be, like, fifty years old?" I asked.

"Doesn't matter to Nettie," Myrtle said. "He's a distant relative of the Mueller family, which makes it even worse."

"Like Romeo and Juliet."

"Only far less attractive," Myrtle said. "And a lot older. Evidently they had a crush on each other in high school, and it took thirty-five years for either of them to do anything about it. Largely because of Nettie, I imagine."

"Love is a good thing at any age," I said. I sure hoped so; I was thirty-seven and still waiting for my Prince Charming. My mind wandered to Tobias, and the companionable time we'd spent on the porch the day before, before I yanked it back to the library. Too early for romantic fantasies. I barely knew the man, after all. And besides, my future was looking a little shaky right now.

"Poor Flora," Myrtle said. "She's spent her whole life living under her mother's thumb. I don't know how she's going to figure out what to wear without her mother to tell her."

"Based on the outfit she had on at the festival, it might not be a bad thing," I said. "Besides, it sounds like she's been finding her way pretty well lately, if she's defied her mother enough to take a suitor. She's never been married?" I asked.

"No, but from what I hear, things with Roger are getting pretty serious; he proposed a few weeks ago. Nettie wanted her daughter to get a prenup signed."

"Does the sheriff know about this?" I asked, feeling a swell of hope. Not that I wished Nettie's daughter ill; it was just that someone in Buttercup had skewered Nettie, and at least I now had an idea of who might have wanted to.

"Of course," she said. "But what's he going to do? Make his cousin—or his cousin's fiancé—a suspect?" She snorted. "You haven't been in Buttercup very long, have you?"

"Still. There are lots of people who had a bone to pick with Nettie Kocurek. You just listed . . . what, a half dozen off the top of your head?"

"And those are just the ones we know about," Myrtle said. "That woman made a career out of steamrolling everyone around her. It's a wonder no one stuck a fork in her twenty years ago."

• • •

It was early evening by the time I arrived home with two books on cheese making and three on jam, as well as a few new cozy mysteries by Ellery Adams and Susan Wittig Albert. Chuck greeted me at the door, licking my hand and then waddling back to the fridge, where he sat down with a hopeful look on his face. I fished out a cooked carrot slice, which he declined, then grabbed a few eggs from the refrigerator and a tub of the goat cheese Peter Swenson had given me in exchange for a candle at the last market. I headed outside and pulled a few spring onions and some baby spinach, then returned inside to toss them into a pan with a small knob of butter. While the veggies softened, I formed a few loose balls of goat cheese and laid them on a plate.

I thought of all the librarian had told me as I whisked a few eggs together with a bit of water. Nettie wasn't at all popular in town, it seemed. Nancy Shaw definitely had frustrations with her, but were wayward pesticides worth killing over? I knew she was protective of her bees. But how protective?

Peter Swenson was another intriguing possibility, I reflected as I added more butter to the pan, swirling it as it melted. His farm adjoined some of Nettie's property. What had they been arguing about? I wondered. He hadn't mentioned any disagreement at the Founders' Day Festival, though—and had struck me as too mild-mannered to attack an old lady with a bratwurst skewer. Still, I thought as I salted the wilted vegetables, you never could tell. Ted Bundy's neighbors always said he "seemed like a nice guy."

And then there was Nettie's daughter, Flora, and her fiancé, Roger Brubeck. Had Nettie pushed too far when she demanded Flora call it off with her beau? Had she perhaps threatened to take Flora out of the will unless she put her boyfriend aside? It sounded as if the daughter had been growing a backbone recently. And skewering someone with a bratwurst fork in the middle of a festival didn't exactly smack of planning. More passion than premeditation—although along with the risk of being discovered, the murderer was at least assured a plethora of likely suspects, since the entire town was in attendance. Had Nettie and Flora had a showdown in the jam tent? Or had Roger confronted his fiancée's mother and lost his temper?

And why, of all the jam jars in the tent, did she have to pick up mine?

I sighed and poured the eggs into the pan, pulling the edges back with a spatula as the yellow liquid began to turn custardy. If it was Flora who killed her mother, there was probably no way Rooster would ever arrest her; after all, she was his cousin.

I poured the veggies into the pan with the eggs

111

and laid the goat cheese rounds on top of them, then flipped the pan so that the omelet folded over and cooked it for another minute. As I eased the golden omelet onto a plate, another cool breeze wafted through the kitchen, raising goose bumps on my arm. The paper on the table flipped open with a rustle. Chuck barked once, then settled back down in front of the fridge.

The paper had flipped open to the article on Thomas Mueller's death.

Chapter 10

I set down my plate and took a deep breath. For a moment, I fancied I caught a whiff of my grandmother's lavender scent in the air; then I glanced at the article again, shaking my head at my active imagination. Doubtless the air conditioning had just kicked on. And there was nothing unusual about an old paper being stuffed up in an old hayloft. Chuck had probably just barked at a noise.

Even so, I found myself combing the article more carefully as I ate my omelet, which was a delicious mix of creamy and crisp, with the tang of goat cheese and a welcome touch of bitterness from the spinach. I smoothed the paper out as I read. Was there something relevant in the yellowed pages? It did, after all, involve the murder of one of the Bacas' rivals: an odd coincidence, to be sure. Thomas Mueller, twenty-five years old, had been discovered next to the train tracks in Gruenwald, the next town on the rail line, with multiple contusions and a hole in his chest that appeared to have been caused by a shotgun. His wallet was missing. According to the article, the theory was that he had been robbed by a hobo or a migrant train worker. He was survived by parents, Tom and Uschi Mueller, and two sisters.

The article gave facts, but little else. Had more been discovered later on?

I forked up another bite of omelet, ignoring Chuck, who had now stationed himself at my feet, and chewed it thoughtfully. It was odd that there should be two unsolved murders—and that the paper detailing the first had been the only one left in the barn. Had my grandparents kept it for some reason?

And if so, why?

I finished my omelet and set the plate down for Chuck to lick—after all, a few smears of goat cheese couldn't be that bad for him, I told myself—then grabbed a flashlight and headed out the screened door. I had assumed the paper was a random dropping from the past, but what if it weren't? What if there was something else up there? Something that maybe linked my grandparents to Thomas Mueller's murder?

The thought made my stomach churn.

The barn was silhouetted against the sky—a tapestry of peach, orange, and gold fading to a deep, almost robin's egg–blue—and a warm breeze brought the scent of my grandmother's roses to me on the evening air as I stepped outside. Chuck sniffed the air appreciatively, glad to be at my side. Normally, I'd leave him behind, but since Blossom wasn't near the barn, I decided to take him with me for moral support.

He trotted a few feet behind me, pausing to

water a tuft of grass, then panted as he hurried to catch up. I was pleased that he showed no hesitation as I opened the barn door—in fact, he seemed to view the whole expedition as an olfactory field trip and immediately started snuffling around the perimeter. I, on the other hand, headed to the ladder leading to the hayloft. If there was some sort of eerie presence in the barn, my chubby poodle wasn't picking up on it.

With my confidence boosted slightly by Chuck's nonchalance, I tucked the flashlight into the waistband of my shorts and climbed the ladder, then clambered onto the loft, where I shone the light into the dim corners of the space.

From what I could see, nothing had changed since the last time I was up here. The pile of hay and mouse droppings still littered the floor, and the windows were still painted shut. The air was warm and still, making me wonder yet again where that stray breeze had come from. The boards creaked ominously as I walked; Chuck, evidently not noticing that I had adjourned to the upper level, growled. I hushed him gently and pushed the straw around with my feet, wondering where the newspaper could possibly have come from.

Dust poofed up in clouds as I shifted hay with the toe of my boot. As I lifted one wad of hay, a small furry body skittered away, and I almost jumped out of the hayloft. I uncovered several more mice as I pushed through the straw—was the hay from 1940, too? I found myself wondering—and was about to give up when my toe hit something solid tucked up into a corner, between two studs.

I cleared the straw away to reveal a metal lockbox. It was mint green, heavy, and about the size of a shoebox, with a keyhole at one end. I tried the lid, but it was locked. The box wasn't empty, though; when I picked it up and shook it gently, I could hear something solid slide back and forth, hitting the metal sides. Unfortunately, the key was nowhere to be seen.

I sifted through the dusty hay for another twenty minutes, searching for the key, until the sunlight seeping through the dirty, cobwebbed windows faded to nothing, and the narrow flashlight beam was pretty much the sole source of illumination. I pushed the last of the dry straw aside and sneezed. If it was here, it wasn't where I was going to find it—at least not tonight.

With the flashlight tucked into my shorts and the box under one arm, I climbed back down into the dimly lit barn to join Chuck, who was eyeing me with concern. Blossom snorted from just outside the barn; it must be milking time. The cow formerly known as #82 might be an escape artist, I thought to myself, but at least I didn't have to track her down twice a day. She didn't like to miss meals.

I took the box and Chuck back to the house, then returned to the barn, where I pulled the string on the sixty-watt bulb that dangled from the tall ceiling and opened the door that led to the pasture. Blossom came readily, walking into her stall and nosing around, looking for cow chow.

As I milked her, my thoughts kept turning to the hayloft. Who had left a lockbox up there—and what was in it? My mind turned to the breeze that had blown the newspaper down the day before. Almost as if the barn had wanted me to find it. Did the lockbox have something to do with the unsolved murder by the railroad tracks? How long had it been in the hayloft? And why had no one found it earlier?

After finishing up with Blossom and turning her out to pasture, I turned off the light and lugged my bucket of milk to the house, where I poured it into sterilized jugs and stowed it in the refrigerator. The milking chores done, I turned my attention back to the box, which I'd left on the kitchen table.

I attacked it with a screwdriver, a hammer, and finally even a saw, but the box refused to give up its secrets. Frustrated, I stowed it on a shelf above the fridge and looked at the old newspaper once more, my eyes skimming over the article.

A Mueller and a Kocurek dead, both at someone else's hands. Were the two connected somehow?

I'd have to ask Quinn about it tomorrow, I

decided, and headed up the creaky stairs to the small bedroom with its homemade quilt and the nightstand my grandmother had painted blue thirty years ago.

"I hear Rooster wasn't impressed with our discovery," I told Quinn the next morning as I handed her a carton of eggs. Now that the hens were laying, I was sharing the wealth with friends.

"Nope," she said. "But I did convince him to go and collect the jam jar and the pin."

"How did you do that?"

"I suggested the paper might like to hear about the evidence the sheriff had missed," she said with a slight shrug as she put the eggs into the refrigerator.

"I'll bet that went over well."

"At least he collected the evidence," she said. "Whether or not he'll do anything with it is something else again."

"Does he have any suspects other than me?" I asked.

"Not that I've heard," Quinn said. Her curly hair was tied up in a frizzy knot on top of her head today, and the kitchen smelled deliciously of cinnamon, yeast, and maple syrup. She wore a yellow checked shirt and denim shorts that made her look like she was sixteen. "I heard he stopped by your place, but Dr. Brandt scared him off."

"How did you know that?" I asked.

"Small town," she said, measuring confectioner's sugar into a large mixing bowl and glancing up at me. "I also heard you owe Rooster a new pair of pants."

"Yeah," I said. "Chuck kind of went crazy—like Rooster was a threat to me. I've never seen him act like that around anyone else."

"His instinct's good," Quinn said. "Rooster always gave me the creeps in high school." She shivered. "When I told him I wouldn't go to the prom, he started spreading nasty rumors about me. And his wife sure does end up with a lot of bruises." She gave me a pointed look.

I thought of Crystal Kocurek. She was a nice-looking woman, with a nervous habit of twisting her light-brown hair between her fingers when you talked to her. She did wear a lot of makeup. I had always attributed it to personal taste, but now I wondered if she might have a different motive. Had she used it to cover the signs of abuse? I hadn't noticed any bruises, but we'd only met a few times—and besides, I didn't know what to look for. But Quinn had spent three years married to an abusive spouse. If anyone knew the signs, she would.

"Has she ever reported him?" I asked.

Quinn sighed. "Who would she report him to? He's the sheriff."

"That's awful," I said. "We should do something about it!"

"I've tried to talk to her, but she doesn't want to hear it," Quinn said, adding a teaspoon of maple extract to the bowl. "She won't even come here for lunch anymore."

"How does a man like Rooster end up in that kind of position?" I asked.

"Family connections," she said, adding a dab of butter and turning on the beaters. "Nepotism."

"No wonder Chuck went after his pants. The pecan tree by the driveway dropped a limb on his car, too. It's almost like the farm doesn't like him."

"Your grandmother never liked Rooster, either."

"Was it because he was Nettie's nephew?"

"No," she said. "There were a few issues up at the farm—someone was messing with her chickens. Turns out it was Rooster and a couple of his buddies."

"What did she do?"

"Fired a few rounds from a shotgun in the air next time she caught them." Quinn grinned. "They never came back."

"I'll bet not," I said, trying to imagine my grandmother with a shotgun in her hands. I'd grown up with a kind, generous woman who was a whiz in the kitchen and kept everything on the farm humming, seemingly without effort. It was hard to imagine her with a shotgun, but she was nothing if not practical. I imagined if that was the only way she could come up with to keep kids from messing with her chickens, she'd do it.

"I'd watch your back, if I were you."

"Thanks," I said, thinking I did need to stop by the station with a check. I just hoped Rooster would let me leave again. "On the plus side, the attorney told me they can't drill on my land until Nettie's will is probated."

"Think Flora will go forward with it now that her mama's gone?" Quinn asked. A timer buzzed; she turned it off and pulled a tray of fragrant, golden-brown twists out of the oven. My mouth watered, but I knew it was best to wait until she'd glazed them.

"You'd know better than me," I said. "How's she taking it?" I asked, still staring at the tray of golden pastry. It was no wonder people came from as far as La Grange to sample Quinn's wares.

"Hasn't left the house, from what I hear."

I looked up sharply. "Guilt, or grief?"

"Could be both," she said. "She's been under her mama's thumb for so long it may be she doesn't know how to get out the front door."

"How'd she ever end up with a boyfriend, then?"

"Flora's been sweet on Roger since high school. She saw him in town after church one Sunday when her mother wasn't well. He asked her to dinner, and it just kind of went from there."

"Does she go to the Brethren Church?" I asked.

The local folks of Moravian—that is, Czech— descent attended the hundred-plus-year-old church at the corner of Kramer Lane and Giddings Road. Since Dewberry Farm was on Kramer Lane, I passed the small, white wooden building with its short steeple every time I came into town. I'd seen Nettie's enormous Cadillac there more than once.

"That's the one," Quinn said, turning on the beaters and running a spatula around the bowl. My mouth watered as the sugar, milk, butter, and maple extract were transformed into a thick creamy glaze.

"And Roger Brubeck's German, right?"

"His father's German," she said, "but his mother's a Czech. Last name was Zapalac."

"If he was half Czech, what was Nettie's problem with him?"

"He's still German—and a Mueller, besides," Quinn shrugged. "It was worse during the wars, but there's still a lot of bad blood in some families."

I would never understand small-town prejudices, I decided. "Speaking of the Brethren Church, Rooster said something about that lamb pin we found," I said, tearing my eyes from the glaze Quinn was making. "He suggested I'd planted it to throw suspicion on one of the Brethren."

"Of course he would."

"What does the lamb represent?"

"It's the lamb of God, just like it is in all churches," Quinn told me.

"So what does it have to do with the Moravians?"

"It's the particular symbol of the Brethren," she said. "I think it has something to do with God's grace."

I leaned forward. "So whoever killed Nettie was one of the Brethren."

"If the pin came from the murderer, then it's likely, yes."

I thought of the scrap of fabric attached to it. "And he—or she—was wearing red." I cast my mind back, trying to remember who had been dressed in crimson. Unfortunately, it being Founders' Day, just about half the town had been in some shade of red. Had I seen that gold pin anywhere?

"Unfortunately, Rooster's right—there's no way to know. Lots of people were in and out of that tent."

"But someone ripped it off of a shirt or a dress. Who would do that if they weren't defending themselves?"

"True," she said. "But we can't prove it."

I sighed. "I just wish they'd do DNA testing on that jam jar."

"Not in the budget, Rooster told me."

"Whoever she hit is likely to have a cut or bruise, though, don't you think?"

"Yes—but it could be covered by clothes, or if she hit him or her in the head, it might be hidden under hair."

"You're a regular ray of sunshine today, Quinn."

"Sorry," she said, pulling another tray out of the oven and putting it on a cooling rack. I realized suddenly that she was looking more tired than usual; there were circles under her eyes, and her face was wan.

"You don't look like yourself this morning. Is everything okay?" I asked.

"Just fine," she said, but her voice was tight.

"You don't sound fine." She said nothing. "Does this have something to do with Jed calling?"

She let out a burst of air. "Yeah. It shouldn't bother me, but it does."

"Don't you have a restraining order against him?"

She nodded. "He's been calling a lot in the last few weeks. At three in the morning. Drunk." Her lips tightened into a thin line as she picked up the glaze-filled mixing bowl.

"What does he want?"

She looked at me as if I had asked her what color the sky was. "To apologize, of course. To tell me he's changed." She thwacked the bowl onto the counter. "And, of course, to ask for a loan."

"I thought he was from a wealthy family."

"Evidently his parents have cut him off. He seems to have a bit of a gambling problem."

"Liquor, too, if he's drunk-dialing you. What did you tell him?"

"What do you think? There's no way I'm giving him five thousand dollars. Even if I wanted to, I couldn't. I'm just scraping by as it is." A shadow passed over her face, and I felt a cold lump form in my stomach.

"He threatened you, didn't he?"

She turned around quickly—but not so quickly I didn't see the fear in her eyes. "He told me he needed five thousand dollars," she said quietly, still turned away from me. "And that if I didn't lend it to him, he might have to come and take it."

I shivered. "Quinn, that's awful. Did you tell Rooster?"

"What good would that do?" She turned around to face me, looking more upset than I'd ever seen her. I could understand why. Jed Stadtler was six foot two, with the physique of a linebacker and the temper of a two-year-old. He'd put Quinn in the hospital twice, and had abused her badly enough that even his family's high-paid attorneys couldn't keep Quinn from getting a restraining order. "Rooster's still got a grudge from high school. Besides, it's not like Buttercup's got enough cops they can spare one to guard me every night."

"Stay with me, then, out at the farm," I offered. "He won't know where you are, and Chuck will warn us if he turns up."

125

She looked up at me. "What if he comes and destroys the shop?"

"If he wants you to lend him money, why would he threaten your livelihood?"

She snorted. "That implies he's capable of rational thought."

"You have insurance if anything happens," I said, hoping she would take me up on my offer and come stay with me for a few days. I knew what Jed had done to her before, and I hated the thought of it happening again. "Shops can be replaced. You can't."

She bit her lip and considered it for a moment, then let out a long sigh. "Thanks for the offer, Lucy, but I don't want to turn tail just because Jed decided to be a jerk. He's spent too many years controlling my life already."

"I understand," I said. I would hate having to leave my space because someone threatened me physically; it would bother me to hand over that power. On the other hand, I hated the thought of anything happening to my friend even more. If she didn't tell Rooster what was going on, I definitely would—even if he did think I was a murderer.

"Can I think about it?" she asked.

"My door is always open," I said. "But no matter what you decide, I'd definitely tell Rooster. If for no other reason than to document that your ex is defying the restraining order."

"I'll call him," she promised, glancing at the back door of the bakery. "I think I may have a dead bolt installed, too."

I followed her eyes to the back door. Nothing would stop an angry man from shoving his hand through the glass pane of the half-light door and unlocking a dead bolt, but I didn't say anything.

"So," she said, turning back to me with a forced smile, "now that that's settled, do you want one of these maple twists?" She scooped up a spatula of creamy maple glaze and began slathering it onto the tray of pastry.

Everything was far from settled, and both Quinn and I knew it. But I smiled as if nothing was wrong and said, "I thought you'd never ask."

Chapter 11

I was still worried about Quinn when I pulled into a parking space in front of the sheriff's office a few minutes later. It was only a few blocks from the Blue Onion—I could have walked—but by 11:00 a.m., it was already getting warm. Although Quinn had promised me she'd tell Rooster about Jed's threat, I wanted to make sure they knew to keep an eye on the bakery.

Besides, I still had to write a check for a new pair of polyester pants.

The station looked more like a house than a sheriff's office; it was a small white bungalow, its front door painted a cheerful red. The wood door stuck a bit as I pushed it open, and a small bell jingled above my head.

A woman looked up from a big metal desk on which were arrayed a number of photos of children—grandchildren, I was guessing—alongside a bowl of cinnamon apple potpourri that made the station smell disconcertingly like a gift shop. A country singer warbled about his cheating girlfriend from a small radio on the windowsill.

"You must be Lucy Resnick," the woman said, smiling at me. Her hair was short and professionally styled into a halo of hair-sprayed blonde curls, and large turquoise earrings dangled from her ears. Her thin lips were painted cotton-candy pink. "Your grandma taught me how to play bridge, you know." She took off her reading glasses and squinted at me. "Aren't you just cute as a button!"

"Thanks," I said.

"I'm Opal Gruber," she said, smiling up at me. "I do my best to keep Rooster in line here at the station. Keep the files organized, answer the phone . . . you know."

"I'm sure he appreciates the help. Especially with the loss of his aunt. He asked me to come in," I said, not mentioning that he wanted to question me, although I was sure she already knew.

"He's out on a call right now, I'm afraid."

"Tell him I stopped by, please. Is he holding up okay?" I asked.

"Oh, you know Rooster," she said.

I didn't, but just smiled and nodded. "Any new developments?"

She seemed to close up a bit. "You'll have to ask Rooster; he likes to keep that stuff close to the vest, if you know what I mean. Tragedy for him, though."

"Were they close?"

"They were family," she said, neatly evading the question. "It's funny you should turn up here, though. Heard a lot about you this week."

My stomach did a little flip-flop, but I pasted

on what I hoped was a relaxed smile. "Hopefully all about how good my dewberry jam is."

"Not much about your jam, to be honest, although I understand you took a silver," she said. "I hear your dog had a run-in with the sheriff's pants." She cocked an eyebrow at me.

I held up a checkbook. "That's part of the reason I'm here," I said.

"If you want to talk about evidence, your friend Quinn came in and told him all about what you two found down by where the jam tent was."

"Good," I said. "Did he go back and pick it up, or send any of it to a lab?"

"He did, but he wasn't too happy about it," she said. "Said it was a waste of time, since he wasn't even sure it was evidence."

Of course. At least he'd sent it to the lab, I told myself, trying to boost my sinking spirits.

"Anyway," Opal continued, "you'll be wanting to know how much a new pair of pants will cost." She put on her reading glasses and flipped through a notebook on her desk. "Let's see. I looked it up this morning: forty-two waist—used to be thirty-eights, but he's been hittin' the pecan pie a bit hard these past couple of years—khaki polyester. That'll be forty-eight dollars and fifty-three cents," she said, looking up at me over the rims of her glasses.

I blinked. "Forty-eight dollars? For a pair of polyester pants?"

"He likes a certain style," she said. "Fits him better in the seat."

I wrote out the check and handed it to her, trying not to think about the balance of my checking account and reflecting that it might not be a bad idea to stop by the *Buttercup Zephyr* and ask about a job after all. "Will the sheriff be back after his call?" I asked.

"He has a lunch meeting," she said. "Should be back in about an hour. Would you like to leave a message for him?"

I considered coming back for the sake of privacy but, based on everything Opal had just told me, decided that was probably pointless. "I just wanted to let him know that Quinn's had some difficulty with her ex; he's been asking for money and threatening her, calling at all hours. She's got a restraining order against him, and he's violating it."

Opal's eyes got big. "I knew she never should have married him. Easy on the eyes, of course, but that temper of his! Runs in the family," she said. "His daddy was just as bad."

"I think she wants to keep this quiet," I said, already regretting that I'd told her.

"Oh, of course!" She mimed locking her mouth and tossing the key over a well-padded shoulder. It was not convincing. "Tell her she needs to come in and file a complaint," Opal said.

"I hope she will. In the meantime, could you ask Rooster to keep an eye on the bakery?"

"Don't you worry, sugar," she said. "Rooster'll make sure nothing happens to your friend."

"Thanks for passing it on. I'll ask Quinn to come down to the station when she gets a minute."

"You do that." She tucked the check into a little blue lockbox. "I'll tell Rooster you dropped by. I'm sure he'll be real interested to hear it."

I'll bet he would, I thought with a chill of foreboding. I could feel Opal's eyes on me all the way to the truck.

Before heading back to the farm, I decided to swing by the office of the *Zephyr*. The offices were lodged in a pink, brick 1950s ranch several blocks from the center of town. In the front yard, a sign advertising *The Buttercup Zephyr, est. 1876* swung in the breeze. Although the building was far from picturesque, it was well taken care of, with trailing rosemary flanking the brick walk and pink-blooming hawthorn under the windows. A plastic hummingbird feeder was stuck to one of the windows with suction cups.

Although it was being used as an office, the interior had a homey feel. The entry hall had a coat rack and a table on which recent issues of the *Buttercup Zephyr* were mixed with *Southern Living*, *Good Housekeeping*, and *Texas Monthly*.

"Hello?" I called, peering into the room to the

right of the entry hall—formerly a dining room, I guessed, now an office with a blonde wood corner desk covered in neatly stacked papers.

"Be there in a sec!" a woman called. She appeared a moment later, holding a tall glass of iced tea in one hand and an iPhone in the other. I was surprised to see she was about my age, with black shiny hair cut into a bob. When she spotted me, her pleasant smile flickered for a second, replaced by something else. Curiosity? Or suspicion? "I was wondering when you'd pay us a call," she said, setting down her iPhone and extending her right hand. "I'm Mandy Vargas, editor of the *Zephyr*."

"Lucy Resnick," I said, shaking her hand. Her skin was cool and dry.

"What can I do for you?" she asked.

"I wanted to introduce myself," I said. "And let you know if you're ever in need of freelance work, I might be able to help out."

"You worked for the *Houston Chronicle*, didn't you?"

"For fifteen years," I said.

"Took the buyout and got out of Dodge, I hear," she said. "Can I get you a glass of iced tea? We can sit on the back porch—the roses aren't in full bloom yet, of course, but it's still nice out there."

"Thanks," I said, following her back to the kitchen, which featured mustard countertops and bright green cabinets. For some reason, although the finishes were obviously dated, the effect was homey and comfortable. I looked around; it really did feel more like a house than an office.

"Sugar and lemon?"

"Just plain," I said. I took the glass and followed her out to the back patio, where we perched on metal chairs at a small, bistro-style table. The view was lovely; the backyard had been fenced, and Carolina jessamine trailed over the wooden slats. Pansies and nasturtiums bloomed in pots around the patio, and although they were nearing the end of their growing season, they still looked like bright jewels. A mountain laurel perfumed the air with its grape Kool-Aid scented blossoms, and I could hear the bees buzzing as they gathered nectar. Were they from Nancy Shaw's hives? I wondered.

"Beautiful yard," I said to Mandy. "You must like to garden."

She was seated across from me and had carried a pen and a notepad with her, I noticed. "I do. I love being able to work outside," she said, crossing her jean-clad legs. Evidently the *Zephyr* wasn't big on formal business attire. Mandy looked very comfortable in a button-down red blouse, a white camisole, and form-fitting blue jeans. She must work out, I thought, conscious of the few extra pounds I'd gained since moving to Buttercup. As much time as I spent working around the farm, it wasn't enough to counteract Quinn's generosity with the maple twists and homemade bread.

"Isn't it just lovely out here?" Mandy asked. "It won't last, but the flowers are always so beautiful —and fragrant."

"They are," I said. "I love all the pinks and blues and purples this time of year. It tends to all turn to yellows and oranges when it heats up, doesn't it?"

She nodded and turned her gaze from the mountain laurel to me, an appraising look behind her pleasant smile. "How are you finding Buttercup? A little different from Houston, I imagine."

"It's a nice change," I said. "I fell in love with the town when I was a girl visiting my grand-mother, and I still feel the same way."

"Do you?" she asked. She paused. "I understand Rooster Kocurek questioned you yesterday regarding Nettie Kocurek."

"He did," I said guardedly.

She picked up the pen and turned to a fresh page in her notepad. "Mind if I ask you a few questions about that?"

"I'd really rather you didn't, to be honest."

"Are you a suspect, then?"

"No," I said, too quickly.

"A person of interest, at least?"

"If so, he didn't tell me. I'm afraid you'll have

to take that up with Sheriff Kocurek. I know as much about her death as you do." I took a sip of my tea and leaned back in my chair, determined not to let her throw me. The last thing I needed was an article in the paper about how Mandy had interviewed the prime suspect in the death of Nettie Kocurek. In fact, I was surprised she hadn't started grilling me already; it seemed small-town reporters were nicer than their city colleagues. Perhaps dropping by the office of the local paper hadn't been such a good idea, I realized belatedly.

"I understand you found a few bits of evidence the sheriff overlooked."

"Like I said, I don't think I should talk about that. It might interfere with the investigation."

"So you did find something."

"You'll have to talk with Sheriff Kocurek about that." I leaned forward, anxious to change the subject. "Opal Gruber says you've got copies of the *Zephyr* all the way back to when the paper started."

"We do," she said. "Up in the attic. Why?"

"I found an old newspaper in the barn," I said. "It had to do with the death of a man named Mueller. It seemed like a funny coincidence, what with the Muellers and the Kocureks being rivals, and I wanted to find out more about it."

"You know, I remember hearing about that," she said, distracted from the more recent murder—at least for the time being. "People talked about it for years. Down by the railroad tracks in Gruenwald, wasn't it?"

"It was in 1940," I said, and took a sip of my tea. A blue jay alighted on a small bird feeder dangling from the mountain laurel, then noticed us and flew off in a hurry.

"Do you think the two deaths might be connected?" Mandy asked, and I could see the curiosity sparking in her eyes. Good. If she linked the crime back to one that had happened more than half a century ago, maybe she'd think about finding someone else to suspect.

"I don't know," I said. "It just seemed like an odd coincidence." I didn't tell her about the eerie breeze that had blown it down out of the hayloft.

"Lots of history at Dewberry Farm," Mandy said. "Some folks even say it's haunted."

Chapter 12

I swallowed. "Haunted? What do you mean?"

"After Nettie bought the place from your grandmother, she moved her sister, Berta, into it. She didn't last two nights."

"What happened?"

"She said there were all kinds of noises—and that she didn't feel welcome. In fact, she told Nettie that somebody kicked her out of bed one night."

I almost choked on my tea. "You're kidding me. Really?"

"Really." Mandy's voice was animated. Now that she wasn't interrogating me, she was warming up to me. "It was very exciting at the time; the grapevine was very active."

"I'll bet," I said.

"She ended up in a home with a serious case of dementia not long after that, though, so I wouldn't put much stock in it. I wondered if there wasn't something to it at the time, but in retrospect, I'm just guessing she didn't want to live there." She looked at me with dark eyes. "Still, rumors do fly—Nettie couldn't find anyone to buy the place after that." She jiggled the ice cubes in her tea, then slid her eyes up to me. "You haven't had any paranormal experiences, have you?"

"No," I said quickly. I wasn't comfortable talking about the newspaper and the hayloft, which was probably just coincidence. "I sometimes think I can feel my grandmother there, though," I amended. "I get a warm, comforting feeling, and I can almost smell the lavender she used to wear." I shrugged. "Although it could just be the good memories I have associated with the place."

"She seemed to be a wonderful woman, from the little I knew of her. But your grandmother couldn't have been the ghost—she was still alive when Berta moved in."

"Maybe Grandpa Vogel kicked her out of bed," I said, half jokingly.

She laughed, tipping her head back. "Wouldn't surprise me. He didn't like the Bacas—or the Kocureks—much, that's for sure."

"No?" I asked. "I know he and Nettie had some problems, but what was his issue with the rest of the family?"

"I think your grandfather thought they were destroying the fabric of the town. He didn't like the way the Bacas had pushed the Muellers out of the cotton business. And the Kocureks charged crazy rent to anyone they didn't like. Almost chased my parents' restaurant out of town, until my dad bought his own building out on Pecan Street."

"You mean Rosita's?" I asked.

She smiled. "Yup. I grew up in that restaurant. When they first opened, it was hard to get business —they didn't serve Czech or German food—but once people tasted my mother's enchiladas suizas, they couldn't get enough of them. And when my father got a liquor license and started selling margaritas . . ." She grinned. "Always a line for a table. They come all the way from La Grange for his frozen strawberry 'ritas."

"Why didn't Nettie like your parents?" I asked.

Mandy gave me a crooked grin. "Maybe because they don't serve kolaches."

For such an unassuming-looking old lady, I thought, Nettie Kocurek had been pretty darned nasty. "Who else did she raise the rents on?" I asked. "Maybe that's something Sheriff Kocurek should be looking into."

"He won't listen to suggestions," she said, "but I could always ask around. It's been a while since I've had a chance to do any investigative reporting."

"Where were you before you came to the *Zephyr*?" I asked.

"I worked for the *Dallas Morning News*," she said. "I did the crime beat for two years before I couldn't handle it anymore, and moved on to covering local politics. When the job came up at the *Zephyr*, I took it." She shrugged. "My parents aren't getting any younger. They'll need someone here to look after them."

"They're lucky to have you," I said.

"I'm lucky to have them," she said, then took a last swig of her tea and stood up. "Well, I hate to run, but I've got some phone calls to make. It was nice to meet you, Lucy."

"You too, Mandy," I said. "Before I leave, though, mind if I take a look through the archives?"

Mandy glanced at her watch. "I don't have time to dig right now, but can you come back tomorrow afternoon?"

"Sure," I said. "How about two o'clock?"

"I'll put it on my calendar," she said, tapping on her iPhone.

"Thanks. And if you need any freelance work done, please keep me in mind."

She hesitated for a fraction of a second, then smiled. "I will."

Blossom was still in the pasture when I got home in midafternoon, loaded down with a bag of groceries along with another fresh loaf of Quinn's bread and a small box of maple twists, half of which I'd already eaten. To my relief, the thumper truck wasn't back in my driveway—and the sheriff's car wasn't, either.

Chuck came trotting out of the bedroom as I tossed the ground beef I'd gotten on sale into the freezer and lined up a few pale tomatoes on the windowsill. I stowed the maple twists in a basket at the end of the counter, then cut two thin slices of the bread and layered on some of the turkey I'd bought that afternoon at the store. I was able to use lettuce from the garden behind the house, but the tomatoes were nowhere near ripe. I hated spending money on groceries, but I didn't want to live on eggs, milk, and lettuce alone.

It seemed counterintuitive for a farmer to buy meat at the grocery store, but all the books on homesteading I'd read advised me to start slow, so I'd winnowed my beginning farm down to a few varieties of vegetables, some chickens, and a cow, supplemented by home crafts such as jam making, candles, and soap. I made a mental note to stop by and ask Peter Swenson about raising goats; they seemed to do well without a lot of upkeep.

Although I'd planned my budget carefully and still had a nice nest egg in the bank, the unexpected expenditures I'd had the last week— attorneys, for starters, not to mention buying a new pair of pants for the sheriff—had been unsettling. If the last several days were an indicator of things to come, I needed to find more ways to bring cash in the door if I had any hope of making a go of the farm.

I could always make more of my candles—they were always popular—and soon, the next crop of lettuce would be ready for the market. But the dewberries wouldn't last forever, and I needed to make sure the peaches didn't fall prey to some disease or pest.

I spread some mayonnaise on my sandwich, grabbed a handful of dewberries from the blue bowl in the refrigerator, and settled myself at my grandmother's table, Chuck stationed optimistically at my feet. A part-time job would certainly take some of the pressure off, at least until I could get the cheese-making part of the enterprise together. I had enough acreage for two cows, according to my research, assuming we didn't have a major drought. Should I plan to get another? I could count on twelve ounces of cheese per gallon of milk, evidently, which was just over two pounds a day. If I managed to sell it for $8 a pound, that was maybe $200 per week—$400 with a second cow.

Which would cover about two hours of attorneys' fees.

It would be a good idea to pick up a bit of freelancing work, I thought as I bit into my sandwich. I knew from my research that many homesteaders supplemented their small farm income with outside work. Unfortunately, the look on Mandy Vargas's face told me that wasn't going to happen until my name was cleared in the case of Nettie Kocurek.

I finished my sandwich, tossing a scrap of turkey to Chuck, and made a plan for the rest of the day as I washed the plate and put it in the dish drainer. I didn't have a part-time job at the moment, but I could pick dewberries and make another batch of my (now silver-medalist) dewberry jam. I could also make a few more pounds of cheese from the milk that had been collecting in the refrigerator—plus, it was time to water and weed the gardens. If I was feeling particularly energetic, I could clean out the chicken coop, too. I still had several batches of soap, so soap making could wait, but it wouldn't hurt to whip up some more candles. I'd also seen a recipe for natural beeswax lip balm I'd wanted to try; if I liked it, I could sell it alongside the soaps and candles.

Feeling more optimistic now that I had a plan, I grabbed the tin bucket I kept by the back door, slipped on my boots, and headed outside to the garden, Chuck waddling behind me.

I checked the lettuce and arugula for aphids— none so far, thankfully—and set up the sprinklers, thankful that at least it was well water, so I wasn't racking up a big utility bill. I'd have plenty of beautiful lettuce—red oak leaf, deliciously bitter arugula, green leaf lettuce, and my favorite, "Freckles," which was pale green with red polka dots—to sell at the next market on Saturday. The larkspur was doing well, too—I should be able to sell bunches for weeks, and the zinnias I'd planted were starting to come up for bouquets later in the summer.

Should I consider doing one of the Wednesday markets, too? I wondered. Or maybe we could start one here in Buttercup. Another question for Peter the goat farmer, I decided, turning from the lettuce and inspecting the cucumber vines that were poking up out of the soil, looking for any sign of squash bugs, the dreaded orange prehistoric-looking insects that could devastate a cucumber crop in days. I was looking forward to making and selling my grandmother's half-sour pickle chips. The tomatoes, too, were thriving, growing lush in their metal cages. I surveyed the lines of plants, flourishing in my care, with a feeling of hope and satisfaction. This land had sustained my grandparents. I'd spent years learning how to grow vegetables and take care of chickens.

I'd make it, wouldn't I?

I looked down at Chuck, who was blissfully unaware of the concerns swirling around both me and the farm like a summer storm, and rubbed his head. If I didn't figure out who had killed Nettie Kocurek, chances were I'd be in jail or dead broke from paying a criminal defense attorney.

Possibly both.

Chapter 13

I finished my chores and ended the day in the milking parlor, where Blossom produced a healthy two gallons before strolling back out to the pasture. Tobias's fence fix had held, and she hadn't gone gallivanting since her trip to town, but I knew from the insolent swish of her tail as she stepped out of the barn that I hadn't heard the last of Harriet Houdini.

The scent of my grandmother's antique roses perfumed the air as I walked back to the farmhouse, the full bucket swinging in my hand. Despite the beauty around me, though, I was preoccupied with the issue of Nettie Kocurek.

While it was possible that the unsolved murder of Thomas Mueller was related to Nettie's death, it seemed like a long shot. I still planned to stop by the *Zephyr* the next afternoon, though.

I put the milk in the fridge and pulled out the two pints of strawberries I had picked earlier that afternoon from the small patch I'd planted near the fence. I popped one into my mouth and almost groaned with pleasure; unlike the Styrofoam-flavored berries I usually got from the store, these were the perfect mix of sweet and tart. I reached for my grandmother's cookbook; as if it knew what I wanted, it opened right to Strawberry Custard Pie.

I smiled, remembering eating a big slice of that sweet-tart, creamy pie on an early summer evening, a mason jar filled with fireflies on the pine table beside me. I scanned the recipe, then set about assembling the ingredients. Eggs and milk were no problem, that was for sure; I had plenty of strawberries, too. I just needed to whip up a crust, and my grandmother's kitchen would be filled with the heavenly scent of pie in no time.

As I measured flour into a bowl, my mind turned back to the problem of Nettie Kocurek's death. I thought of those closest to her: her daughter, Flora, topped that list. Although she'd evidently lived under her mother's thumb for half a century, the fact that she was branching out and dating a man her mother considered unsuitable was definitely a mark of burgeoning—if belated—independence. Was it enough for Flora to put her mother out of commission? I wondered. If Mama threatened to change her will, I decided, it might be. If given the choice between her mother and her lover, might Flora have chosen her lover?

I scooped shortening into a measuring cup and mused on the fact that I knew very little about Roger, other than the fact that Nettie didn't like him. He was a definite possibility, too. Although he and Flora had been quite obviously attached during the Founders' Day Festival, could it be that he didn't want Flora without her substantial inheritance?

Peter Swenson, too, had evidently had it out with Nettie over something. Was it over her less-than-organic farming practices? If so, would that be worth killing over? It was hard to imagine, but strange things did happen, and I couldn't afford to discount anything. Nancy Shaw had been unhappy, too; Nettie's pesticide use had been affecting her livelihood. Had her refusal to stop spraying poison driven Nancy to murder?

And then there was the Moravian lamb pin Quinn and I had found near where Nettie had been killed. It looked as if it had been ripped from clothing; something a woman defending herself might have done. If so, that seemed to take Peter out of the equation; after all, he was of avowed German heritage, not Czech. Nancy Shaw didn't sound Czech either, and Roger Brubeck was German through and through; he'd been wearing lederhosen that day, after all. And the pin had only been given out to people attending the Czech church. I remembered Flora wearing a bright red fancy outfit; had she worn a pin on her dress?

I patted the dough in the pie plate and tucked it into the oven, then set to work on the custard part of the pie, cracking an egg into a bowl and mixing it with sugar, butter, and flour. When the piecrust was ready, I hulled the strawberries and folded them into the batter, then poured them into the crust. I tucked the pie into the oven, a vintage white Frigidaire from the '50s—the same oven the pie my grandmother made had been baked in, all those years ago.

I washed the bowls and mixers as the pie baked; before long, a heavenly scent filled the kitchen, and Chuck moved from the rug in front of the refrigerator to a spot right in front of the oven, tail wagging hopefully. After drying the last bowl, I sat down and made a schedule for the next day. I'd stop by to talk with Nancy Shaw and Peter Swenson in the morning, then swing by the *Zephyr* in the afternoon. The person I really needed to talk to, though, was Flora Kocurek. How was I going to manage that?

The timer buzzed, and I removed the pie from the oven, admiring the rich red of the berries against the creamy yellow custard. Although I was dying for a piece now, I knew it was best to wait, so I put it on a cooling rack next to the stove, then poured myself a glass of Blossom's milk and sat back down at the table, turning the glass on the scarred wood surface.

I hardly knew Flora—but there was nothing that said I couldn't be neighborly and bring her a casserole, or a pan of brownies, was there? I even considered taking over the strawberry custard pie, but I couldn't bring myself to do it; I'd worked too hard on it to give it to Nettie's daughter.

Whatever I made, it had to be with what I had on hand; I wasn't in a position to spend money.

I was deciding between brownies and a cobbler when the phone rang. I picked it up on the third ring, filled with both hope and dread—hope that it might be Tobias, dread that it might be Rooster Kocurek or the oil-exploration company.

"Hello?"

"Lucy, how are you! It's Molly."

I breathed a sigh of relief. "Fine, thanks. How are you?"

"Better than you, from what Alfie tells me," she said in an ominous voice. Then she brightened. "Now, I know it's late notice, but Alfie told me you'd talked about coming over sometime this week. I was wondering if you would join us for dinner tonight? I made chicken and dumplings and I've got enough for half the town."

"Thanks for the invitation, Molly. I'd love to." I leaned against the wall and looked at the berry-studded pie on the cooling rack. "And I just pulled a strawberry custard pie out of the oven, so it's perfect timing."

"You don't have to bring anything but yourself," she said.

"I know, but if I don't get some help, I'm going to eat the entire pie myself."

She laughed. "You'll have many willing helpers here. See you at six thirty?"

"Can't wait!"

• • •

"Glad you could make it," Molly said as she opened the front door. The family's giant Lab, Barkley, gave a deep-throated woof, then wagged his tail. I handed Molly the pie and reached down to pet him.

"Smells wonderful in here," I said as I stepped into the front hall of the Kramers' beautiful farmhouse. Before they had kids, Molly and Alfie had refinished all the pine floors so they glowed honey-gold, and furnished the place with an eclectic mix of antiques both from her family and from the antique show that took place down the road at Round Top twice a year.

"Come on in." Molly led me down the hallway, which was covered in photos of their kids—Brittany, Ethan, and Nick—toward the kitchen. The house smelled intoxicatingly of cooking chicken, and my mouth watered. "This pie looks yummy. What kind is it, again?"

"Strawberry custard," I said. "I got the recipe from my grandmother's cookbook."

"Then it's guaranteed to be delicious," Molly said, taking a sniff. She wore denim shorts and a T-shirt from Marfa, Texas. Her brown hair was streaked with silver, and she had a solid, comforting presence to her. Although she was always bustling around, taking care of her kitchen, her kids, or the farm, she had a deep, calm energy that made me feel peaceful. I could see why Alfie was so devoted to her. "Can I get you a drink?" she asked as she slipped the pie into the refrigerator. "A glass of wine, or some tea?"

"A glass of wine would be great, if you have a bottle open," I said.

"I do." She winked at me and reached for the bottle—a half-empty pinot grigio. "I always cook with wine." As I sat down at Molly's long table, she poured two glasses and handed one to me. Her kitchen was a comfortable room, with open shelves filled by Fiestaware in a rainbow of colors, a collection of ceramic chickens pecking their way across the windowsill, and white lace curtains that looked European. Barkley had settled himself on his dog bed, which was next to the back door.

I took a sip of the wine, which was cool and crisp, and leaned back in my chair. "Where is everyone?"

Molly lifted the lid of the pot on the stove and took a sniff, then pushed a wayward lock of brown hair behind one ear. "The kids are out feeding the chickens, and Alfie's checking the fences." A big bowl of dough rested beside the stove: future dumplings, I guessed.

I leaned forward in my chair. "Can I help with anything?"

"Just relax. Everything's just about done. I just have to toss the dumplings in at the last minute and dress the salad before we sit down."

After one last check on the chicken, she pulled up a chair across from me. "You've had a heck of a week, from what I've heard. How are you holding up?"

"Okay, for now, anyway." At least I hoped so. "I haven't been charged with anything, at least."

Molly's brow was furrowed above her brown eyes. "Rooster really thinks you did in Nettie?"

I shrugged. "Quinn says I'm an easy target. He's not looking much further."

"I don't know why not." Molly crossed her arms and made a sound that resembled a harrumph. "Half the town has wanted to put her six feet under at one time or another."

"That's what I keep hearing, too. I'm going to go talk with a couple of people tomorrow, and see what I can find out."

Molly leaned forward, curiosity in her brown eyes. "Like who?"

I told her what I'd heard about Peter Swenson's argument with Nettie—and about Nancy Shaw. I took another sip of wine. "I also want to talk with Flora. I hear Nettie was thinking about changing her will if she married Roger."

Molly shook her head. "Lots of bad blood between those two families. Goes back for decades."

"I found an old newspaper in the barn about a Mueller who was murdered back in the '40s," I said.

"You must mean the guy found by the railroad track—wasn't his name Thomas Mueller?"

I nodded. "That's the one."

"They always figured it was one of the Bacas who killed him, but no one ever proved it."

"Why?"

She leaned forward and spoke in a low voice, as if Nettie Kocurek might jump out of the pantry and chide her for spreading rumors. "The story goes that Thomas Mueller was sweet on one of the Baca girls. Old Josef Baca warned him off, but he didn't listen."

"So he killed him because he wouldn't stop seeing her?" I swallowed. "Jeez. It's like the Capulets and the Montagues, only with Germans and Czechs."

Molly shook her head and chuckled. "I know. Crazy, isn't it? Of course, nobody ever proved it. Helps that there was a Kocurek in the sheriff's office then, too. The Bacas and the Kocureks have always been tight."

"So it was never officially solved, and somebody got away with murder." I shook my head, thinking about it. Then I remembered the lockbox I'd found in the hayloft. "I almost forgot—I doubt it's related, but I found something else with the newspaper in the barn." I told Molly about the green metal box.

"Ooh, how exciting. Did you bring it with you?" Her brown eyes sparkled with curiosity.

"I didn't think to," I said.

"You should; I'll bet Alfie can get it open."

"I'll bring it next time I come." I took another sip of the wine, and Molly reached over to top off my glass. "I just can't think why anyone would have hidden a lockbox in the hayloft."

"It does seem a bit odd," Molly said, refilling her own glass. "Everybody who had things to hide used to bury them under trees."

"Really?"

"Oh, yeah. The old folks didn't use banks. There have to be tens of thousands of dollars stashed in boxes under trees in Buttercup; people have been poking around on their properties for years." She rolled her eyes. "Alfie spent six months digging up this place when we bought it fifteen years ago."

"Did he find anything?"

"Nothing but a few rusty nails and an arrowhead or two," she said. "He's still convinced there's money out there, though. I bought him a metal detector for Christmas, but he still hasn't found anything of value."

As if he'd heard his name, Alfie appeared at the kitchen door, opening it but not stepping inside. His boots were caked with mud, and his face was grim.

Chapter 14

Molly sat up straight in her chair. "What's wrong?"

"One of the cows is down," he said. "I'm hoping it's just milk fever."

Molly shot up out of her chair and hurried to the phone. "I'll call Dr. Brandt."

"When he gets here, tell him we're in the lower pasture, near the stock tank," Alfie said, closing the door behind him and heading back outside.

Molly dialed the number from memory and passed the information on, then returned to the table looking worried.

"What's milk fever?" I asked, thinking of Blossom and all the things I didn't know about cows. And of Tobias, who would be here shortly. Why hadn't I taken a moment to fix my hair before running out the door?

"It happens around calving time," she said. "Low calcium—easily fixed with an injection. Assuming that's what it is."

"What else could it be?" I asked.

She sighed. "Any number of things, I'm afraid. The important thing is, when they go down, get help fast. The longer they're down, the less likely they are to get back up again."

I slumped back in my chair. "I sometimes think I'm crazy for buying Dewberry Farm."

"Nah," she said. "You'll get the hang of it. And on the plus side, if you have trouble, our veterinarian is pretty easy on the eyes."

"True." I couldn't argue with that.

"He's quite a catch, in fact."

I felt my cheeks warm, and she chuckled. "I thought we were talking about cows, not vets," I protested.

"I'm just teasing," she said. "We'll see what develops with our vet; I hear he helped with Blossom the other day."

"He did. Ed Zapp didn't mention the cow he was selling me was an escape artist. Tobias—Dr. Brandt—helped me fix the fence."

"First-name basis, eh?"

"Isn't everyone here on a first-name basis?"

"More or less," she admitted, then stood up to check on the chicken again, using a potholder to protect her hand from the heat. The scent was divine; my stomach grumbled as she put the lid back on the pot and turned back to me. "For the record, I'm glad there's a Vogel in Dewberry Farm again, and I have no worries that it'll work. You'll get the hang of it before you know it."

"But your family's been doing this for generations," I said.

"We have, and we're here to help you if you need it," Molly said.

"If the Kocureks decide to go through with the drilling, there might not be much you can do, unfortunately."

Molly twisted the potholder in her hands. "I'd be more worried about staying out of jail, to be honest, Lucy." Her voice was suddenly low and solemn.

I swallowed, but it did nothing to get rid of the lump that had formed in my throat. "You think?"

"Rooster seems to have you in the crosshairs."

"Why not Flora?" I asked. "She's got more to gain than I do."

"She's family, Molly. He won't go after family."

"There was a Moravian lamb pin at the site." The words tumbled out of me. "Torn off of red fabric. Do you know anyone who wears one of those?"

Molly sat down in the chair across from me and picked up her wine glass, taking a big swig. "Just about half the town, unfortunately. The Moravian half, anyway. And since it was Founders' Day, almost everyone was wearing red."

"I know the Kocureks and the Muellers have had a feud going on for decades. Do you think one of the Muellers might have killed Nettie?"

"I doubt it," she said. "Most of them left town to look for work elsewhere. The only one left is Ursula Mueller—she runs the Daughters of the German Republic. She'd be second cousin of the guy who died, I guess," she said, doing some kind of mental genealogical analysis in her head, "and she didn't have too many dealings with Nettie. And I guess there's Jacob Mueller, too."

"He runs the Art Guild, right?" I remembered walking in and admiring several large canvases depicting the rolling Texas countryside.

She nodded. "He does great rural paintings. They sell for a mint in Houston."

"I'll bet," I said. "They're gorgeous—I wish I could afford one."

"That's a lot of beeswax candles," she grinned.

"Tell me about it. What about Flora's boyfriend—Roger Brubeck?"

"I don't know much about him, to be honest," Molly said, pursing her lips. "He's only been back in town a few years, and keeps to himself, for the most part. Moved into his parents' house when his mom went into Sunset Home."

"How did he and Flora end up getting together?"

"Got together not too long after the Founders' Day Festival last year, believe it or not. He took her out for Bubba's barbecue, and those old flames reunited."

"I heard they were sweet on each other in high school."

"That's the rumor. At that time, though, Nettie wouldn't have allowed it. He ended up heading to Texas A&M." She got up and peeked under the pot lid, then adjusted the heat before returning to the table. "He got a degree in accounting," she said as she sat back down across from me. "I hear he did taxes in Houston until he moved back to his parents' house. He still works as a CPA; he hung out a shingle on Magnolia Street."

"So he's not desperate for cash."

"No, but he likes money. There were a lot of rumors that he was dating Flora for her money—and that he was seeing someone on the side."

I leaned forward, feeling a spark of hope. "Who?"

She glanced around, as if one of her children might be hiding behind a cabinet door, then spoke in a low voice. "Somebody young, is all I heard."

The mention of somebody young made me think of the teenager I'd met at the festival. "That reminds me of something. Alfie tells me you think Teena Marburger's got some kind of second sight."

Molly nodded, her brown hair bobbing. The sapphire stud earrings Alfie had just bought her for their anniversary twinkled in the light from the windows. "She does. Her grandmother did, too."

"How do you know?" I asked.

"She knew I was pregnant before I did." Molly grinned. "Twice."

"What about the third time?"

Molly's grin widened. "She was too young to tell me."

Goose bumps rose on my arms. "What other kinds of things does she—'know'?"

"It varies. She says things just pop into her head,

and sometimes she doesn't know what it means until later. She told Edna Orzak to watch out for pecans last fall, and a week later she slipped on one in the back room of the Red and White and broke her hip. Laid her up in the hospital for six months."

"Not very helpful," I said.

"Not that time," Molly admitted. "But last April, she told Alfie he should put off going to Houston—he was going to look for a new tractor."

"And?"

"She had no way of knowing he was going that day—he hadn't told anyone but me."

"What happened?"

She fingered the gold band on her left hand. "He decided to listen to her, and I'm thankful for it. There was a twelve-car pileup on SH 71 that day. Three people died."

I shivered. "She told me that someone was trying to reach me the other day."

"Any idea what that might mean?"

"Unfortunately, no." I was about to say more when there was a knock at the door. My heart did a little jig in my chest as I followed Molly down the hallway.

Tobias was there, in blue jeans and a Luckenbach T-shirt, holding his bag. Our eyes met and held for an electric moment before he focused his attention on Molly. "Where is she?" he asked in an urgent voice.

"In the lower pasture, near the stock tank."

"Can I come?" I asked impulsively.

"I'd love the company."

Molly's eyebrows flicked up as she looked at me, then turned to Tobias. "Thanks so much for coming out, even though it's late. We're having chicken and dumplings, and there's plenty; I hope you're planning to stay to dinner."

"Thanks for the offer, Molly. If it's something easy like milk fever, which it probably is—Alfie knows his stock—I'll gladly take you up on it." His voice was friendly and calming.

Molly smiled at him. "I'll just put the dumplings in then, and set an extra place at the table. Even if it is a complicated case, you'll still need to eat."

"You've convinced me. And it smells terrific."

"Thanks so much for coming out." Molly grabbed a spoon and reached for the bowl of dumpling dough as I slid into my sneakers; a moment later, Tobias and I were headed across the backyard toward the lower pasture.

"How's Blossom doing?" he asked as we hurried down toward the murky pond at the lower end of the property, where we could see Alfie kneeling over a dun-colored cow.

"She's stayed close to home, thankfully. Those cuts look good, too; thanks for treating them."

"I should come by and walk your fence with you sometime soon. Just to be sure." He glanced over at me, and a rakish grin spread across his face. "That cow's got a reputation."

"Just my luck." I smiled back at him. "Thanks for the offer of help; that would be great. As long as you let me cook you dinner."

"Two dinners in a row? This is my lucky week." His voice was gravelly in a way that made my heart skip a beat, and I found myself wondering if he was referring to the two home-cooked meals, or two evenings in a row with me.

"Tomorrow night okay?" I struggled to keep my voice light.

"Office hours end at six; will that work?"

"Perfect," I said, mentally thanking Alfie and Molly for the invitation to dinner tonight—and for the luck that had brought Tobias to their farm. I was worried about the cow, though; as we approached, I could see she was disturbingly still on the ground, her head turned back at an awkward angle. A small brown calf bleated nearby, his cries pitiful. As glad as I was that he was here, I hoped Tobias hadn't arrived too late.

"Thanks for coming so quickly," Alfie said. "She calved two days ago. I think it's milk fever, but I want to be sure."

"Looks like it," Tobias said, whipping a stethoscope out of his bag and pressing it to her side, then looking at his watch. "Slow heartbeat. How long has she been like this?"

Alfie shifted from one booted foot to the other,

looking worried. "Less than an hour. I saw her and her calf at around four this afternoon. She was a little unsteady on her pins, which is why I came out to check on her."

"Staggering a bit?"

He nodded. "A bit."

Tobias looked at the cow's eyes, then felt her ears. "Looks like you got it right," he said. "We'll know in a few minutes, but I'm pretty sure it's milk fever. Glad you called me when you did." He put the stethoscope back into his bag and pulled out a syringe and a bottle. She shivered as he injected her, but didn't change position. Tobias gave her a pat on the side and stood up. "If that's what it is, she should be up and around in a few minutes. How many other cows have calved or are in calf?"

Alfie shifted his ever-present lump of snuff from one side of his lip to the other. "Five have calved in the last month or so, and there are another half dozen on the way."

"We should probably supplement them just to be sure." Tobias scanned the other cows in the pasture; they looked normal to me, but then again, I wasn't a vet. "I don't have any in the car, but if you'll swing by the clinic tomorrow, I'll give you something to add to their feed."

Alfie looked down at the cow, which still hadn't changed position. The calf was still bleating nearby, upset; I had the urge to go and comfort him, but when I took one step toward him, he skittered away nervously.

"How long until we know?" Alfie asked.

As if she'd heard him, the cow suddenly lurched to her feet, looking a little surprised at the audience.

"Looks like we pegged it." Tobias watched as she took a few careful steps toward her calf and nuzzled its head. Then he turned back to Alfie. "Start in on those supplements and keep an eye on her—and the rest of them. Call as soon as you see anything—even a bit of staggering."

"Should I be supplementing Blossom, too?" I asked.

Tobias turned to me. "Not unless she's in calf. Speaking of which, have you thought about that?"

"Not yet," I said. I knew I had to but was worried about what I'd do if she had a boy calf. Or how I'd manage two Harriet Houdinis if she didn't. I didn't have enough pasture for more than a couple of cows; I was hoping that at some point, I could sell extra calves to the Kramers.

"You can do IVF," Alfie suggested, adjusting his worn straw cowboy hat, which Molly told me was his "summer hat." I knew enough to know that IVF was artificial insemination, but I had no idea how to go about doing it.

"Who would I call?" I asked.

"George Skalicky is your man," he said. "But the thing with that is, you have to be able to tell if she's in heat before you call, which can be hard to do when you're starting out. If I were you, I'd borrow Brawly."

"Who's Brawly?"

Alfie pointed to a hulking black mass in the next pasture over. "My bull," he said, his voice tinged with pride. "He's a beef/dairy cross. That way you're covered either way."

I looked at Brawly, who was frighteningly large, then turned and watched as the bleating calf ducked under his mother and began pulling at a teat. "I am so out of my depth," I murmured. Even if I did manage to stay out of jail and keep the Kocureks from erecting an oil well on my farm, the amount I had to learn was daunting.

"That's what you've got us for," Alfie said, clapping a hand on my back. "Now, let's go see if Molly's got those dumplings ready. I hope you'll stay for dinner, Tobias."

"Absolutely. Molly already invited me." Tobias zipped up his vet bag and slung it over his shoulder. "I'd be a fool to refuse her chicken and dumplings."

Together we headed back to the farmhouse, Tobias on one side of me and Alfie on the other. As we walked, I felt a wave of gratitude for my companions. Despite the worry hanging over my head, the company and support of these two strong, good men gave me hope.

Chapter 15

Dinner was delicious—Molly promised to give me the recipe for her chicken and dumplings, which came with a gravy so scrumptious I considered licking the plate. The strawberry custard pie was a big hit, particularly with the kids, all of whom had seconds. It was a rowdy dinner until Molly shooed everyone upstairs to finish their homework. She grimaced as I cleared the empty pie plate from the table. "Sorry there wasn't any left over to take home with you."

"I wasn't planning on it," I said as I carried the plate to the sink. "Besides, I'll have enough strawberries to make another in a day or two."

Tobias brushed by me with two plates in his hand and grinned. "How about tomorrow?"

"What's tomorrow?" Molly gave Tobias an inquisitive look.

"Tobias is coming over to walk my fence with me, so we don't have any more unplanned cow escapes," I answered. "I promised to feed him dinner." I glanced at Tobias, who was returning to the table for more plates. "Hope you like enchiladas."

"Like them? They're my favorite."

Molly cast me a speculative glance, which I ignored.

Alfie was either oblivious or more subtle than his wife. "Blossom been behavin'?"

I was thankful for the opportunity to change the subject. "She hasn't gotten out again, if that's what you mean. And I finally figured out how to keep her from kicking over the milk pail."

Alfie laughed. "You're learnin' fast. You'll be an old hand in no time."

"Maybe. If I can keep the Kocureks from mucking with the farm long enough to learn."

Worry creased Alfie's forehead. "Any word on that?"

"It's on hold until the will is probated, apparently. I've got an attorney, but she charges a fortune."

Molly, who was sitting down while the rest of us cleaned up, took a sip of her iced tea. "How are things with Rooster?"

"I don't know," I said, feeling my stomach tighten as I opened the dishwasher. "He hasn't called me, at least. I'm hoping no news is good news."

"I wouldn't count on it," Tobias said. "He's not the most professional detective."

"I've been asking around town," I said, "trying to figure out who could have done it."

"What have you turned up?" Molly asked.

"Well, Flora and her fiancé are obvious possibilities. But I understand Nettie's irritated half the town at one point or another." I took a sip of cold tea and then a deep breath. "I know both Nancy Shaw and Peter Swenson had words with her recently, but have you heard anything else?"

"Peter?" Alfie blinked. "You think he might have killed Nettie?"

"I'm not saying that," I said quickly, regretting my candor. I knew Alfie and Peter were friends. "I'm just finding out who else might have been upset with her." Someone in Buttercup, after all, had skewered Nettie Kocurek, and I knew it wasn't me.

"Hmm," Molly said. "I know someone was sugaring all their gas tanks."

I rinsed a plate and put it into the dishwasher. "I'd heard that. Does Rooster know about it?"

"I'm sure Nettie told her nephew about it right away," she said, "but that doesn't mean he's connected it to her murder."

"If it *is* connected." Alfie transferred the remaining chicken and dumplings—which wasn't much—to a small dish. "Like you said, lots of people were upset with her. Besides, I think someone put sugar into our tractor tank not too long ago, which would mean it wasn't just directed at Nettie."

"What? Is that what was wrong with the tractor?" Molly's voice was tight.

"That's what Fred Sanger thinks." Fred Sanger was the local mechanic. I hadn't had to go see him yet, which was evidently a good thing, as I drove a Toyota. From what I'd heard, he viewed purchasers of Japanese cars with suspicion bordering on hostility.

Molly crossed her arms. "Why didn't you tell me?"

Alfie put a lid on the dish and tucked it into the refrigerator. "I didn't want you to worry."

"Alfie, that's not your decision to make! If there's a threat, I should know about it, don't you think?"

"You're probably right, sweetheart." He closed the refrigerator door, then walked up behind her and put his big, work-roughened hands on her shoulders.

Molly reached up and put her smaller hands on his. "Why would someone do a thing like that?"

Alfie shrugged. "I don't know. Why would someone stick Nettie Kocurek with a bratwurst skewer?" No one said anything. "Okay, there are lots of reasons someone would stick Nettie Kocurek with a bratwurst skewer. What I meant to say was, sometimes there's no good explanation for things."

"Do you think the kids are safe?" Molly's round face looked worried. "I mean, if whoever it was was willing to vandalize our farm equipment, what else would they do?"

Alfie shrugged again. "It was a month ago, and that's the only thing that's happened. Besides, it's happened at multiple farms—not just ours."

"Did you tell Rooster?"

"No. What's the point?"

Tobias, who had gotten up to clear the table, set a plate on the counter next to me. "I think he should know. If it's happening at other farms, he may be able to identify a pattern."

Alfie patted Molly on the shoulder again, then reached in his back pocket for his can of Skoal. "I'm not sure Rooster could identify a pattern on a Flying Geese quilt, Tobias."

Molly sighed. "I'm afraid he's right. Rooster's strongest skill is handing out tickets to out-of-staters on FM 955."

Tobias wasn't swayed. "Tell him, at least, will you? So he can tell his officers to keep an eye out?"

Alfie tucked a bit of snuff in his lip before answering. "I'll drop by tomorrow and let him know."

"And ask him to keep an eye on the farm and the kids, too." Molly looked up at her husband. "Promise?"

"Promise. Now, I'm going to go check on that cow. Just in case."

"I'll go with you." Tobias rinsed his hands under the faucet as I put the last plate into the dishwasher.

"You sure?"

"Absolutely," he said.

"He's cute," Molly said when Alfie and Tobias had closed the door behind them.

"He is," I agreed.

She cocked an eyebrow. "And you're feeding him dinner tomorrow?"

I felt my face color. "He's checking on my fence."

"Mmm." Molly grinned.

"Oh, stop." I wiped my hands on a dish towel. "If I end up in jail for murder, it won't make a difference whether or not I feed him dinner."

"Well, I want to see how this budding romance develops, so we'd better get to work figuring out who skewered her."

I sighed and sat down across from my friend. "You mentioned a rumor that Flora's fiancé had someone on the side. Any idea who that might be?"

"I know Alfie's seen him flirting with one of the waitresses at Rosita's. And I do see his truck parked there a lot." Molly pursed her lips. "On the other hand, it's the only Mexican restaurant in town."

"Whose truck?" Brittany, Molly's sixteen-year-old daughter, stood at the kitchen doorway. She wore shorts and a Buttercup Bandits T-shirt, and her long brown hair was pulled back into a ponytail.

Molly jumped guiltily—I knew she didn't like the kids to hear her gossip—and when she spoke, her voice was stern. "How's the homework going?"

"Done with my math and almost finished with my English paper." Brittany was on track to be valedictorian of Buttercup High, and sharp as a tack. Not to mention persistent. "Whose truck?"

Molly sighed. "We're talking about Roger Brubeck," she said.

"Flora Kocurek's fiancé?" Brittany shook her head. "I wouldn't marry him."

Brittany's mother pulled the tablecloth off the table and balled it up in her hands. "I should hope not. He's over fifty, and you're not even seventeen!"

Brittany shot her mother a look that clearly translated as "duh."

"Not *me*. I meant Flora."

"Why not?" I asked.

"My friend Marta works at Rosita's on the weekends, and she told me he's down there all the time, hitting on Tammy Beck."

"Even since he got engaged to Flora?" Molly asked as she tossed the tablecloth into the laundry room.

"That's what she says."

"Tammy's one of the waitresses, isn't she?" I asked. I remembered her; I'd splurged on a taco salad a few weeks back and had talked with my bubbly server about the upcoming Founders' Day Festival. I could see why Roger would be

173

interested; she was vivacious, with a pretty face and a curvy figure. She'd mentioned she'd be serving tacos at Rosita's stand at the festival, but had hinted she preferred Bubba's barbecue.

Brittany walked to the fridge and grabbed a Diet Coke. "Yeah. She's worked there for a few years."

"Do you know if she ever went out with him?" I asked.

"I'm not sure," Brittany said, "but Marta told me Tammy told her she thought he was kind of cute." The teenager shuddered as she popped the tab on her soda. "Which I don't get at all."

I had to agree with her. Roger might have been a nice guy, but he wasn't exactly *GQ* material. Although if he was two-timing Flora, he might not have been a nice guy, either.

Brittany fixed me with an innocent blue-eyed stare. "I've heard Rooster thinks you did in old Mrs. Kocurek."

Molly paled. "Brittany!"

I held up a hand. "It's okay." My voice sounded calm, but I felt as if I'd been doused with ice water. "Who told you that, Brittany?"

"It's all around town," she said. "But not everyone believes it."

I swallowed. "Well, that's a relief."

"You should tell them not to gossip," Molly chided.

"Yeah, right." Brittany took a swig of her Diet

Coke. "That's about all there is to do in Buttercup. I can't wait to get to UT."

"First you have to graduate," Molly called after her as she drifted out of the kitchen. She turned to me and rolled her eyes. "Teenagers."

Despite the excellent food and company, I felt my stomach churn as I drove up the long drive to Dewberry Farm that evening. Blossom, thankfully, was waiting by the barn door rather than gallivanting around downtown, and as I stepped out of the truck, I could hear the chickens chuckling as they settled down for the night.

I hooked up the soaker hoses to give the tomatoes a good watering, then checked on the chickens' food and water. There were a few hens in nesting boxes, but the rest were roosting. Already the days were growing long; soon it would be light until nine.

The sun was down by the time I finished my chores and let Chuck out for a waddle around the garden. He didn't go far—just visited his favorite rosebush and then headed back to the kitchen, where he parked next to the food dish. I measured out his kibble. He sniffed at it, then gave me a plaintive look.

"Doctor's orders," I reminded him. "It's good for you." He continued to look at me. "All right," I finally said, fishing a bag of shredded cheese out of the fridge and dusting the top of the dry kibble. "Just don't tell Tobias," I muttered as he gulped it down.

I glanced at the clock; it was almost eight thirty. Enough time to whip up a quick batch of brownies to take to Flora's tomorrow, I decided. With my chunky poodle looking on hopefully, I measured out flour and cocoa, mixing them up with eggs, melted butter, and a healthy dose of dark chocolate chips. I dropped a chocolate chip on the floor. Chuck lunged for it, but I was too quick for him.

When the pan was in the oven, filling my grandmother's house with the cozy smell of baking, my thoughts turned again to the lockbox I'd found in the loft. I set it on the table and looked at it, running my fingers around the sides and trying to figure out how to open it. After a few minutes, I grabbed a flashlight and headed toward the shed behind the house.

After a good bit of digging through cobwebs and rusted tools, I found a decrepit chisel. I carried it to the back porch, then grabbed my hammer and the box and sat down on one of the rocking chairs, propping the box up between my feet.

I don't know why I didn't think of using a chisel earlier. The box opened like a clamshell on the third whack.

If I had been hoping for gold, I would have been disappointed. All I could see in the box was a bouquet of long-dead flowers, held together by a moldering piece of string. As I lifted the fragile bouquet from the box, something fell onto the floor of the porch. Setting the flowers down gently, I stooped to retrieve it; it was a small picture. I picked it up; there was a faded photo of a lovely young woman with dark brown hair.

I turned the box right-side up, wondering what the significance was of the flowers and the lockbox—an old love of my grandfather's, maybe?—and why someone had hidden them in the loft. Why not in the house, or the attic? It was very strange. As I put the photo back in the box, I noticed a piece of paper wedged into the bottom of the box.

I pulled it out gingerly and unfolded the brittle page, which was stained with brown splotches. Emblazoned at the top of the page, in very fancy script, were the words *Marriage License*. Unfortunately, just about everything else on it was lost to water damage.

Disappointed, I took the page into the kitchen and held it up under the light. It looked like one of the names began with an "M." The other name on the certificate was completely indecipherable. I squinted down at the page. Although the month had been swallowed by water, the year was still legible: 1940. The same year as the newspaper that had blown down from the loft. Coincidence? Or had that piece of paper somehow not made it into the box?

I glanced up at the top of the certificate again and noticed that the county name had been written under the florid script. Fayette County—which was the county Buttercup was in.

The timer rang, bringing me back to the present. I tucked the certificate back into the lockbox and pulled the brownies out of the oven, leaving them on the stovetop to cool. Chuck eyed me with interest, but I informed him that there were no treats forthcoming and headed up to bed. Reluctantly, he followed, and fell asleep promptly at the foot of my bed.

I, on the other hand, stared at the ceiling for hours, wondering about the lockbox—and wondering how in the world I was going to clear my name.

Chapter 16

The Kocurek homestead was not what I'd call picturesque, but it certainly was imposing.

It was just before ten when I pulled up outside the gates, which were two square, red brick pillars spanned by an imposing black gate of wrought iron. The oversized gate looked out of place beside the low barbed wire fence that seemed to stretch out for miles on either side of it.

Most people in these parts had gates you could open manually—if they had gates at all, since cattle guards were more common. But attached to one of the rather ugly brick pillars near the entrance was an intercom, along with something that looked like a security camera mounted to a post just inside the gate. I wondered if the camera had been added since the sugaring.

I pushed the red button and waited, stealing a glance at the plate of brownies beside me. I had originally put them on a paper plate but decided instead to use one of my grandmother's china platters, so I'd have an excuse for a second visit to retrieve the plate if necessary.

"Who is it?" The voice was male and surly.

"A neighbor," I said. "Lucy Resnick. I brought a plate of brownies for Flora."

There was a long pause, during which I feared

the gates wouldn't open. Then, without any further communication through the speaker, there was a click and a whir, and the iron gate swung slowly open.

I took a deep breath and put the truck in gear. Rocks from the drive pinged against the under-carriage as I drove down the straight dirt road toward a compound of large farm buildings. In the center of the compound sat a squat, red brick ranch unsheltered by trees.

Where most of the farmhouses in Buttercup were a hundred years old and constructed of wood, Nettie Kocurek's house appeared to date from the 1950s and included a series of white-painted columns on a narrow front porch that wasn't deep enough for a rocking chair. The square of lawn surrounding the house was protected from cattle by a wrought-iron fence that matched the front gate, and the expanse of shorn Bermuda grass was interrupted only by a line of square-trimmed boxwoods that stretched across the facade of the house. It was anything but welcoming, I thought as I bumped over another cattle guard.

I pulled into a gravel parking area to the left of the house, wedging my truck in between a shiny red Ford F-150 and Nettie's Cadillac. Wherever the barn and outbuildings were, I thought as I walked across the gravel drive to the ranch's bright white front door, they were nowhere near the Kocurek homestead.

Despite the intercom, nobody came to the door when I rang the bell. I waited a minute, then rang again, adding a knock in case the ringer was broken. I shifted the platter of brownies to my other hand as the time crawled by; finally, I heard the deadbolt snick back, and the door opened about three inches.

"Hi." I addressed the eye that peered out at me suspiciously. By its color—brown—and the mass of frizzy brown hair above it, I guessed it was Flora's. "I'm so sorry for your loss. I brought some brownies."

The eye blinked, still regarding me.

"Flora?" It was the voice from the intercom, and it came from somewhere behind the eye. I heard footsteps, and a moment later the door opened wide, releasing a strong whiff of tuna casserole.

"Hi," I said again, this time to the man standing in the doorway. His thinning hair had been combed over a shiny pate, and his western-style shirt and blue jeans looked oddly out of place on his paunchy frame. Flora, who was wearing a red floral housedress and matching lipstick that made the rest of her face look even more wan, had crossed her arms and was looking at me through narrowed eyes.

"I'm so sorry about Mrs. Kocurek," I said, holding out my grandmother's platter. "I brought some brownies."

"That's mighty kind of you." Roger squinted at

me from behind thick glasses. "I don't believe we've met. I'm Roger Brubeck, Flora's fiancé."

"I'm Lucy Resnick." I smiled. "I moved to town a few months ago—bought a piece of property from Mrs. Kocurek." I shifted the platter and thrust out my right hand. "Dewberry Farm," I said.

"She's the one Rooster thinks killed my mama," Flora spat, pulling her arms tight around her. "Brownies are probably poisoned, too."

Roger patted her on the shoulder. "Now, now, Flora. No need to be ornery. She's just payin' her respects."

But Flora was not about to be mollified. "Mama knew she was trouble. Of course she was trouble, being the granddaughter of that Vogel woman. If she'd a known that's who it was, she never would have sold her that piece of property."

Roger shot me an apologetic look. "I'm terribly sorry about all this. It's been a shock." He put an arm around Flora. "Did you remember to take your medicine this morning?"

"Shock?" She shook his arm off of her. "I'm not in shock, Roger," she said, glaring at me. "I just don't like people who offer sympathy but don't mean it."

"She's just being neighborly, Flora."

"Well, tell her to take her poisoned brownies and go be neighborly somewhere else," she said, and stomped off into the darkened house.

"Don't mind her," Roger said quietly when

she'd gone. "Ever since . . . well, the incident, she hasn't been herself."

"I'm so sorry. It must be tough."

"I think once Rooster . . . I mean, once the crime is solved, things will be better." His eyes darted away from my face, and I realized with a sinking sensation that he had been about to say "once Rooster arrests someone."

Meaning, most likely, me.

"Thanks for the brownies," he said, and I handed him the plate. He reached to close the door, but I stopped him.

"Can I ask you a question?"

"Yes?"

"I heard someone put sugar in the tanks of some of your farm machinery. How long ago did that happen?"

A groove appeared between his eyebrows as he considered the question. "It was right after Christmas," he said.

"Any idea who might have done it?"

He shook his head. "Not a clue. Now, if you'll excuse me, I need to attend to my fiancée."

"Of course," I said. "Let me know if there's anything I can do to help." And with a strained smile on his sallow face, he closed the door.

I walked back to my car slowly, taking in what Flora had said. Her mother had held a grudge against me—and I was more than willing to bet that her sudden interest in oil exploration had started when she'd discovered who I was. Why else would she let the property sit fallow for fifteen years?

As I walked around to get into my truck, I glanced into the bed of the Ford pickup next to mine. There was a paper bag in the back, half covered by a plastic tarp. I darted a swift look back at the house—the window shades were all closed—and reached in to pull the tarp aside.

Underneath it was a paper sack with a label—COMPOSTED COW MANURE. Not exactly the kind of clue I was looking for. I flipped the tarp back, then got back into my truck.

As I bumped across the cattle guard and down the dirt road to the gate, I felt anger and frustration rise in me. Nettie Kocurek didn't like me because of who I was—and had tried to ruin my farm to wreak revenge on me.

Unfortunately, unless my instincts were wrong, whoever had killed her had done an even better job.

My mood was still dark when I pulled up in front of the *Buttercup Zephyr*, the newspaper I had found in the barn on the seat beside me. Mandy Vargas greeted me at the door, wearing jogging shorts and with her dark hair pulled up in a pony-tail, earbuds slung around her neck. "I'm on my way out for a run, but I pulled some of the files for you. You're welcome to stay and go through them —there's a copier in the back if you need one."

"Terrific," I said. "Remember that old news article about the Mueller murder I told you I found up in the barn?" I said. "I also found a marriage certificate."

"A marriage certificate?" she asked, a furrow appearing on her brow.

"I can't read it, but it's from the same time period. Since I found it in my grandparents' barn, I'm curious about it." I smiled at her. "I was wondering if maybe the two were related."

"Hmmm," she said, not seeming too interested. "Let me know what you find out." She reached for her earbuds.

"Speaking of finding out," I said before she could wedge the first earbud in, "remember those things the police missed down at the crime scene?"

Mandy grimaced. "Yes. Are you ready to tell me what they were?"

"A scrap of red fabric with a gold lamb pin. Also, a smashed jam jar." I swallowed. "I don't know who the pin belonged to, but unfortunately, the jar was mine."

"There were lots of jam jars in that tent," Mandy said. "Besides, just because it was yours doesn't mean you smashed it."

Although her words buoyed me, the reality was that her opinion didn't carry weight in the justice system of Fayette County. "I wish Rooster felt the same way," I said.

"The lamb pin is interesting," she said. "It's a Brethren Church thing, so it might limit the pool of suspects. It might not be a bad idea to talk to Father Mikeska and find out who got one." She pursed her lips, looking thoughtful. "Assuming Nettie ripped it off the murderer's clothing."

That would put me out of the running for top suspect—I wasn't Czech, I'd only been here for a few months, and I'd never seen a lamb pin before finding one on the town square. "Rooster won't believe me, though. He thinks I planted it to implicate someone else."

"It would have been better if someone else tracked it down," she agreed, which did not give me a warm and fuzzy feeling.

"One more question. Do you have any idea who's been putting sugar in gas tanks?"

She perked up. "Is there another case?"

"The Kramers mentioned it happened to them," I said. "I think the Kocureks were hit, too."

"I did some research and ran a little article on it a few months back. Nobody found out who it was, and I thought it had died down," she said. "It was mostly small farms that suffered; I was surprised when the Kocureks were hit. Their farm is bigger than the average target, and pretty well fenced."

"With a radio-controlled security gate, too. Did that come before or after the problems?"

"It's been there for years," Mandy said. "I'll give them a call and follow up on it. Thanks for the tip. Now, if you'll excuse me, I'm going to run before it gets too hot." With a smile, she tucked the earbuds into her ears and jogged away.

I let myself into the small house, thinking about the pin I'd found and wondering a little at Mandy's willingness to let me walk right in when nobody was there. I was still used to city living, where everything was locked up tight. I still hadn't adjusted to the trust in small communities—and realized with a warm rush that that must mean she didn't believe I had murdered Nettie Kocurek.

As I walked past the front desk, the headline from the most recent issue of the *Zephyr* screamed up at me: PROMINENT BUSINESSWOMAN STABBED, KILLED AT FESTIVAL. On the front was a picture of Flora Kocurek and Roger Brubeck, decked out in their Czech outfits. Flora wore a white blouse and a lace-trimmed apron, her hands over her mouth as if she had just received shocking news (which I supposed she had), and Roger stood beside her. One arm was wrapped around her protectively, but he was looking somewhere else, distracted. Had he killed her? I wondered. He was wearing lederhosen, though, and not a scrap of red, and I reflected that the lamb pin knocked him off my suspect list. Besides, he looked disappointingly unmussed.

A quick scan of the article revealed nothing I didn't already know. The one bright spot was that

Mandy hadn't named me as the prime suspect.

Yet.

Making a mental note to check in at the Brethren Church and inquire about lamb pins, I headed to Mandy's desk and picked up the folder she'd left for me. The first headline blared LOCAL MAN FOUND DEAD AT GRUENWALD TRAIN DEPOT. A large photo showed the station as it had been years ago. A police officer in a crisply pressed uniform stood in front of the depot, looking grim; off to the side, standing in the shadows, was another person. The words "Gruenwald Station" were crisp and freshly painted.

I scanned the faded newsprint. Thomas Mueller had evidently been the son of Uschi and Tom Mueller, who owned the Mueller cotton mill. Although I knew all of the details already, rereading them made my heart hurt.

After reading the story, I flipped through the rest of the pages in the folder. The crime had never been solved; it had been assumed to be a robbery, since the man's wallet was missing. I found myself wondering who had stored all of those articles in the barn. I'd heard of murderers keeping mementos of their crimes. Had someone living at Dewberry Farm killed young Thomas?

My stomach did a little flip-flop as I considered the unpleasant truth. If the murderer had been at Dewberry Farm, there was a good chance it was a member of my family.

Chapter 17

I was still brooding on Nettie's death twenty minutes later, when I swung by the Blue Onion to pick up another loaf of Quinn's yeasty white bread. The dining room was full as I walked in— it was lunchtime—and the conversation was animated as I opened the front door. Which made the awkward silence that fell the moment all eyes landed on me even more uncomfortable. With a brittle smile, I scurried to the back of the restaurant—even Tori, the waitress with whom I shared a passion for maple twists, paused, iced tea pitcher in hand, to stare at me.

By the time I reached the kitchen and closed the door behind me, I could hear the hum of conversation starting again. Only this time it sounded like a hive of angry bees.

"Lucy!" Quinn looked up from the counter, where she was mixing fresh tarragon into a big bowl of chicken salad.

"That may have been the most uncomfortable ten seconds of my life." I glanced over my shoulder at the door to the front of the restaurant.

She raised a quizzical eyebrow. "What do you mean?"

I let out a big breath and leaned against the wall.

"The moment I walked in, everyone stopped talking."

"Oh." She brushed a stray curl out of her eyes with the back of her hand and dismissed it. "It's because of what happened to Nettie, of course. Don't worry about it. It'll blow over."

"Easier said than done. Can I help?" I asked, surveying the list of tickets clothes-pinned to a cord above her head.

"Sure. Would you mind warming up three slices of quiche for me? The oven's preheated."

"Got it." I retrieved a quiche from the fridge— Quinn's ham-and-leek quiche was legendary in Buttercup—and cut three generous slices, transferring them to a warming pan. "Want me to plate the greens, too?" I asked.

"That would be great. I use a little Dijon vinaigrette," she instructed, "and toss in a few cherry tomatoes."

As I arranged the greens on the plate, thankful for something to busy my hands, I glanced over at my friend. "It looks like I'm turning into a pariah," I said, trying to keep my voice light.

She gave the chicken salad a vigorous stir, but didn't look up. "As soon as Rooster arrests the right person, it'll all die down."

"But will he?" I asked.

"Let's hope so. Hey, can you grab me the plastic wrap?" She pointed to the roll on the edge of the counter. Despite her cheerful yellow tank top and her bright red apron, she looked pale, and there were dark circles under her eyes.

"Sure," I said, feeling a twinge of worry for my friend. I reached for the roll of wrap and handed it over to her. "How are things with Jed?"

Her eyes flicked to me, and I saw fear in them. "He's drinking again," she said flatly.

"Oh, Quinn." I sucked in a breath. "I'm so sorry."

She folded her lips into a grim line and thrust the spoon into the bowl, stirring hard. She looked spooked. And it wasn't too hard to figure out why.

"He threatened you again," I said quietly.

She stopped stirring for a moment, but didn't raise her eyes.

"Stay with me," I said. "Just until you can work things out with the attorney."

Quinn looked up at me. Despite the fear in her eyes, her jaw was set. "I'm not going to let him control me anymore, Lucy." She pushed her shoulders back and stirred harder. "I spent five years living in fear. No more."

"Okay," I said, backing off and reaching for the jar of dressing. "The offer's open, though. Any time, day or night." I gave the bowl a pointed look. "And you might want to lay off on the chicken salad, or you're going to have chicken pâté instead."

She stopped and blinked down at the contents of the bowl, then laughed. "Another casualty of my awful ex," she said, then retrieved four slices of bread from the freshly cut loaf on the board next to her and spread them with chicken salad. As I drizzled the greens on the plates in front of me with dressing, she sliced the sandwiches in two and arranged them on plates, then retrieved a bowl of sliced berries and melon from the fridge and spooned some into small bowls. "But enough about him. What's new with you?"

"Well, I'm not in jail yet, so that's good news."

Tori bustled in and filled a cup with soup from the pot on the stove, then added a crouton and a slice of Swiss cheese and tucked it into the oven next to the quiche.

"How's it going, Tori?" I asked.

"Busy, busy." Her dark eyes glinted. "Everybody's talking about you out there."

"All good things, I hope."

"Edna Orzak said you did the town a service."

Quinn's voice was sharp. "What do you mean?"

"When you . . ." Her voice trailed off as she realized what she'd said. "I mean, when you bought that farm," she said feebly, then clipped two more tickets to the clothesline that hung over the counter. "We're going through iced tea awfully fast," she told Quinn, avoiding my eyes.

"There's another jug in the fridge," my friend told her. We waited in uncomfortable silence as she filled the pitcher, shooting me a sidelong glance, then retrieved the bowl of soup from the oven and set it on a tray alongside the chicken salad sandwiches. When she pushed through the swinging door back into the dining room, Quinn apologized to me. "She's only here for another couple of days, anyway," she said. "She gave her notice last Friday."

It was on the tip of my tongue to offer to take the job—after all, I needed the money and Quinn needed help—but then I remembered the reaction in the dining room and bit the offer back. Quinn had enough on her plate with her ex-husband's threats. She didn't need a suspected murderess scaring off her customers in the dining room, too.

I slid the tray of quiche out of the oven and plated them, then asked what else needed to be done.

"We've got an order for two buttermilk pies and a dewberry cobbler," she said.

"A few fresh berries and a mint sprig on the pies?"

She smiled as she stretched plastic wrap over the bowl of chicken salad. "Exactly," she said as she stowed the chicken salad in the fridge and pulled out a bag of washed greens and a tray lined with rounds of breaded goat cheese. I grabbed a pie and shut the door, then selected a knife from the block. Quinn glanced up at me as she dropped a knob of butter onto the griddle. "No thumper truck?"

"Not yet, anyway," I said, slicing through the creamy golden custard and flaky piecrust. My mouth watered; Quinn's buttermilk pie was to die for. "Not until they probate the will."

She sighed as she arranged four goat cheese rounds on the griddle. The smell of sizzling butter filled the kitchen, making my mouth water. "I wish Rooster would follow up on that evidence you found."

"Well, he did point out that the label on the broken jam jar was mine," I said, plucking two mint sprigs from the mason jar on the windowsill. "So I guess that's something."

"So? Anybody could have picked that jar up." She flipped the goat cheese rounds. "The lamb is the big issue. There can't be that many of those pins running around town."

"I'm going to stop by the Brethren Church and see if I can get a list of who had them," I said as I placed berries on the slices of pie and reached for the cobbler pan. As I opened the oven to put a bowl in to warm, the cheesy smell of quiche wafted out. I pulled the tray out and replaced it with the cobbler. Although I'd waited tables one summer in college, I'd forgotten how busy working in a restaurant was.

"It's a start," Quinn said as I set the tray of quiche on a rack and reached for the plates of greens. "And at least we know the killer was probably Czech."

"Which cuts the suspect list to only half of Buttercup," I groaned.

"We all have to start somewhere." She put the bowl into the fridge and turned to me with a sly grin. "Speaking of starting somewhere, I hear you have a dinner date tonight."

I felt my cheeks turning pink. "Where did you hear that?"

"It's a small town, Lucy." Her grin widened into a real smile. "I'm happy for you. Tobias is a good man."

"It's only dinner," I reminded her.

"We'll see what happens. What are you making?"

As we filled the orders on the clothesline, we talked recipes. Quinn became animated as she helped me plan out dinner, and I could feel the tension leaving her. "I made extra vinaigrette yesterday," she said, pausing in the assembly of a sandwich to open the fridge and pull out a mason jar filled with golden-yellow dressing. "Why don't you use this on the salad? You've got lettuce in the garden, right?"

"Unless Blossom's gotten to it," I told her.

"So. Salad, a loaf of bread . . ." She pointed to one of the fresh loaves cooling on racks at the end of the counter.

"And enchiladas," I said.

"Sounds great. How about dessert?"

"I was planning on making a chocolate icebox pie," I told her.

"If the way to a man's heart is through his stomach," she said, placing sandwiches on plates and adding little bowls of berries and cut fruit, "you should be a couple by tomorrow."

"How about you?" I asked. "Anybody catch your eye?"

She snorted, but all of a sudden the drawn look was back. "I'm too busy dealing with my last romantic disaster."

"What's going on?"

"He wants to get back together. He called me yesterday afternoon and told me he'd changed." She busied herself with the plates and didn't look up at me.

Tori scurried into the kitchen, and I waited until she had filled a tray with plates and disappeared back through the door before responding. "What did you tell him?"

"That it's over." Her voice was flat and hard.

"How did he take it?"

"Not well."

I pulled the bowl of cobbler out of the oven, inhaling the rich berry scent. "Have you told the attorney?"

The noon sun glinted off her red hair as she nodded. "She told me to document it."

"You still have a restraining order, right?"

"For all the good it's doing," she said. "When he drinks, that all goes out the window."

I glanced at the back door of the restaurant,

which had a big glass window on the top half—and was easy as pie to break into. "As I said, you're welcome out at the farm. Just until things settle down."

She lifted her chin. "Thanks, but I'm going to stay put. I'm not letting him chase me out of my home."

"Are you sure? We could ask the cops to keep watch on the restaurant . . ."

"Rooster Kocurek?" She gave a bitter laugh. "If you recall, I'm not exactly on his good list right now. No," she said, shaking her head. "I've thought about it, and I've made my decision. I'm not going to let Jed Stadtler affect my life any more than he already has."

I didn't argue, but foreboding filled me as I sliced another piece of buttermilk pie for a new order.

I hoped I was wrong, but I had a feeling Jed wasn't going to stick to phone calls.

Chapter 18

Six o'clock rolled around faster than I'd ever thought possible. I'd spent another hour helping out Quinn before heading home to do my own chores. By the time I'd weeded the cucumbers, picked lettuce, fed the chickens, made pie, and tucked the enchiladas into the oven, Tobias was due in just under thirty minutes and I still hadn't showered.

I had just pulled on a pair of jeans and a white linen blouse when I heard the sound of a truck rumbling up the drive. I ran my fingers through my damp hair, put on a hasty touch of mascara and lip gloss, and checked to make sure my blouse didn't have too many wrinkles. I was on my way to the kitchen to peek at the enchiladas when the doorbell rang.

Chuck raced to the door barking, but transitioned to wagging as soon as he recognized Tobias. I opened the door and smiled, feeling my heart thumping inside my chest.

"Howdy, ma'am," he said with a grin, then bent down to rub Chuck behind the ear. "Hey, buddy." Chuck slathered him with kisses, and Tobias looked up at me. "How's it going with the Light 'n' Lean?"

"He eats it, but he's not happy about it."

"And the carrots?"

"Not a fan, I'm afraid. Come on in."

He stood and walked into the house, Chuck at his heels. "Can I get you something to drink? Shiner Bock?"

"That sounds terrific," he said. "Smells great in here."

"Chicken enchiladas," I said. "And chocolate icebox pie for dessert." I pointed to the cutting board as I reached into the refrigerator for two beers.

"I've heard your grandma was a good cook, too," he said. "Must run in the family."

"You haven't tried the enchiladas yet," I reminded him. "You might want to reserve judgment."

"I sampled your pie yesterday, so I'll trust my instinct."

I laughed. "I've got some chips and salsa. Why don't we sit on the porch until the enchiladas are done? I think we're about twenty minutes out."

He carried the chips and salsa, and I carried two longnecks out onto the porch. The chickens chuckled in the background, and a cool breeze carried the scent of my grandmother's roses to our noses.

I handed him a Shiner and settled into the rocker across from him, taking a sip of the cold, dark beer. Chuck settled between us, eyeing the chips. "So," I said. "How's Alfie's cow?"

"Doing just fine," he said. "He's a good stockman; he caught it right away."

"Is milk fever common?"

"Can be," he said, taking a pull off the bottle. He wore a pair of worn cowboy boots under his faded jeans. Unlike many of the locals, who wore belt buckles the size of billboards, he wore a plain, understated brown belt and a light blue button-down shirt that brought out the color of his eyes. "Especially after calving."

"It must be nice to make a difference in your work."

"It is," he said. "But you know what that's like, too. Weren't you in the newspaper business?"

"Yes, but it's a dying industry," I told him. "And I'm not sure how much of a difference I made. I reported what I saw, but things never really seemed to change because of it. It's not like giving a cow a shot and seeing it make a miraculous recovery."

"I do like it when it goes well," he told me. "But I'm not always so lucky. We get a lot of dogs hit by trucks around here. It can be depressing." He bent down and rubbed Chuck on the head. "You stay out of traffic, okay?"

I laughed. "I have a hard enough time getting him to walk down to the mailbox, much less romp around in the road. Walking him is like walking a thirty-pound anchor sometimes."

"Well, he should be a little lighter soon," Tobias said, giving him a final pat.

"Here's hoping." I took another sip of beer.

"How are things with you?" Tobias asked. "Still glad you moved to Buttercup?"

"I think I am," I said. "I just hope I can stay."

"Worried about the thumper truck? I thought that was put on hold when Nettie died."

"It was," I said. "But I'm still worried about it. I'm even more worried about taking a one-way trip to Huntsville, though."

"You think Rooster's going to charge you with murder?"

"The rest of the town seems ready to." I told him what had happened when I dropped by the Blue Onion that afternoon.

He waved it away. "People love gossip. It doesn't mean anything."

"I'd feel more comfortable if Rooster had a few more suspects."

"Surely there are a ton of people who would have wanted to put Nettie out of commission," Tobias suggested.

"She wasn't exactly Ms. Popularity around here, was she?"

"She ruled by fear," Tobias said. "And did whatever she pleased, regardless of the consequences."

"I know she had it out with at least a couple of people from town recently," I said. "But do you know anyone—other than the Muellers—who had reason to want her dead?"

"I've always wondered about Flora," he said.

"Why would she kill her mother?"

"Because she was the only one standing in the way of marrying her beau and inheriting the farm?"

"I thought they were engaged."

"They were," Tobias said. "But rumor has it Nettie was changing her will. Flora was going to have to choose between marriage and money."

I leaned forward. "Do you know for sure if she changed it yet?"

"I don't know," he said. "Rooster should, though."

"I may have to go down to the sheriff's office and ask," I said. "He'll love that. Who inherited if Flora was cut out?"

"Lots of rumors going around," Tobias said. "Some people say she was going to leave the whole thing to Texas A&M."

"Think they'd want to drill for oil on my land?" I asked.

He laughed. "First, let's worry about getting you off the hook for murder, okay?"

"Okay," I said, feeling a warm glow inside. The folks at the Blue Onion might not be with me, but Tobias was making it clear he was on my side. I knew Molly was, too. And Quinn.

"So. It might be a good idea to find out what was up with her will. If she hadn't changed it yet, that gives us two potential suspects."

"Flora," Tobias ticked off on one finger.

"And Flora's fiancé," I added. "So we have two potential suspects. Three, if you put any stock in the rumor that Nettie and Peter Swenson had an argument the other day."

"An argument doesn't mean motive for murder," Tobias pointed out.

"Not necessarily," I said. "But until we know what they argued about, we don't know."

"True," he said.

"I also know that Nancy Shaw wasn't too happy about her using pesticides."

"Think she'd kill Nettie over bug spray?"

"If it were messing with her livelihood, she might," I said.

"I can tell you've done this before."

"Done what?"

"Investigative reporting," Tobias said. "You're good at it."

"Thanks." I felt my cheeks turn pink. "So, we've got four suspects so far. What about that old feud with the German contingent?"

"The Kocurek-Mueller thing? It's still going—always has—but I can't think that would be motive for murder."

"Besides, whoever did it was probably Czech."

"Why do you say that?"

"There was a Moravian lamb pin on a scrap of fabric near Nettie's body."

"Not likely that a German would be wearing that," he agreed.

"Of course, there was also a jar of my jam," I said.

"So? It was the jam tent. Just because it was yours doesn't mean you did it. In fact, you'd be more likely to use someone else's jam, don't you think?"

"That's what I thought, but Rooster appears to think otherwise. Thanks again for pointing out the chain of evidence issue the other day," I said. "I was too flustered to think straight."

"Don't mention it."

I thought about Nettie. "I wish I knew more about Nettie Kocurek. I know she felt strongly about her great-grandfather's statue, and was really pushing the Czech heritage. But was she doing something else that upset someone? Some kind of business dealing?"

"It would be interesting to find out what she and Peter were arguing about," Tobias said.

"Maybe I'll drop by to talk farming," I suggested.

He was about to answer when the buzzer sounded from the kitchen. "Sounds like dinner's about done. Let me go check on the enchiladas, and I'll be right back."

"I'll keep an eye on Blossom and Chuck," Tobias said, nodding toward the heifer, who had drifted close to the fence and was eyeing my roses.

"Harriet Houdini, you mean? Good luck with that," I laughed, and headed into the house.

•••

Dinner was delightful—the enchiladas were the perfect mix of cheese, chicken, and spicy chilies, and Quinn's salad dressing was tangy and fresh, complementing the delicate lettuce from my garden. Tobias regaled me with stories of his youth—and the list of places Blossom had ended up, which included the lumberyard, the middle of State Highway 71, and the parking lot of Hruska's Bakery. I had laid the table with my grandmother's flowered tablecloth and put a couple of sprigs of larkspur in a vase in the middle, and the kitchen felt cozy and warm and companionable. It was good having company—especially handsome, humorous company—and as I finished the last bite of chocolate pie, I realized I hadn't enjoyed a meal in my grandmother's kitchen as much since I was a kid.

"That was amazing," Tobias said, putting down his fork. "I'm doing the dishes."

"No you're not," I protested. "You're the guest."

He shook his head, eyes glinting. "You cook, I clean." And before I could say another word, he had swept up the plates and started the water in the sink.

I relented in the face of such efficiency and pulled a dish towel off the hook on the wall. "Okay. But I'm drying."

We stood side by side at the sink, talking about his burgeoning vet practice and my hopes for my fledgling farm, our arms brushing from time to time. I felt a tingle at his touch—he seemed to be charged with energy somehow. An energy that drew me in and made me feel cared for and special and beautiful. The dishes were done all too soon, and I was loath for him to go, but couldn't think of a reason to make him stay.

"Has Chuck had his walk yet?" he asked, eyeing the bald poodle, who had been watching wistfully as I put up the food.

"Not yet," I confessed.

"Well, then, let's leash him up," he suggested. Happy for an excuse to keep Tobias longer, I clipped the leash to Chuck's collar and together we headed for the door.

Although Chuck dragged his heels when I took him out, he, too, had evidently come under Tobias's thrall and trotted happily after him as we headed down the driveway. The sun was setting in beautiful orange and pink streaks over the bluebonnet-strewn hills, and the ozonic smell of rain was in the air, mixed with the green smell of fresh spring grass.

"What happened to the thirty-pound anchor?" Tobias asked as Chuck sprang over a rock in the gravel driveway, looking spry as a puppy.

"You must have the magic touch," I told him. "Everyone likes you—even Blossom."

"Not everyone," he said.

"What do you mean?"

"My ex-wife wasn't one of my biggest fans," he told me.

"Ex-wives usually aren't," I agreed. "But I think she must be crazy."

"Do you?" He gave me a sidelong smile. "That's a comfort."

"What happened?" I blurted unthinkingly, then cursed my lack of tact. "I'm sorry; that was a really personal question," I added, blushing.

"Not much to it, really. She left me for her sports medicine doctor," he said.

Ouch. "I'm sorry," I said. "How long ago?"

"Five years," he said. "That's when I moved out here. Nothing holding me in the city anymore." He sighed. "I think she expected a bigger salary. She was what you call 'high maintenance.'"

I couldn't imagine anyone leaving this kind, funny, handsome man. Then again, I hadn't known him that long. He claimed salary was the dividing factor, but there were always two sides to every story. "There's more to life than money," I said.

"I'm glad you agree," he told me. "Because neither of us is likely to get rich out here in Buttercup."

I laughed. "Even if I do strike oil, none of it belongs to me." I fervently hoped the rolling hills that had been my family's home for so long would not be flattened in search of profit. I'd heard horror stories about some of the fracking operations that had sprung up around Texas, poisoning both water and land. I could feel my blood pressure rise just thinking about it.

Tobias turned the conversation back to me. "And what about you? Ever been married?"

"Came close," I confessed, "but no, I've never walked down the aisle."

"What happened?" he asked. "If it's not too personal," he added with a grin.

"It's not," I said. "I don't know what happened, really. We got along well enough, but as the day got closer, I started getting cold feet. Then, two weeks before the wedding, he showed up at my doorstep at 2:00 a.m. and told me he wanted to call it off."

"Wow," Tobias said. "How did you feel about that?"

"Relieved," I said. "And hurt, too, even though I felt the same way. Isn't that funny?"

"It's natural," he said.

"I think it's for the best," I told him. "He's working for the *Times* in New York now. Foreign correspondent. We still keep in touch."

"Did he marry?"

"No," I said. "Neither of us did. We've both been in relationships, but neither of us have ever found the right person."

"I hope that changes for you."

There was a quiet electricity in the air between us as we walked down the dusty road. Tobias stopped and turned to face me, his blue eyes on mine. He reached for me, and I felt every cell in my body respond, like iron filings drawn to a magnet. As his arms closed around me, his phone rang. He swore under his breath and reached for it.

"Tobias Brandt," he answered. He was quiet for a moment, and his face tensed. "I'll be right over."

The house seemed particularly empty when I returned to it. The phone call—a golden retriever had been backed over by a Ford F-150 and needed emergency surgery—had put everything on hold. Tobias had promised to call and let me know how things went; I would have gone with him, but he was going to be in surgery for hours, likely, and there were chores around the farm that needed doing.

Chuck lazed on the front porch as I milked Blossom, who still did her level best to knock over the milk pail and eyed me balefully when her attempts were unsuccessful. I was still stirred up by Tobias's visit, and the way things seemed to be going. I felt something for him that I hadn't felt for anyone in a long, long time—and on some level, it was unsettling. I'd come out here to make my own way, not to become embroiled in a relationship. What if things went wrong? We'd be cheek by jowl in the town for years—there was no way to leave your past behind in a town as small as Buttercup.

On the other hand, a little voice reminded me, unless I managed to find my way out of the number one slot on Rooster Kocurek's suspect list, it didn't matter how well things were going between Tobias and me. I'd be living in Huntsville, not Buttercup. And it's hard to have a relationship when there's a wall of bars between you.

My eyes drifted to the shadowy loft above me, and my thoughts turned to the lockbox with the photo and marriage certificate. Why had someone hidden that in the loft, of all places? And was my family somehow involved in Thomas Mueller's murder?

It took an hour to feed and water the chickens, water the vegetable patches, set up the irrigation for the peach orchard, and walk down to check on the dewberries; it was time to pick another batch in the morning. The phone still hadn't rung when I put on my cotton nightgown and crawled between the blue sheets of my grandmother's bed, Chuck at my feet. I prayed the Marburgers' dog would be okay; she couldn't have a better vet than Tobias to put her back together.

I picked up one of the library books I'd checked out: *Mourning Gloria* by Susan Wittig Albert. Her tales of China Bayles switching gears from her career as an attorney to the owner of an herb shop in Pecan Springs had been an inspiration to me when I was considering moving to the country myself. Tonight, though, my thoughts kept veering from the murder on the pages to the operation that was going on in the vet clinic—and, even more disturbingly, the murder in my own small town. Who had killed Nettie Kocurek, anyway? And why couldn't the officer in charge of the investigation be at least a little more professional in his investigation? As China worked in her herb garden and made a mental list of suspects, I decided it was a good idea and began constructing one of my own. Talk to Peter Swenson and Nancy Shaw. And stop by the Brethren Church and ask about that pin.

I was about to pick up the book again when the phone rang. I bolted out of bed, anxious to find out how the golden retriever was doing.

"Lucy."

"Quinn?" I felt my adrenaline spike. Her voice was all wrong. Panicked. Breathy. "Are you okay?"

"He broke in," she said. "I kicked him in the knee, and he took off . . . but the back door's all shattered, and I'm afraid he's coming back."

Chapter 19

"Are you okay?" I repeated.

"I'm fine," she said. "I called Rooster, and he's heading right over."

"I'm coming to get you," I said. "You can't stay there tonight. I've got plenty of room, and I'd love the company."

She was quiet for a moment. "Okay."

I stayed on the phone with her until she told me a sheriff's car had pulled up outside, then I threw on shorts and a T-shirt and raced out to the truck.

The black-and-white car was parked right in front of the Blue Onion, and all the lights were on in the building. The front door was unlocked, and I let myself in, calling out to identify myself.

"We're back here," Quinn called from behind the dining room. Then, in a lower voice, she said, "It's okay. I called her."

Quinn stood in the kitchen, leaning against the counter and hugging herself. She wore a tattered blue bathrobe, and Rooster stood a few feet away from her, looking rumpled in his uniform, as if he'd just gotten out of bed. Which he probably had.

"Evenin', Miz Resnick," he said, the suspicious look in his eye belying the polite greeting.

"Good evening, Sheriff. Thanks so much for

coming out." I looked at my friend, whose eyes looked haunted, and then at the shattered window that stood out in the cheerful room like a jagged, broken tooth. "I'm so sorry, Quinn. I'm so glad you're okay." I crossed the distance between us and put a hand on her shoulder. My instinct told me she was too rattled for a hug—particularly in front of Rooster Kocurek.

"You're sure it was Jed Stadtler?" Rooster asked, as if I weren't there.

"I was married to him for five years," she said. "He threatened me on the phone today. Plus, I'm guessing his fingerprints are all over this place."

"Don't you have a restraining order against him?"

She nodded. "Doesn't seem to be doing a lot of good, though, does it?"

"So he broke through your door and let himself in."

"That's what woke me up," she said.

"Then what happened?"

"He came up the stairs and into my bedroom. He tried to hit me in the head."

"Tried?"

"I blocked it," she said, raising her right arm. A large bruise purpled her freckled skin, and I felt anger boil up in me.

"That's right. You do that tae kwon do stuff."

"Karate, actually," she corrected him.

"So. He tried to hit you, and it didn't work. Then what happened?"

213

"He yelled at me. Called me a . . . a bitch," she said. "Reared back to hit me again."

"And then?"

Quinn lifted her chin. "I kicked him in the crotch." Rooster winced a little bit. "And his knee, too," she added. "I may have broken it. Then I ran to the bathroom, locked the door, and called you."

"Did he follow you?"

She shook her head. "He left. I heard him go downstairs, and heard the truck engine out back."

"Thank God he didn't have a gun," I said.

"He does, though," she said, in a voice that chilled me.

"Maybe you'd better think about getting one," Rooster said.

"I don't like having them around," she said. "Bad things happen with guns. Accidents."

"Might change your mind next time your ex comes around with a sawed-off shotgun," Rooster pointed out.

"Hopefully he'll be in jail for breaking and entering and it won't be an issue," she countered.

The sheriff hitched up his belt and sighed. "I suppose I'd better get this all written up." He squinted at the jagged shards of glass in the door. "You're going to need to replace that, or at least board it up. Are you staying here tonight?"

"I thought I'd go out to Dewberry Farm and stay with Lucy," she said.

Rooster eyed me. "Are you sure that's a good idea?"

Quinn eyed him levelly. "Can you spare an officer to park outside my back door every night?"

He took a shuffling step backward. "Budget's kind of tight. Maybe not all night, but we'll be sure to swing by and keep an eye on the place."

"Then it's a better idea than staying here."

Rooster sniffed. "Out of the frying pan into the fire, if you ask me."

"I didn't," Quinn said, her voice cool. "Are you going to be taking fingerprints tonight?" she asked. "I need to get this cleaned up so I can open tomorrow."

Rooster let out a heavy sigh. "I'll call Ed, see if I can get him over here tonight."

"Thank you," she said.

It was almost two in the morning by the time Rooster finished in the kitchen and we were able to sweep up the glass. His technician had gotten several prints, and I hoped at least some of them were Jed's; so many people came in and out of the kitchen, they could be anyone's. They also took Quinn's prints; they'd already taken mine from the day that Nettie was killed.

After we'd nailed up a piece of plywood I'd found in the shed out back and poured the last of the broken glass into the trash can, we double-checked the locks on the windows—"Like that's going to help," Quinn added jadedly—and I kept her company while she packed a few days' worth of clothes.

She followed me out to the farmhouse, which was only a few minutes away from the town square. I'd left the lights on, and the house looked cozy and welcoming as we bumped up the long drive. "Thanks for letting me stay," Quinn told me as she carried her suitcase into the house.

"My pleasure," I told her. "Like I said, I'll enjoy the company."

Once we'd dropped her suitcase in my old bedroom, Quinn and I checked all the doors and windows and lingered in the kitchen for a minute. "Piece of pie?" I asked.

"I can't eat yet," she said, leaning up against the door frame. "Still too riled up. I forgot to ask, though; how did dinner go?"

Although only a few hours had passed, it felt like dinner with Tobias had been weeks ago. I wondered how the surgery had gone; when Quinn went to bed, I'd check my messages. "Great," I said. "Your salad dressing and bread were terrific."

"I wasn't talking about the food, silly."

"Oh. Things seem to be . . . progressing. We had to cut the evening short, though—the Marburgers' golden retriever had a run-in with an F-150, and Tobias had to go and do emergency surgery."

"Poor Sadie," Quinn said. "She's a sweetheart,

but has a bad habit of chasing cars. Is she okay?"

"I don't know yet," I said. "But I'm glad you're okay. That must have been terrifying."

"It was," she acknowledged. "I wish I'd never met him. All I can hope is that this will put him behind bars and I can rest easy for a while. I hate always having to look over my shoulder."

"What did he want?"

She shrugged. "Same thing he always wants. To control me. He can't stand that I'm living my life without him. I keep hoping he'll move on, but he just can't seem to let go. And when he drinks . . ."

"You're welcome here for as long as you want," I said.

"Thanks." She looked up at me with haunted eyes. "But how long will it be before he figures out where I am now?"

Chapter 20

The night passed without any further disturbance, and after milking Blossom and checking on the chickens, I accompanied Quinn to the Blue Onion to open the next morning. There was no sign of Jed, thankfully, and once Tori turned up to start the lunch service, I took my leave. "I'll see you tonight, right?" I asked.

"Yes. Thanks again," she said.

"Let me know what Rooster comes up with."

"I'm going to call him in a minute," she said. "Right after I call the glazier. The sooner I get that window fixed, the better."

"Have you thought about a security system?"

"Too expensive."

I sighed. "I wish I could help."

"You're doing more than enough," she said. "Now, go and find out who murdered Nettie Kocurek, so we can prove Rooster wrong."

I put on a brave smile that I didn't feel and set off to pay a visit to Peter Swenson.

If driving up to Nettie Kocurek's house felt like time traveling to the 1950s, following the winding drive to Peter Swenson's was a little like pulling up to Tolkien's Shire. His property was tucked back behind a stand of oaks, and the rolling hills were verdant with crops: I recognized a variety of greens and the feathery tops of carrots, as well as rows of the velvety green of young tomato plants. About half the property was a sizable pasture, filled with goats in a variety of colors and bounded by barbed wire and cedar posts.

But it was Peter's house that commanded your attention. Nestled among a swath of fruit trees and half-built into a hill was a small, rammed-earth home with a grassy roof and round windows that would not have looked out of place in Hobbiton. The door was made of cedar planks, with what looked like hand-forged hinges, and tufts of rosemary and lavender flanked the limestone walk. I knew Peter had built the place himself, but had imagined a wooden shack, not the quaint hobbit-esque home built into a hillside. The only thing that linked the place to current-day Texas was his fry oil–powered school bus, which was parked about fifty yards from the house. He had painted it green, with the logo MOVEABLE FEAST painted along the bottom, amid what appeared to be a veritable cornucopia of vegetables. Nowadays, he used it to transport his produce to the Austin farmers' markets. Quinn had told me he lived in it while building his home; apparently he'd removed the seats and put in a futon and a small kitchen.

As I opened the door of the truck, a rooster crowed, and a few hens scuttled out from behind the lavender. The front door of the cottage opened before I got there, and Peter's lanky frame emerged.

"Howdy, neighbor!" he said in an exaggerated Texas accent. Which was kind of funny, since he came from the Pacific Northwest.

"Howdy yourself," I replied, wondering exactly how I was going to ask him about Nettie Kocurek without sounding like I was trying to implicate him. "Your house is amazing," I told him. "I can't believe you built it yourself!"

"Would you like the tour?" he asked, obviously proud of his handiwork.

"I'd love one."

The interior of the house was just as quaint as the exterior, with low, beamed ceilings and rustic cabinets that looked like he'd made them himself.

"What made you decide to leave Seattle and build a hobbit hole in Buttercup?"

He gave me a rueful smile. "A girl," he said. "I'm a hopeless romantic. I met her at South by Southwest in Austin, and she seduced me with her vision of an organic farm in the countryside."

"Well, you've got the organic farm."

"But not the girl," he said with a crooked grin that showed his white teeth. "She moved to Portland six months after I bought the property. Didn't like living in a bus and making bricks out of mud."

"Reality can be a lot harder than the dream, can't it?" I asked, thinking of my own troubles since moving to town. I looked around at the rustic yet beautiful interior. Hand-laid wood floors, whitewashed walls, and thick oak beams gave the house a fairy-tale feel that was enhanced by the open shelves of handmade mugs and plates in the cozy kitchen. He invited me to sit down at a small, round wooden table that, like everything else in his house, I suspected he'd made by hand. I ran my hand over the smooth surface. Pecan, I was guessing. "She should have hung around a bit longer, though. The results are spectacular."

"Thank you. But there are still goats to be milked, and it turned out she wasn't too fond of that, either."

"I can understand that."

"I'll bet you can. But if you think your Jersey girl is a challenge, you should meet a few of my nanny goats."

"At least none of them have consumed the town square geraniums yet," I pointed out.

"Only because I invested in a solar-powered electric fence six months ago," he said with a grin. "Before that, Nettie Kocurek was threatening to shoot them and serve cabrito to her farm hands."

"Ah, Nettie. Quite a charmer, wasn't she?"

"She won't be much missed. At least not by me." He took a sip from his tumbler. "Can I get you a glass of kombucha?"

"No, no thanks," I said. I'd tried his kombucha once at market days. Despite his assurances that it was a health elixir and delicious, it tasted like dill pickle juice, only worse.

"How about some mint iced tea? I picked a bunch and brewed it yesterday."

"That sounds terrific," I confessed.

As he filled a tumbler with mint tea for me, adorning it with a fresh sprig from a jug on the windowsill, he said, almost idly, "So, what brings you out for a visit?"

"I actually wanted to ask you about Nettie," I said, figuring that honesty—or at least partial honesty—was the best policy. "Since you and she were neighbors, I was wondering if you had any idea who might have wanted her . . . well, you know."

He gave me a sharp look. "Dead?"

"Yeah."

He sighed. "I'm sure you've heard we had an altercation a few weeks back."

"I'd heard a rumor," I confessed.

He shook his head and handed me the tumbler, then sat down in the handmade chair across from me. "Small towns. Everyone knows everything, it seems."

"What was the disagreement about?" I asked, taking a sip of my tea, which was lightly sweetened with honey and had a lovely, fresh kick from the mint.

"She was spraying weed killer along my fence line," he said. "A few of my goats took sick.

Plus, it was jeopardizing my organic certification."

"What was her response?"

He cocked an eyebrow. "She said she was welcome to do whatever she wanted on her property, and that if I could prove her chemicals had killed any of my goats, she would pay the replacement value."

"Which isn't very much," I said.

"Not enough," he said bitterly. "I look after my goats. I know them by name, and I take great care to make sure they're only eating what nature intended." He shook his head. "Sometimes I wonder if she wasn't doing it intentionally. She didn't like having a hippie living next door."

"She did like to get her way, didn't she?"

"By whatever means possible," he agreed. "A bunch of my nanny goats took sick a few months back; Dr. Brandt told me it must have been something they ate."

"Any idea what?"

He shook his head. "Unfortunately not. I lost two of them—Bridget and Tufty—but Nettie claimed she had nothing to do with it."

"Did you believe her?"

"Of course not," Peter said. The anger, I could tell, was still fresh. "But I couldn't prove it, so I was out of luck. I've kept a close eye on them since, though."

"I'm sorry," I said. "I know what it is to lose an animal you love."

He shrugged. "I should get used to it—I'm a farmer, after all—but somehow, I never do." He took a pull of his kombucha as if it were whiskey.

"Do you know if she was arguing with anyone else?" I asked.

He gave me a twisted grin. "Well, she wasn't crazy about her daughter's choice of husbands," he said. "But everyone knows that." He thought for a moment, and then said, "I think she was working on some kind of deal."

"She was sending a thumper truck out to my property to look for oil," I told him.

"I know about that," he said. "But there was something else."

"What makes you think that?"

"Maybe the Kocureks are trying to buy more property."

"But Nettie just sold me Dewberry Farm six months ago," I said. "That doesn't make sense. Why would she be buying more?"

"Good question," he said, taking another swig of kombucha. "Maybe Faith could tell you. I've seen her car out there several times these past few weeks. Hard to miss a pearly white Escalade with BUYBUTT on the license plate."

I almost choked on my tea. "Buy Butt? Really?"

"You didn't notice?"

"I guess I was too busy worrying about spending my life savings to look at my real estate agent's license plate." My list of people to question kept getting longer. "I'll have to stop by her office this afternoon," I said.

"You've had a rough time since you came to town," Peter said. "The Kocurek family seems to have it in for you."

"A lot of people seem to think I have it in for them," I pointed out.

He laughed. "Rooster in particular. He glommed onto you immediately, didn't he?"

"I guess I'm an outsider."

"I know that feeling," Peter said, and looking around at his hand-built house, I could understand his meaning. "Not too many rammed-earth houses around Buttercup," he said, echoing my thoughts. "And at least you have roots in this town—you're living in a house that belonged to your grand-parents."

"That's true. But you seem to be integrating quite well."

"I think they're getting used to me, but I'm never quite sure."

"Teena Marburger certainly likes you," I said, grinning.

He blushed. "I know. I don't know what to do about it, either. She told me the other day that the splinter would soon be gone."

"What's that supposed to mean?"

"I wish I knew," he said. "She seems to have some weird sight into the future. Only problem is, people aren't quite sure what she meant until after the fact, so if anything, her predictions just make everybody nervous."

"Maybe I should ask her whether I'm going to jail or not," I half-joked.

"It wouldn't help," he said, taking me seriously. "She doesn't take questions, unfortunately. Just spouts things out." He shrugged. "Some people call it a gift, but I'm not so sure." He took another swig of kombucha and changed the subject. "How's the farming business going? Anything I can help with?"

"I noticed your vegetables are looking terrific. Any organic gardening tips you can share?"

"I'm a firm believer in compost tea," he said, and for the next twenty minutes, he loaded me up with tips for growing tomatoes and dealing with the cucumber beetles that would soon be descending upon my squash plants. "Wait until summer," he said. "You'll be out there vacuuming leaf-footed bugs off of your tomatoes."

"You're kidding me, right?"

"Well, row cover works, too, but then you have to hand-pollinate."

He wasn't kidding, I realized, and thought—for the hundredth time—that I'd had no idea what I was getting into when I signed the contract for Dewberry Farm.

By the time I left, I was full of mint tea and glad I'd stopped by—I now had another new lead. As we stepped out of the little house, the goats all began clamoring at the fence.

"Feeding time?" I asked.

"They just want me to pet their noses," he said, walking over and stroking a brown nanny goat between the eyes. Four others pushed toward his hand.

"They really like you."

"The feeling is mutual," he said, stroking a velvety ear. "Sorry, girls," he said, "but I've got to weed the lettuce patch."

"Thanks so much for talking with me—and for the tips," I said.

"My pleasure," he replied with a sunny smile. "We outsiders have to stick together." It was a lovely visit, but I still found myself wondering if he felt strongly enough about his goats to do in Nettie Kocurek.

Chapter 21

My next stop was Faith Zapalac's office, which was on the corner of the town square, catty-corner from the Blue Onion, and with a lovely view of Krystof Baca's pickle-nosed statue, which still squatted in front of the courthouse, flanked by the decimated geraniums. I still hadn't gotten around to replacing those, I realized, and added them to my mental list.

First, though, I wanted to talk to Faith and see what I could find out about any of Nettie Kocurek's land deals. Which was going to be a challenge. I hadn't seen the real estate agent since the Harvest Festival, and things hadn't exactly been cordial between us; after all, she sold me Dewberry Farm without making clear that the mineral rights wouldn't belong to me.

I knew Faith was in the office—her white Escalade with its BUYBUTT plate was parked in front, and as I walked by, I could see her head bobbing up and down behind the plate glass window advertising "Buy a Piece of Buttercup Today!" She was facing away from the street, the phone pressed to her hair-helmeted head. I opened the front door quietly, not wanting to interrupt her animated conversation.

"I know," she crowed into the phone, oblivious

of my entry. "We've only got a few more to go before we can break ground, and I think one of the ones we were interested in is going up for sale next week." She was quiet for a moment. "I've been working on that one for months, but they keep holding on. What?"

She listened for a moment. "They're probatin' the will right now. Who knows?" She sighed. "I suppose we'll have to wait and see how everything settles out."

The person on the other end spoke loudly; I could hear the agitation even from across the room.

"Even if she does know something, what does it matter?" There was another loud response, the upset in the caller's voice even more urgent. "She won't want to shoot herself in the foot, and nobody's gonna be able to prove anything. And I promise you, my lips are sealed." As I watched, Faith drew herself up in her chair. "Are you threatening me?"

At that moment, she became aware of my presence. Faith swiveled around, her black-mascaraed eyes widening, her lipsticked mouth slackening into an "o" before pressing into a thin line as I pretended to study the listings taped to the wall. "I'm sorry, but I'm going to have to call you back," she said firmly. "A client just walked in."

She hung up and sat back in her pink vinyl

chair, adjusting her white rayon blouse. Her eyes blinked nervously, her eyelashes thick with clumpy mascara. "I didn't hear you come in." There was more than a hint of accusation in her voice. Maybe even fear?

"I just walked in," I said.

"If this is about those mineral rights, there's nothing I can do," she said in a flat voice.

"I do want to talk to you about that," I said. "You said there wasn't any problem."

She shrugged. "Caveet enter, you know?"

"You mean *caveat emptor*?"

"Whatever," she said.

"You should have advised me about the mineral rights. That's what I paid you for—to represent my interests."

"Seller paid commission, actually. Now, if you'll excuse me, I have an appointment."

"Too bad," I said. "Now that my land may be taken over by oil wells, I was going to ask if there were other properties for sale."

She blinked. "Other properties? You mean, buying more land? But I thought we stretched that loan as far as we could just to get you into your grandma's old place!"

"We did," I said, "but, uh . . . I may have come into a little more money."

Now I had her interest. "Oh? How did that come about?"

"My aunt died," I said without thinking.

So had Rooster's, I realized as soon as I'd spoken, and she did, too. It hung between us for a moment. "Anyway," I said, "I wanted to talk to you and see if there was anything new out for sale."

"Well, then," she said, softening. "I'm glad you can put that mineral rights thing behind you. You might want to think about selling that property—of course, with the Kocureks doing exploration, you might take a bit of a hit, but if you've got more resources now . . ."

I swallowed hard, as if I could swallow back my anger, and forced a smile. "These things happen," I said in what I hoped was a light tone. "Real estate is never a sure bet."

"I'm so glad you understand that," she said, looking relieved. "Now then. I've got a few new parcels that just came on the market. This one's about fifty acres—a bit more than you've got now. Of course, the price is a little steep . . ." She showed me the listing price, and I stifled a gasp before remembering that I wasn't actually in the market for property. "But it's got a pond, and frontage on a wet-weather creek. Lots of good pasture."

"It's nice," I said. "Mineral rights?"

She gave me a tight smile. "Don't want to make that mistake again, do we? Looks like they'll convey, but we'll do a double-check. And then there's another piece coming up on the market in the next week or two, but I think I already have a buyer for that."

"Whose property?"

"Well," she said in a conspiratorial tone, "it's not official, but the Chovaneks are considering selling up and moving to Houston. It's a big tract, and like I said, I've got some interested buyers, but you might be able to divide it and take a portion for your farm."

"The Chovaneks? Haven't they been here for more than a hundred years?"

"Well, you see, they've had a lot of bad luck lately. A few of their tractors gave up the ghost not too long ago, and their stock seem to have gotten into some bad pasture; they lost about a hundred head of cattle. Some kind of nightshade poisoning, I think I heard."

"That's a shame," I said.

"Happens sometimes," she said. "It's always tough with cows—they eat anything that isn't nailed down, practically. Almost as bad as goats. In fact," she said airily, "a few farms seem to have been having trouble this last year. I wouldn't be surprised to see a few more properties on the market shortly. Here's what's listed currently, and recent sales, too," she said, pushing a photocopied list toward me. "Of course," she added, "you might have some competition. I've got a few clients looking for something special."

"I heard the Kocureks were looking to expand a

bit," I said as I glanced at the page, even though I hadn't heard anything of the sort.

"What gives you that impression?" she asked.

I shrugged. "Just rumors." I waited a moment, and then threw out what I hoped would be a hook. "Somebody told me you and Nettie were planning something together."

"Well, I'll be," she said, blinking rapidly.

"You weren't working with Nettie?" I asked.

She crossed her arms over her chest. "Just because somebody is my client doesn't mean they fill me in on everything. Besides, she hadn't been in touch with me since you bought your farm." Her defensive posture made me wonder if she was telling the truth.

"Huh. I thought I'd seen your Escalade out there a few times recently."

She shook her head. "Must be somebody else's."

"With BUYBUTT on the back of it?" I asked.

Instead of answering, she shuffled the stack of listings together. "I might have stopped by to do client relations or something; I don't keep close track of everything." She pushed a flyer toward me. "Why don't you look through these and see if there's anything that interests you?" she said. "What did you say your price range was again?"

I hadn't, but I threw out the first number that popped into my head, and it was a big one.

Her eyebrows rose, but all she said was, "Your aunt must have liked you a whole lot, honey."

"She did. She was my father's sister—other side of the family. We were very close."

"I'll see what I can do." She arranged her face into a bright smile. "I hate to run, but I have a lot on my plate this afternoon, so why don't you let me know if you'd like me to show you one of those properties. Do you want me to set up an appointment with the mortgage broker?"

"I think I'd rather find the right property first," I demurred.

She nodded thoughtfully. "All right, then. You just let me know, okay?"

"Sure," I said, letting myself out the door and heading to my pickup truck. The shades were now down in the front office of Buttercup Properties, and I wondered what business Faith had to attend to.

Something told me it had to do with the phone call she'd been on when I arrived. I just wished I knew who she'd been talking to.

My next stop was to visit Quinn. Instead of parking in front of the cafe, I drove the pickup around the back of the Blue Onion, where the plywood over the door was a stark reminder of what had taken place last night. I knocked on it, identifying myself in a loud voice, and Quinn peered out through the window over the sink, her curly red hair pulled back from her drawn face with a blue bandanna. A moment later I heard the deadbolt snick back, and the door opened.

"Sorry to freak you out," I said. "I just thought it would be better if I came through the back."

"I don't care who knows you're here," she said.

"Well, I do," I replied as Tori walked through the swinging door from the dining room, her dark eyes filled with curiosity as they fixed on me. Everyone would know I was at the restaurant within five minutes, I realized, stifling a groan. But at least I hadn't flaunted my presence—and I hadn't had to walk the gauntlet of curious eyes and whispers.

The plywood over the door cast a shadow over the sunny kitchen. "Did you get in touch with the glazier?"

"He'll be here tomorrow," she said. "I called for a quote on a security system, too."

"Good." I knew it was expensive, but considering the circumstances, I wouldn't feel comfortable if Quinn stayed here without it. I was nervous enough about her staying here at all—at least until Jed was behind bars. "I just wanted to swing by and check on you," I said as Quinn slid a slice of quiche into the oven.

"I'm doing okay," she said. "Thanks again for letting me stay over."

"It's nice having the company," I said.

She smiled, but there were dark circles under her eyes.

"Any word from Rooster?"

"Nothing yet. I let my attorney know what happened, though. She alerted the Houston police, and I'm hoping they have enough evidence to arrest him for breaking and entering."

"Not to mention assault and disregarding a restraining order," I added dryly.

"I've learned not to get my hopes up." Tori pushed through the door to retrieve a tray, and we both fell silent, aware of her curiosity. Quinn busied herself washing another bunch of salad greens and I leaned against a counter and smiled at the waitress. She didn't return the favor.

When she disappeared through the door again, I pushed myself away from the counter and headed toward the door. "I've got a few more stops to make this afternoon," I told her.

"Any luck this morning?"

"Maybe," I told her. "We'll talk about it over dinner," I suggested, glancing at the door to the restaurant. Quinn nodded in understanding.

"Thanks for stopping by."

"I'll see you tonight, okay? Be safe," I warned her.

She glanced over at the corner, and for the first time I noticed the baseball bat leaning up against the wall. "I'll do my best," she said.

The sun was high in the sky, the rising mercury a hint of what I knew was to come in July and August, as I drove out toward the Bees' Knees, the window of the truck open and the smell of grass and baking soil in the air. As I turned toward the road leading to Nancy's homestead, a gust of cool wind freshened the air, carrying with it the ozone scent of rain—always a welcome gift in Texas. I glanced in my rearview mirror; sure enough, there was a front advancing from the west, the clouds a heavy gray blue. I sent up a quick prayer that it would continue advancing in Buttercup's direction, hopefully parking over my fields for an hour or two before moving on, as I turned up the lane toward the Shaws'. Nettie Kocurek's red ranch was next door. I recognized Roger Brubeck's truck outside, and parked next to it was a white SUV. Faith's Escalade? I wondered, squinting to see if I could make it out.

The road veered away and my view was obscured by a stand of mesquite before I could identify it, but I found myself wondering if Faith Zapalac was at the Kocureks'—and if so, what business she was conducting with Flora now that Nettie was gone.

Another cool breeze gusted through the window as I pulled in next to Nancy's truck. The air felt fresh on my skin as I opened the door, and all around me I felt a sense of expectation and electricity, as if the trees themselves were waiting for something to happen. What did bees do when it rained? I wondered as I walked up the flagstone path to the little house Nancy shared with her husband, Martin. She had landscaped it with lots of bee-friendly plants, most of which were native—a hummingbird darted in and out of bright red cherry sage flowers, and a number of bees and butterflies were busy collecting nectar from a swath of purple and white lantana. I knocked on the blue-painted door, but nobody answered.

I knocked a second time and waited a few minutes before heading around back toward the honey house.

A rumble of thunder sounded behind me, rolling across the sky, and the smell of rain intensified. The first fat drops of rain fell, making poofs of dust as they hit the ground, and I broke into a trot.

The honey house door was ajar, but there was no light on. "Nancy?" I called, standing and knocking at the door. The wind picked up and the raindrops multiplied, turning into a sudden downpour. I pushed the door to the honey house open and stepped inside.

Although it smelled of warmed honey and beeswax and rain, there was something disquieting about the shadowy barn. I stood inside the doorway for a moment; the only sound was the rain drumming against the metal roof, as if demanding to be let inside. The path outside was quickly turning to mud, and the clouds filled the sky; it looked like the rain was going to stick around for a while. I hovered by the door, trying to decide if I should make a run for the pickup truck—Nancy obviously wasn't here—but when a flash of lightning filled the sky, followed almost instantaneously by a bone-shaking crack of thunder, I decided I'd at least wait until the initial fury died down before heading back to the truck.

I turned the light on, hoping to dispel the eerie feeling in the shadowy space. The honey extractor gleamed, and the beeswax on the shelves glowed gold. I felt a cool breeze from a vent overhead, and looked up to realize the air conditioner was on. Which made the open door a bit odd; Nancy would have been careful to close it, to make sure her product wasn't compromised. Where was Nancy, anyway? Had she and Martin gone somewhere in his car?

I walked past the shelves toward the table and chair Nancy kept under the window, for when she was making labels or dipping candles. As I approached, I noticed a blanket crumpled on the floor in the corner, next to the separator. I took a step toward it, stooping down to pick it up, and froze.

It wasn't a blanket. It was a blue chambray shirt, and there were arms coming out of the shirt, and a tumble of silvery hair. Only the chambray shirt was stained dark, sticky red. Red, I realized with growing horror, from where it had soaked up Nancy's blood.

Chapter 22

What happened next I recall in bursts, like stop-motion photography. Something inside of me took over, propelling me through the mud to the house, traipsing through Nancy's clean kitchen to the phone, and dialing 911. Had I taken her pulse? No, I hadn't taken her pulse. I had known, just known, she was dead. There was so much blood. Could I stay on the line? The phone was corded and I'd left my cell phone in the truck, so no, I couldn't stay on the line. I had to go back, check her pulse, stay with her until someone came to care for her. To take her away. I recall seeing my muddy footprints on the Saltillo tile floor, and thinking I'd have to clean that up before Nancy came back—and then remembering that Nancy would never set foot on that floor again.

I returned to the barn out of duty, dreading what I had to do. I put my fingers to Nancy's pale, exposed wrist—I couldn't bear to be near the blood pooling around her head. The skin was still warm, but there was no steady beat beneath my finger. Nothing at all. Fighting back the urge to retch, I put her hand down gently and retreated to the chair, wrapping my arms around my body and waiting for the whine of sirens.

As I breathed in the scent of honey—tinged with

the coppery scent of Nancy's blood—my eyes swept the clean concrete floor of the honey house. A torn-off label caught my eye; it was about six inches by three inches and looked like it had been torn off another bag. The front of the label said COMPOSTED COW MANURE and seemed to have been printed on a laser printer. Underneath, on the sticky side, there was a bit of whatever it had been stuck to. I could make out the letters "MIK," along with "15 mg" and the words "Brand Aldi." I'd seen the same label in the back of the truck at the Kocureks' house, I realized with a jolt. It hadn't occurred to me then, but now I wondered who would keep manure in a paper bag; I'd only ever seen it in plastic bags. Maybe it wasn't cow manure, after all.

I found a scrap of paper and a pen, jotted down what I saw on the label, and put it back on the floor, wondering what the label was covering—and whether it was connected to Nancy's death.

"So." Rooster was staring at me, and I could see in his eyes that he thought I was a murderer. They'd taken the body away—taken Nancy away—in a black body bag, the rain spattering the plastic as they carried her to the ambulance. I watched from the covered porch on the back of Nancy's house. Where was Martin? I wondered. How would he take the loss of his wife? They'd been married thirty years; it was going to be an awful shock. This place was going to be lonely without Nancy. My eyes strayed to the line of hives under the cottonwoods near the creek, back behind the property. Who would take care of the bees now that Nancy was gone? My heart ached thinking about it.

The ambulance and Rooster's car had pulled up right outside the honey house, and the flashing lights seemed surreal in the serene country scene. The cherry sage still glowed scarlet against the wet green leaves, and as they loaded Nancy into the back of the ambulance, I found myself thinking of the hummingbird I'd seen just a little while ago. So much had changed in such a short time. Poor Nancy. They'd take her to the morgue in Houston, probably, far away from her comfortable home in Buttercup. I watched them close the doors behind her and hugged myself.

"Mizz Resnick?"

"What?" I swiveled, startled. Rooster stood there, his round face stony. "Oh. I'm sorry. I didn't see you there."

I hadn't noticed him leave the barn; I'd been too focused on the body bag. Thunder rumbled in the distance as I looked at him, solid and somehow menacing. His hair and his polyester shirt were wet from the rain, which seemed to be slowing down a bit.

"I asked what brought you out here," he said

in a slow, measured voice that somehow managed to be menacing.

"I . . . I thought . . ." I was about to tell him I thought Nancy might have known something about Nettie's murder, but decided referencing Nettie's death was a bad idea. "I wanted to talk about another order of beeswax," I said. "And maybe ask about setting up a hive of my own," I added. I had considered it, after all, although it wasn't in my plans for the near future.

"Beeswax?"

I nodded. "She sells it to me, along with honey. I use it to make candles."

He scribbled down what I'd said. "Beeswax," he repeated, not sounding at all convinced by my story. "And what time did you arrive here?"

"I don't know," I said, feeling numb. I had no sense of time right now. "Probably around thirty, forty-five minutes ago."

"Hmm. Did she know you were coming?"

"No," I told him. "I just swung by."

"What were you doing back here?" he asked, nodding toward the honey house.

"She didn't answer the door, and I saw her truck here, so I thought she might be working."

"You let yourself in?"

"The door was open. I went inside because it started to rain, and then . . ." I shuddered, remembering the dark stain on the blue chambray, the tumble of hair against the concrete floor.

"You came inside," he finished for me. "Very convenient."

"Convenient?" I didn't like the way this was going, I decided. Not at all.

"Well," he said, rocking back on his booted heels, "I don't know if you've noticed, but it seems that ever since you rolled into town, dead bodies are piling up all over the place."

A burst of anger shook me free of the numb feeling. "Excuse me, Sheriff. Are you suggesting I killed Nancy and then called you to come and get the body?"

His eyes glinted. "You said it, not me."

"You have got to be kidding me." I ran my fingers through my hair. "If I were the murderer, why on God's green earth would I call the police to tell them I'd found the body?"

He shrugged. "Maybe to explain why your fingerprints and DNA evidence are all over the place."

I couldn't believe it. The man was serious. "And are they?"

"Maybe. Too early to say." He gave me a nasty smile. "We're still conducting the investigation."

"Even if you did find my DNA—which you won't, since I just got here—what possible motive would I have for killing poor Nancy?"

He cocked a bushy eyebrow. "Maybe she saw you doing in Nettie. Maybe she was blackmailing you."

I almost choked. Although I'm not usually a violent type, I had a strong urge to wring Rooster's fleshy neck. Instead, I took a deep breath and tried to sound calm. "I'm afraid there are a few problems with that theory, Sheriff. First, I didn't kill Nettie, so there's no way Nancy could have seen me doing it." I forced a polite smile. "And second, I don't have any money. I spent it all on the farm." Which your aunt did everything in her power to destroy, I thought but didn't add.

He smiled, exposing his teeth. Which, I couldn't help noticing, needed brushing; there was a piece of lettuce stuck between his incisors. "That's not what Faith Zapalac tells me."

I blinked. "What?"

His smile broadened, and I started to get a very bad feeling. "I ran into her just before your call came in. She told me you had come into some big money."

Which is the trouble with lies, I reflected, feeling sick to my stomach. When you tell them, they have a nasty habit of coming back and biting you in the butt.

Chapter 23

By the time I got home, I was feeling like I needed about a quart of whiskey. Instead of emptying what was left of my bottle of bourbon, I let Chuck out to water the roses and poured myself a big glass of iced tea before helping myself to a slice of chocolate icebox pie. Sitting in my grandmother's kitchen was usually a comfort to me, but today, I felt too agitated to relax. As I finished the last bite of creamy chocolate pie, the phone rang.

I set the plate on the counter as I picked up the phone. "Hello?"

"I'm glad to hear your voice." It was Tobias. "I thought I'd scared you off last night."

"I'm so sorry," I said. "It's been a crazy twenty-four hours." I glanced down at the answering machine and realized the light was blinking. "I haven't checked my messages. What happened with Sadie?"

"She looks like she'll pull through," he said. "I called last night, but you didn't answer."

"I was at the Blue Onion," I told him.

"Midnight snack?"

"I wish." I told him about Quinn's run-in with her ex, and then about finding Nancy.

He let out a long, low whistle. "And I thought I'd had an exciting day."

"I could go for a bit less excitement, to be honest. Rooster now seems to think I've murdered two people."

"He thinks you killed Nancy and then called the police?"

"He seems to think I killed Nettie, then killed Nancy because she knew something about it."

"And then called the police. Maybe things have changed, but that's not usually how it works, in my experience."

"I said that's what I thought, too, but he didn't seem convinced." I slumped against the wall. Two titmice fluttered around the feeder outside the window, and the swath of bluebonnets beyond the fence rippled like water in the breeze. Blossom was investigating the gate at the far end of the pasture. Looking for a way to open the latch, I was sure.

"How did Nancy die?" Tobias asked.

"I don't know, but there was a lot of blood. I checked her pulse," I told him, shivering at the memory, "and her skin was still warm. I don't think she'd been gone long." I considered telling him about the torn label I'd found, but decided not to bother. It wasn't much to go on.

"I'm sorry you had to find her like that," he said. "How is Quinn doing?"

"She's staying here for a few days. Rooster took fingerprints—Jed broke the back door and let himself in—and she called her attorney. We're hoping he gets arrested, so she doesn't have to worry."

"Doesn't she have a restraining order?"

"Yes, for all the good it does."

"I hope Rooster's got someone keeping an eye on her place." There was the sound of a bell, and voices. "Looks like my next appointment's here. I'm going to have to let you go."

"Thanks for checking in on me," I told him. "I'm sorry I didn't call earlier."

"No worries," he said, then paused. "I'd love to take you out to Rosita's sometime soon, if you're up for it."

"I'd love to," I said.

"Maybe tomorrow for lunch?"

"That would be great," I said. We settled on a time, and as I hung up the phone, I found myself smiling. At least one thing had gone right today.

Unfortunately, however, that did not negate the several things that had gone wrong.

I sighed and checked the pie safe, where I kept the jams and candles I took to market on Saturdays; murder or no murder, I needed to have something to sell this weekend at the market. There were only six jars of Killer Dewberry Jam left, and with all the excitement, I hadn't picked since the day the thumper truck had come. I grabbed a basket and a stick and headed down to the dewberry patch down by the creek.

Even though the muddy ground squished under

my feet, I was thankful for the cool air the rain had left in its wake—and the water. Already the lettuce seemed greener; I was going to have plenty of heads to pick for the market this Saturday, and the broccoli plants were going strong. I'd have to plant one or two more rows of lettuce over the next few days, I decided, and maybe some arugula; we were moving into the warm season, but I might be able to eke out a few more cool-season crops. I smiled with satisfaction at the neat lines of healthy green plants. I'd have to try composting the chicken poop like Peter recommended —it was supposed to be a great natural fertilizer—and as I walked down to the creek and made plans for future plantings, I felt the tension seep out of me.

The creek was lined with cottonwood, sycamore, and willow trees. The dewberry vines were clustered under them, glistening with raindrops and hanging low to the ground, heavy with fruit. I used my stick to move branches aside as I picked the fat, ripe fruits—partially to avoid the poison ivy that tended to sprout up among the canes, and partially to look for any snakes that might be hiding among the brush. The breeze rustled the leaves above me, showering me with rainwater from time to time, but the whispery sound was soothing. The creek was already running a bit higher, and as I worked, I heard an occasional plop as a startled frog leaped into the water.

It was good to be outside, away from the house, away from people, focusing on the simple and nourishing task of picking berries and filling my basket. No snakes today, and only two sprouts of poison ivy—my luck was improving—and it took less than an hour to fill my basket. There were several more berries blushing; they'd be ready in a few days. I took a detour through the small peach orchard on my way back to the house, pleased to see the boughs heavy with fuzzy green fruit. With any luck, it would be a good harvest.

I could only hope I'd be around to take advantage of it.

Pushing that thought away, I headed into the kitchen, where I put my big canning pot on the stove as I rinsed and measured the berries, pouring them into my jam pot and adding sugar, water, a touch of lemon juice, and my grandmother's secret ingredient—vanilla. As the mixture heated, a sweet smell filled the kitchen, and I found myself turning things over in my mind as I stirred with a wooden spoon.

Nancy's death had been a real shock, but I was sure it was related to what had happened to Nettie. Did that label have something to do with her death? Her house, after all, had been right next to the Kocureks. Or did she know something about what had happened at the Founders' Day Festival—something that the murderer was afraid she'd spill?

Peter Swenson had mentioned seeing Faith Zapalac over at the Kocureks a lot recently, and suggested they were trying to put together some kind of land deal. Was he telling me the truth, or was he just trying to divert my attention away from him?

Faith had been talking with someone when I walked into her office, though—and she'd thought someone was threatening her. She'd gotten off the phone quickly when I arrived, but it was entirely possible she'd called back as soon as I'd left. She had almost certainly talked to Rooster at some point—I'd only been away from her office for an hour before Rooster knew what I'd said about an inheritance.

What was I going to do about that, anyway? I'd panicked and told Rooster the inheritance was still up in the air, but it wouldn't take long to discover I had no rich aunt, much less any other relatives who had died recently. Rooster was a lazy officer, but it was too much to hope that he wouldn't check out my story; I knew he was determined to put me away. And he'd confront me with it when he found out it was a lie. In which case I'd have to tell him why I'd said it, and what I was investigating. Something I was loath to do.

As the mixture in the pot started to bubble, I reached in the drawer for my candy thermometer and hooked it to the side of the pot, burying the silver bulb at the bottom into the foamy purple syrup. The smell of berries and vanilla was intoxicating; it was a shame, really, that a jar had been wasted at the festival.

Why had Nettie hit someone with a jam jar? Or, it occurred to me for the first time, had someone hit Nettie with it? I wished there were some way to find out what the autopsy results were. Some-thing told me the murder was a crime of passion—why else would anybody take the risk of killing someone in a tent at the festival?

And I still hadn't figured out anything about that lamb pin on the scrap of red fabric.

I gave the berry mixture another stir, making a mental list of things to do. Talk to Nancy's husband —maybe when I stopped by with a King Ranch Chicken Casserole. Find out about the lamb pin on the scrap of fabric. And figure out what kind of real estate deal Faith was trying to put together with Nettie Kocurek.

As I used a pair of tongs to lower clean jars into the canning pot, I thought about the rash of tractor troubles I'd heard about—and something tugged at my memory. Something Faith had said, about a farm that was coming up for sale. A hundred head of cattle had died of poisoning, and that had made them decide to sell up.

Then again, the Kocureks had had machinery sugared, too—at least that's what the librarian had mentioned—and if Nettie was trying to drive people off their land by sabotaging them, she'd hardly damage her own equipment. I wondered who else had had trouble? I'd have to ask Mandy Vargas down at the *Buttercup Zephyr* for a list. I knew Rooster wouldn't be forthcoming with it.

I peered down at the thermometer; the jam was almost done. I retrieved the jars from the canning pot, setting them down on a dish towel I'd laid on the counter next to the stove, and watched the mercury until it reached 104 degrees. When it hit the point, I pulled a plate out of the freezer and spread some of the syrup on it. It set immediately, which meant the jam had jelled.

I turned off the heat and ladled the mixture into the jars, leaving about a half inch of headspace, then fitted the sterilized lids over all of them and used the tongs to put them back into the pot. I'd boil them for another fifteen minutes before returning them to the dish towel to cool and waiting for the lids to pop down—the sign that the jars were sterile and sealed. I was just shy of a full jar, so instead of filling one more, I scooped myself up a bowl of Blue Bell Homemade Vanilla Ice Cream and poured the dewberry mixture over it.

The taste of tart-sweet berries with creamy ice cream was divine, and by the time the timer rang to tell me to take the jars out, I was wishing I'd kept back enough of the syrup for a second bowl. As the jam cooled, I hand-lettered another batch of labels; I'd put them on the jars when they had reached room temperature and then store them until Saturday.

Once the jars were all lined up on the dish towel, glowing in the afternoon light that slanted through the kitchen window, I took a quick inventory of the pie safe. I still had three dozen candles and about as many bars of homemade soap. With the carrots, greens, broccoli, and green garlic I would harvest, there would be plenty to sell at my stall this Saturday. I still had plenty of milk to process, too; once I got regular cottage cheese production going, with any luck, I'd turn a bit of a profit. Not enough to pay my attorney's fees, perhaps, but something was better than nothing.

I had just finished washing up the pot when Chuck started barking, and I glanced out to see Quinn's truck bumping up the drive. A few minutes later, she knocked, and I walked to answer it, drying my hands on a dish towel.

"Smells terrific in here," she said as she walked in carrying a heavily loaded cloth bag. "Just made another batch of jam," I said. "How did things go at the restaurant?"

"The window guy never showed up," she said. "But he said he'd be there tomorrow."

"And the lunch trade?"

"Busier than ever," she said. "I stayed out of the dining room as much as possible, but Tori told me there were lots of questions."

"I'll bet." Whenever a police car arrived with its lights flashing, questions were sure to follow.

"Any word on tracking him down?"

"Nothing yet," she said. "Rooster is giving me the runaround. Says the evidence is still with the lab, so he can't do anything."

"At least he doesn't know where you're staying," I said.

"I sure hope not, anyway." She put the bag on the counter and started pulling out groceries. "I've got some plums here that need to be used up, so I was thinking of making pork medallions with plum sauce."

"Sounds good to me," I said. "Can I help?"

"You can pour me a glass of wine if you've got any," she suggested.

"Happily," I told her. In truth, I could use a glass—or maybe a half dozen glasses—of wine. The day had not been a triumph, I reflected as I pulled a bottle of inexpensive but not awful sauvignon blanc out of the fridge.

"Do you have ginger?"

I dug in the vegetable crisper and withdrew a slightly wrinkled knob of ginger root.

"That'll work," she nodded as I tossed the ginger over to her. "How was your day?"

"You didn't hear?" I asked as she reached for a cutting board.

"Hear what?"

"I found Nancy Shaw dead."

"Oh, no." Quinn held the knob of ginger to her chest, looking stricken, as I poured us each a glass of wine. "I knew she'd had a heart attack a few years back . . ."

"It wasn't a heart attack." I handed her a glass and told her about the puddle of blood.

"That's awful," she breathed. "Poor Martin. Unless, of course, he did it himself."

"Would he?" I asked. "I kind of guessed this had something to do with Nettie."

"I always thought they were happily married," she said. "I'll have to send up some food. Poor guy." She shook her head and rinsed a few plums in the sink. "Was Rooster there?"

"Of course." I relayed our conversation, and she groaned.

"Lucy Resnick. Sometimes you don't have the sense God gave a goose. Why on earth did you tell Faith Zapalac you were inheriting money?"

"Because I needed an excuse to stop by the office," I told her. "Peter Swenson said he'd seen her at Nettie's a lot recently, and I thought I'd see if I could find out why."

She took a swig of wine and then rinsed a half dozen plums. "What are you going to tell Rooster when he finds out you don't have an aunt?"

I sighed. "I don't know. The truth, maybe?"

"Might have been a nice idea to mention that up front," she said.

I took a sip of wine and offered to chop plums,

but she waved me away. "It's therapeutic," she explained. "Did Peter have anything else to say?"

"She was spraying stuff near his fence line that he was afraid was messing with his goats' organic status," I said, "but I'm not sure that's enough to kill someone for. He did mention that Faith Zapalac was over there a lot recently, though."

"Probably sucking up to Nettie and suggesting she subdivide her property."

"That's a possibility," I admitted. "Peter did say he thought the Kocureks were trying to do some kind of real estate deal."

"Why would Nettie be interested in doing a real estate deal?" she asked. "She was already rich as Croesus?"

"To hear her talk, she was a poor pensioner," I snorted.

A few moments later, the phone rang.

"Lucy, it's Molly," my friend said breathlessly when I answered. "I heard you found Nancy Shaw murdered."

"It's true," I said.

"I also heard that Quinn's ex broke into the Blue Onion last night, and that she's staying with you."

"Also true," I confirmed.

"I'm so sorry," she said. "Please tell her if there's anything we can do . . ."

"I will," I said.

"I can't believe someone killed Nancy," she

said. "I heard Martin was devastated. Came home to find a sheriff's cruiser in his front yard."

"Is someone with him this afternoon?"

"Yes," she said. "He's staying with their daughter out in La Grange. It's such a tragedy. They were expecting their first grandchild, did you know?"

"I didn't," I answered, feeling a pit open up in my stomach.

"Bad times in Buttercup," Molly said. "People selling up left and right."

"I know," I said. "Faith Zapalac mentioned it to me. By the way," I asked, "how's that cow?"

"Doing just fine," she told me.

"I heard the Chovaneks lost a hundred head recently and are selling up."

"There have been a lot of problems with sick cattle recently," she said. "It's been a rainy spring —must be making the weeds grow. They sometimes eat things they shouldn't."

A thought glimmered in my mind. "Are you sure it's not linked with whoever's been sabotaging tractors?" I asked.

"Oh." She was quiet for a moment. "I hadn't thought about that."

"It's worth thinking about," I suggested. I thought of the list of properties for sale Faith had given me. I needed to ask Tobias how many of them had been linked with sick cattle.

"Of course. Anyway, I've been meaning to call

you about the lockbox you found in the loft."

With everything else that had been going on, I'd almost forgotten about the box. "I got it open the other day; there's an old marriage certificate, a photo, and an old bouquet."

"Really? Who was it?"

"I don't know. The certificate had too much water damage to tell the names."

"I'll bet if you take it to the county clerk, they'll be able to help you out."

"Did you find something out?"

"I was talking to Gus Holz the other day, and he mentioned that Thomas Mueller used to work for your grandparents. He didn't have a car or a truck, and it was a few miles to town, so they let him put up in the hayloft of the barn."

"Wait a moment. The Mueller man who was killed over Gruenwald lived here?"

"That's what Gus said."

"That would explain why the lockbox was in the hayloft, at least," I said. "Did he say anything else?"

"Only that he'd been sweet on one of the Baca girls. Unrequited love, I guess; he was just a farmhand, and she ended up marrying one of the Kocureks."

"Did he have any ideas who might have killed him?"

"No," she said, "and it will probably remain unsolved. Almost everybody in town who was around when it happened has moved or passed on."

"Who's still here?"

"Well, there's Anna Kosmetsky, but she's in the Alzheimer's ward. And Liesel Mueller—his cousin, I think—but she's always been what my momma called 'simple.'" She paused for a moment. "Why are you so interested in this, anyway?"

"I don't know," I said. "I like mysteries, I guess. And knowing he lived in the barn . . ." I thought about it for a moment. "But he couldn't have been the one holding onto the article about his death, could he?"

"Maybe your grandmother left it up there," Molly suggested.

"But why put it in the barn?" I asked. "And it doesn't explain the marriage certificate."

"You should go over to the county clerk's office and see if you can get another copy," she suggested. "After you manage to clear your name of Nettie's death," she said. "Speaking of which, I stopped by the Brethren Church today."

"What did you find out?"

"I asked Father Mikeska about the lamb pins. He told me they'd been given out at Christmas to recognize people who were particularly active in the church community."

My hope flared. "Does he have a list?"

"As a matter of fact, he does," she said. "He

showed me a picture that was taken after they were awarded. I wrote down everyone's name. Want the list?"

"Absolutely," I said. "I'll get it from you next time I'm out there."

"Great. Now, what about the pictures Mandy took at the festival?" she asked.

"You mean we could see who was wearing one the day of the event?"

"Just a thought."

"Molly," I said, gripping the phone with both hands. "You're a genius."

I hung up a moment later and explained everything to Quinn, finally feeling like I might possibly escape being charged with murder.

"There's only one problem," she said, looking up from where she was slicing the pork tenderloin into one-inch medallions. The red juice on the cutting board brought back an image of Nancy, and I looked away.

"What's that?"

"How are you going to convince Rooster Kocurek you didn't plant the pin?"

My hope deflated a bit, but I refused to be totally demoralized. I slugged down the rest of the wine, looked at Quinn, and said, "I'll burn that bridge when I get to it."

Chapter 24

Quinn and I shared a relatively jovial dinner together, despite the circumstances, and didn't resume our conversation until after I'd finished my evening chores.

"Have you made kolaches with your grandma's cottage cheese yet?" my friend asked as she reclined on my old overstuffed couch with Chuck stretched out beside her. I sat down in the rocker across from her with a glass of mint iced tea. He and I were both enjoying the company.

"Not yet," I told her. "I made the cheese the other day, though. It was good!"

"Where's her cookbook?" she asked.

"I'll get it," I said, standing up. "Need anything in the kitchen?"

"No. I'm too full of chocolate pie." I retrieved the cookbook from the kitchen and handed it to her, then sat back down in the chair, rocking gently as she leafed through it. She stopped about halfway through. "Oh, you've got a recipe for her bublanina."

"What's that?"

"A really yummy Czech cherry cake. She brought that to lunch at my mom's house one time. It was awesome with vanilla ice cream."

"I still haven't made most of the recipes," I confessed.

"She's got a few good pickle recipes, too. When your cucumbers come in, you should definitely try them." She paused and looked up at me. "It may sound weird, but I keep expecting your grandma to walk in from the kitchen," she said. "It's almost like I feel she's here."

Goose bumps rose on my arm. "I feel that way a lot," I admitted. "And you know that newspaper clipping? The one about the murder at the train depot in Gruenwald?"

"What about it?"

"It fell from the hay loft while I was milking Blossom."

"That could be the wind. Those old barns aren't too tight."

"I told myself the same thing," I said. "The thing is, the window was closed; and there wasn't a breeze that night. I almost felt like . . . like she wanted me to find it."

"Weird." Quinn shivered and looked back down at the book. "Okay, here it is. Cheese Kolaches."

"What do I need?"

"Well, more cottage cheese, for starters," she said, "but other than that, the usual suspects. Yeast, flour, eggs, sugar, butter. Fruit, if you want to add it."

"Let's give it a try tomorrow," I said. She was silent. "If you're still here, that is," I added.

She seemed to wilt a little at the reminder. "I'm afraid I won't be able to go home anytime soon." Anger shadowed her face. "It's not fair. He's the one who attacked me. Why should I be the one who has to rearrange my life?"

"I've thought the same thing," I admitted.

"I made a bad decision when I married him, and now it feels like I'll never be free." I could hear the bitterness in her voice. "And Rooster isn't doing anything to make sure he's put away. He won't tell me, but I know that man. He's making me pay for not going out with him in high school."

"How did he get elected as sheriff, anyway?"

She sighed. "There's always been a Kocurek in the sheriff's office," she said. "It's like a town tradition." She reached for her wine glass—she hadn't yet moved on to tea—and drank down what was left. "I love Buttercup, but some things about it drive me nuts."

"Maybe we can change them," I suggested.

She shot me a look of disbelief. "How are you going to change them from behind bars in Huntsville?" She tossed the words off casually, then clapped her hand to her mouth and blanched. "Oh, God, Lucy. I'm so sorry I said that."

"You're just being realistic," I said, trying to sound casual, but the truth was, hearing her vocalize my fears had hit home. What were we doing leafing through my grandmother's recipe book when odds were good Rooster Kocurek was going to arrest me for murder—maybe two murders—any day now?

I got up and stretched, trying not to show how upset I was. "I should probably hit the sack," I said. "You should, too—you have to get up early."

"Lucy," she said. "I'm so sorry."

"It's okay," I said, and gave her a smile. "See you in the morning."

But it wasn't okay, and both of us knew it.

It took a long time for me to go to sleep that night. I kept thinking about Nettie's murder—and Nancy's—and wondering who was responsible. Who would have wanted both of them dead? Was Nancy killed just because she heard or saw something she shouldn't have? Or did she die for another reason?

It was past midnight when I drifted off, Chuck snuffling lightly at the foot of the bed. I was dreaming about giant thumper trucks advancing on the farmhouse, their bumpers bristling with bratwurst skewers, when Chuck growled.

My eyes shot open just as headlights raked the wall of my bedroom. Chuck barked, and my stomach clenched, adrenaline pumping through my body.

Tires skidded on gravel as I leapt out of bed and hurried to the kitchen, wishing I had plugged my cell phone in next to my bed. Chuck trotted along behind me, still growling low in his throat. As I reached the last step, there was a pounding at the door that sounded like a thunderclap. The windows rattled, and my mouth turned dry.

"Quinn!" Jed bellowed.

I grabbed the phone and dialed 911 with shaking hands as Quinn came down the stairs to join me in the kitchen. The headlights still glared through the windows, making the cozy room look stark and cold. "I'm calling the police!" I whispered.

"I know you're in there! You can't hide from me!"

The voice on the other end of the phone was a comfort. "Nine-one-one, what's your emergency?"

"There's a violent man trying to break into my house," I whispered as Jed started hammering again. The door shook on its hinges; I hoped it wouldn't burst open from the force. "I need the police, as fast as possible."

"What's your address?"

I told her.

"It'll be a few minutes until we can get someone out there; I'm putting in a call right now. Can you stay on the line?"

"Okay, but I'm going to have to put you down."

"I'll be here," she said.

All of a sudden, the hammering stopped. Quinn and I looked at each other; she looked dead white in the reflected glare of the headlights.

266

"Did he give up?" I asked, even though I knew he hadn't.

"Truck's still here," she said. Her eyes darted around the room and landed on the broom by the back door. She grabbed it, holding it like a sword. "I'm so sorry, Lucy," she said.

"There's nothing to be sorry about," I said. "He's breaking the law."

"Yes, but he's breaking the law here. Whatever happens, let me handle it. I married the asshole, not you."

I shook my head. "I'm not going to let you face him alone."

Before she could answer, there was a crash, and the back door window exploded. Jed kicked the glass out and reached through to unlock the door, looking much taller than six foot two. He thrust it open with a kick, hollering, "Where are you? I know you're in here somewhere."

Chuck, who had been growling low in his throat, launched his thirty-pound bald body at Jed's leg, clamping onto his calf with his teeth. Quinn's ex started back, yelling. "What the . . ."

As I watched, he shook Chuck off and kicked him hard in the ribs. "No!" I yelled as my little dog flew across the room and hit a wall, then fell motionless to the floor. "Chuck!" I called, and started toward him, then stopped myself. This wasn't over yet.

"Go home, Jed," Quinn said. She had pulled

herself up and faced him, white-faced in her thin bathrobe, the broom in her hand. Her voice was tight, but rang with authority.

"There you are, you slut. Tryin' to hide. Don't you know you can't ever hide from me? I'll always find you." My stomach turned at the menace in his voice, and at the stench of sour beer and sweat.

"Go home," she repeated as he lurched across the room toward her.

"Sure, bitch. But I'm takin' you with me."

He swung at her, a wide, round swing aimed at her face. She ducked out of the way, and he stumbled forward, crashing into my grandmother's pie safe. I could hear glass breaking as jam jars crashed to the floor. I backed up against the counter, wishing I'd had time to find a weapon. As I clutched the tile countertop, something bumped against my hand. A rolling pin. I grabbed it as Jed reeled away from the pie safe, knocking a bowl off the countertop. It shattered against the wood floor as he advanced on Quinn, who jabbed at him with the broomstick.

The first jab took him in the solar plexus, and he staggered back for a moment.

"You hit me!" he said, sounding shocked.

"Go home," Quinn said again. This time, I could hear her voice tremble.

"Not without my wife," he said, and launched himself at her again. Quinn jabbed with the broom again, but he caught it, shoving it back toward her and knocking her off balance. She gasped and fell backward; he followed, backhanding her across the face before pinning her to the wall.

She yelped, but then kneed him, hard. He grunted in pain, but it wasn't enough to get him to back off. "You'll pay for that," he hissed, and I winced as he gave her a vicious hook to the chin. She managed to block it, but only partially. A few drops of my friend's blood spattered on my rag rug, and anger welled in me, eclipsing the fear.

I gripped the rolling pin in my hand and advanced, raising it over my head. I was about to bring it down when Jed howled, staggering away from Quinn, one hand covering his face. "My eye!" he said. "You tried to rip out my eye!"

"Go home," she said, her voice slurred and breathless. She had crumpled to the floor, her back against the wall. Blood dripped from the right side of her mouth.

Quinn's words seemed to make Jed forget the pain. His voice was savage as he turned and advanced on her, fists clenched. "I told you already, you bitch. I'm not going anywhere without you."

My friend pushed herself to her feet, still leaning against the wall.

"Say goodnight," he said, and launched a ham-sized fist at her just as I started swinging the rolling pin. Three things happened at once: his fist splintered the wall, the rolling pin smacked into his right temple, and Quinn's fist hammered the left side of his face.

He stood upright for a split second before crumpling to the floor, hitting the wood floorboards with a sickening thud.

"Quinn," I said, still holding the rolling pin. "Are you okay?"

"Been better," she said. I ran over and switched on the light.

"Oh, Quinn," I said. My friend's mouth was leaking blood, and her face was already beginning to swell.

"Chuck," she said, gesturing toward the inert poodle. "So sorry, Lucy."

I hurried over to my chubby dog, putting my hand on his tummy. It was rising and falling, but there was a streak of red blood on his muzzle. "He's still alive," I said. "I'll call Tobias."

I reached for the phone.

"Ma'am? Ma'am?" It was the dispatcher.

"I'm still here," I said.

"Is everyone okay?"

"We knocked out the intruder, but we need some medical attention," I said, looking at Quinn.

"I'll get an ambulance out there."

"Thanks," I said. "Are the police on their way?"

"Yes, ma'am. Should be there any minute."

"Good. I appreciate all your help, and I hate to hang up on you, but I have to call my vet."

I hung up and dialed Tobias. He answered on the third ring.

"I'm sorry to bother you, but Chuck just got kicked into a wall. He's breathing, but he's unconscious, and there's some blood."

"What happened?" he asked.

I looked up at Quinn, who had slid back down to the ground and was hugging herself. "Jed Stadtler."

"Damn," he said. "Are you and Quinn okay?"

"We will be," I told him. "Police and EMTs are on their way."

"I'll be right over."

"Thanks," I said, and hung up, looking at Quinn's swelling face. "Those were some pretty awesome moves, my friend. EMTs are on the way, but we should probably get some ice on that." I dug in the freezer for a bag of frozen peas, which I wrapped in a dish towel and held up to her cheek.

"Thanks," she said. "But what about him?" She pointed to Jed, who was sprawled across the floor like a jeans-clad bear rug.

"He doesn't get ice," I told her as I adjusted the peas.

She gave me a weak smile. "Duh. I mean, what if he wakes up?"

I grimaced. "I'll keep my rolling pin handy."

Tobias arrived just as Deputy Metzger cuffed Jed and half-dragged him out to the patrol car.

Rooster, thankfully, had been off duty. It had been bad enough dealing with Jed Stadtler tonight. I didn't need another hostile man in my home. Quinn's ex had started to come to just before the deputies arrived, and was still spouting obscenities at my friend as the deputies struggled to get the cuffs onto him and read him his rights. I hoped this incident would land him in jail, so that this couldn't happen again anytime in the near future.

Tobias knocked on the door just as the ambulance bumped up the road, its blue and red lights illuminating the dark pasture. At least they didn't have their sirens on, I reflected, although I knew news of tonight's events would have circulated through Buttercup by the time I finished my first cup of coffee the next morning.

"Are you okay?" he asked, taking in the deputies, the dented pie safe, and Quinn's swollen face.

"I think we'll be all right," Quinn said, sounding as if her mouth was stuffed with cotton, "but I'm worried about Chuck."

As the EMTs came through the open front door, Tobias hurried over to where my little poodle lay. My attention was torn between my friend and my dog; I prayed both would be okay.

"Did you move him at all?" Tobias asked.

"No," I told Tobias. "I was afraid to."

"Good call," he said, palpating Chuck's side

and looking at his bloodstained muzzle. Poor little dog, I thought; he was just trying to protect us. "He looks like he's got some broken ribs," Tobias told me. "I'm hoping the lung hasn't been punctured."

"Is he going to be okay?" I asked.

"I'm going to do everything I can to make him okay," he said. My heart squeezed as I realized he hadn't said Chuck would be fine. My poor dog couldn't be in better hands, though, I reminded myself. "I've got a board in my car," Tobias said. We'll slide him onto that and strap him down, and I'll take him to the clinic for X-rays."

"Go with him," Quinn said as a young EMT shone a light into her right eye.

As much as I wanted to be with Chuck, I knew I couldn't leave Quinn alone. Tobias knew it, too. He gave his head a small shake. "Stay here with Quinn," he said. "I'll take care of him and call you with updates."

"Thank you so much. I'm sorry to call so late . . ."

"Don't be." He reached out and put a hand on my shoulder. The contact sent a zing of excitement running through me, but was also deeply comforting. "I'm glad you called. Please don't ever hesitate—particularly in a situation lik this."

"Thanks," I said, and my heart seemed to expand when he smiled.

By the time Tobias drove his truck down the driveway with Chuck on the seat next to him, the EMTs had finished examining Quinn; although she'd have bumps and bruises, there were no broken bones, and she'd somehow escaped a concussion. Both she and I gave our statements to the deputies as the EMTs packed up their gear.

"She looks a lot better than the other guy," Deputy Metzger said as he closed up his notebook.

"We should probably check him out, too," the young EMT said.

"Why don't you follow us down to the courthouse?" he said. "We'll get him in a cell and you can take a look at him there."

"Sounds like a plan," the EMT said.

Deputy Metzger lingered at the door for a moment. "I hate to be the bearer of bad tidings, Miz Resnick, but the sheriff's working on getting a warrant."

"A warrant?"

The deputy grimaced. "An arrest warrant," he said.

My stomach turned to ice. "How long do I have?"

"A day or two," he said. "But you didn't hear it from me."

Quinn drew in her breath.

"Thanks," I said, feeling sick as my friend and I followed him out the door.

"That Stadtler's truck out front?" the deputy asked, pointing to the huge truck parked askew in the gravel drive.

Quinn nodded, still holding the bag of peas to her cheek.

"Good thing he was too drunk to remember the gun rack," the deputy said. "He's got a shotgun and two rifles back there."

I shivered, thinking of how much worse it could have been.

Chapter 25

Tobias didn't call until 3:00 a.m., but the news, thankfully, was good.

"He's got two broken ribs, but he'll mend," he told me as I sank onto a chair, limp with relief.

"Thank you," I said. "What was the blood on his muzzle?"

"He lost a tooth, but it isn't anything that'll keep him from the food bowl."

"That's great news," I said. "Thanks again for coming out so late, and for taking such good care of him."

"Don't mention it," he replied. "How's Quinn?"

"She'll be okay, at least physically," I said, "but I'm guessing she'll be sore in the morning."

"You two really handled things well last night," Tobias said. "Things could have turned out a whole lot differently."

I told him what the deputies had said about the gun rack in the back of Jed's truck, and he let out a long, low whistle. "You did get lucky, and so did I. It's been a long time since I've enjoyed anyone's company as much as yours; I'd hate for something to happen to you."

I felt a flutter in my stomach. "Thanks," I said. "I'm still a murder suspect, though. The deputy said Rooster's working on getting an arrest warrant."

"Well then, we'll just have to clear your name," he said easily. "I'm not going to give up our lunch date that easily."

Relief washed over me. "It's good to know someone in town is on my side."

"Always," he said. "I'm going to hit the sack, but I'll keep an eye on Chuck. You can come visit him tomorrow, but I'd like to hold onto him for a day or two to make sure he's doing okay. He'll be on reduced activity for a while."

"He'll love that," I said. "No more forced marches to the mailbox."

"He'll be back on duty soon," Tobias said. "Whether he likes it or not."

We talked for a few more minutes before hanging up. When I climbed between the covers, despite the harrowing events of the night, I was smiling.

I had just finished milking Blossom and was cleaning the milking equipment in the kitchen sink when Quinn limped down the stairs into the kitchen. I had sent her to bed immediately the night before, then cleaned up the glass near the back door and tried to push the dents out of the metal sheets in my grandmother's pie safe as I waited for news from Tobias. It was the second time in a week I'd been brushing glass into a dustpan thanks to Jed Stadtler, I reflected. I hoped he went away for a very, very long time.

My friend looked terrible. Now, despite the ibuprofen and the ice, her face had swollen so much she looked like a hamster storing sunflower seeds. I poured her a cup of coffee, then headed for the freezer to retrieve the bag of peas.

"How's Chuck?" she asked as she lowered herself gingerly onto a chair.

"He's doing okay," I told her as I handed her the bag. "Two broken ribs, and he lost one tooth, but no organs were punctured. He'll be up and around in no time, according to Tobias."

"I'm so sorry, Lucy."

"There's nothing to be sorry for. You aren't responsible for Jed's actions," I said.

"If I hadn't been here . . ."

"I'm glad you were here and not in town; he had two of us to contend with, not one. And now that he's in custody, you can rest easy." I shook two pills out of a bottle of ibuprofen and handed them to her. "I'll make scrambled eggs in a moment—they don't take too much chewing—but take these with your coffee."

"Thanks," she said, wincing as she applied the bag of frozen peas to her swollen cheek. "That rolling pin was good thinking."

"I backed up against the counter, and it just bumped against my hand." I looked at the pin, which was standing up in the crock I used to store baking tools. "Although it shouldn't have; I put it back in the crock after I made those strawberry pies the other day."

"Are you sure you didn't grab it out of the crock?"

"I'm sure," I said. My skin prickled. Why had that rolling pin been on the counter—and why had it rolled into my hand?

"Well, whether it was on the counter or in the crock, I'm glad you thought to use it." She grimaced. "And I'm glad Rooster wasn't on duty last night."

The mention of Rooster reminded me of my dilemma. "Unfortunately, if I don't get this Nettie Kocurek business figured out soon, I'm afraid he's going to show up on my front doorstep with an arrest warrant."

"You think so?"

I poured myself a second cup of coffee and sat down across from my friend. "Unless I figure out who killed Nettie, I am more than likely going to jail. And I'll lose the farm, and the next twenty years of my life. Maybe more." I took a sip of coffee and looked at Quinn. "If that happens, will you take care of Chuck?"

"It's not going to happen," she said fervently. "We're going to look at that list from Brethren Church and talk to everyone on it. And we're going to go down to the *Zephyr* and look at every picture Mandy took at the festival. Maybe she caught the murderer coming out of the jam tent—who knows?" She kept going. "Maybe someone will have jam on their clothes. There are so many things we haven't looked into yet."

My heart expanded at my friend's offer to help. "Thank you for that," I told her.

"I mean it." She looked at me hard. "I'll do anything I can to help prove you're innocent. Because you are."

My first trip to the newspaper office wasn't particularly fruitful; there was no sign of Mandy at the *Zephyr*, so I left her a message and headed over to Molly's house to see if I could pick up the picture she'd called about.

I spotted a few cows grazing contentedly in the flower-studded fields as I drove up to the Kramers' farmhouse. Molly's old Buick was parked out front, and she came to the door a moment after I knocked, drying her hands on a dish towel.

"Hey, Lucy! I was hoping you'd stop by. I heard about what happened last night; is Quinn okay?"

"She's doing all right," I said. Despite my protests, Quinn had headed into the cafe to work, claiming she'd rest if she felt she needed to. I doubted it, but I couldn't force her to go to bed, so I sent her off with ibuprofen and orders for more frozen peas.

"Scary," Molly said. "But I hear you gave better than you got."

"It was mostly Quinn and her karate," I said. "But I'm hoping he'll be off the streets for a while, and Quinn can relax." I handed her a jar of jam. "This is for you, by the way. Thanks so much for tracking down that picture."

"Thanks!" she said. "Come on in. It's in the kitchen with the list; I'm just cleaning up from breakfast."

"Need help with the dishes?"

"Nah. Sit down and relax," she said. "After last night, you deserve a break. Can I get you a cup of coffee?"

"Sure," I said, thinking I needed all the energy I could get. "Only if there's some made."

"There's plenty," she said, pouring two mugs. "Milk and sugar?"

"Both," I told her, and a moment later she handed me a chunky blue mug and gestured to the kitchen table. I thanked her as I sat down, then mentioned that the cow looked like it had recovered.

"It has," she said, "but I've been thinking about what you said yesterday. It might be worthwhile talking to Tobias and seeing if he's seen a trend."

"I'm going to see him at lunch today," I said. "I'm wondering if someone's trying to drive people out so they can pick up property."

"Are you thinking of the Kocureks?"

"Yes, but evidently their farm was hit, too."

She shrugged. "Could be a decoy."

"Expensive decoy."

"No kidding. We're still paying for repairs." She put up the last dish and hung the dish towel on the fridge, then retrieved the list and a four-by-six photo from a stack near the phone. "Here's the picture I told you about," she said. "Father Mikeska let me borrow it to make a copy, but I promised I'd bring it back."

"I'll scan a copy at the library and return it for you," I told her, peering at the photo. There were about fifteen people in the picture, and I recognized most of them. All were wearing bright red sashes with a golden lamb pinned to the shoulder.

"At least that narrows it down a bit," I said. I recognized Edna Orzak, the owner of the Red and White, along with Faith Zapalac, Nettie, Flora, and even Rooster.

I sighed. "I was hoping this would narrow things down more."

"Peter Swenson isn't on there," she pointed out.

"That's true," I said, brightening. "But every other possible suspect is."

"Except you," she pointed out.

"Yeah, but Rooster won't admit the lamb pin as evidence."

She put her hands on her hips. "Because he's a turkey, that's why. I do not understand how that man continues to be elected."

"You know, I was thinking about it on the way over here. Where did the bratwurst skewer come from, anyway?" I asked.

"From George Skalicky's booth," she said. "He runs it every year—it's about three tents down from the jam tent—and he makes all the sausage himself from an old family recipe."

"I thought he just raised cattle."

"He raises a pig or two, too. Keeps enough for his family, and sells the rest at the Founders' Day Festival. All the proceeds go to the town beautification fund."

"Who would have had access to a skewer?" I asked.

"From what I remember, he grills the sausages behind the tent and keeps a big can of skewers back there." She shrugged. "Anyone could grab one."

"So that's no help," I said. "Although if it were three tents away, it sounds like there's premeditation, doesn't it?"

"Yes . . . but why kill her at such a public event?"

I cocked an eyebrow. "Lots of available suspects."

"And lots of potential witnesses," she pointed out.

I sighed. "Any more word from Brittany on Roger and that waitress down at Rosita's?"

"She hasn't mentioned it since the night you came over to dinner, no. I can ask her, though."

"I thought I might go down there for lunch," I suggested.

"I did hear a rumor about Flora and Roger, though," she said.

"What?"

"I was down at the Red and White yesterday, and Mary Elizabeth down at the Enchanted Garden was talking to Flora about the wedding flowers. Apparently Flora's ordered a whole mess of yellow roses, since Roger calls her his yellow rose."

"Romantic," I said dryly. "They're not wasting any time getting married, are they?"

"No," she said. "Apparently Nettie didn't change the will before she died."

I perked up. "Really?"

"That's what Alfie's cousin Willa says. She's a probate attorney, offices in La Grange."

"She shouldn't be talking about clients like that."

"The will's public record now. But that's not the point."

"No?"

"Guess what Edna Orzak said when I picked up a pork roast yesterday?"

"What?"

"She said she wondered if Flora or her fiancé might not have hurried Nettie along somehow. So they could have their wedding cake and eat it, too, so to speak."

As encouraging as it was knowing that not everyone in town thought I was a murderer, unfortunately Edna down at the Red and White wasn't the person with arresting authority. "Does Rooster know all of this?" I asked.

"I don't know, but if he's not checking with Nettie's attorney, he should be. If Edna is right, and she was going to make Flora choose between Roger and her inheritance, then Flora had motive in spades."

"I wish I could talk to Nettie's attorney," I said.

"I wish Rooster would talk to Nettie's attorney," Molly said.

"I could always call Alfie's cousin and suggest that if Nettie was in fact planning to change her will, it could be germane to the investigation."

"You think she'll call Rooster?"

I shrugged and took a sip of my coffee. "I don't know, but it's worth a shot."

It had been a good visit, I thought as I climbed back into the truck a half hour later and headed toward the library to scan the photo. Molly always managed to lift my spirits; she was an eternal optimist. As I bumped over the railroad tracks and passed the train depot, I waved to Bessie Mae, who was in her customary folding chair under the shadow of the roof. She raised a wrinkled hand solemnly in response, then lowered it slowly. I wondered if Flora would follow in her mother's footsteps and continue to help care for Bessie Mae along with a lot of other folks in town. For someone as mean as a snake, Nettie did have a soft spot for the older woman. It made me think better of her, even though it seemed out of character. People can be surprising.

I had just pulled up outside the library when my cell phone rang. I smiled when I saw the number was the vet clinic.

"Hello, Dr. Brandt," I said.

"Hello, Ms. Resnick," he responded. I could hear the smile in his voice.

"Your ears must be burning," I said as I engaged the parking brake. "I was just talking about you with Molly."

"Good things, I hope."

"Always," I laughed, glancing over at the property listings page sticking out of the top of my bag. "How's Chuck?"

"Begging for food," he said.

I laughed. "So, almost back to normal, then?"

"Not quite, but I think he'll be just fine."

"Thank you so much for coming out in the middle of the night," I said. "He looked so bad last night; I thought I'd lost him."

"My pleasure," he said. "Are we still on for lunch?"

"That would be terrific. I wanted to ask you about cattle poisonings around town."

"Cattle poisonings? I must confess that I'm disappointed."

"Sorry about that," I said, feeling my face heat up, "but I heard yesterday that the Chovaneks lost a hundred head of cattle and were selling up."

"It was a tragic case," he said. "I still haven't figured out what they got into. We're looking into everything."

"Have there been a lot of sudden cattle deaths the last few months?"

He was quiet for a moment. "Come to think of it, we have had quite a few recently. I put it down to the wet spring, but do you think there might be something else to it?"

"Somebody's been vandalizing tractor engines, too," I said. "Smaller farmers, mostly."

"Why?" he asked.

"This is just a wild guess, but could it be that someone's trying to make a land grab."

"By wrecking equipment and poisoning cattle?"

"I know it sounds crazy," I said, "but with the drought we've had the last few years, a lot of farmers are really struggling right now. That's the only reason I was able to afford Dewberry Farm, to be honest. We've been really lucky with rain this spring, which has helped the farmers; but maybe that put a kink in the works for somebody who was hoping to buy a lot of land cheap."

"Like who?" he asked.

"I think Faith Zapalac might have an idea," I said.

"I guess that makes sense. She's the only game in town, isn't she?"

"Yup."

"It's an interesting thought," he admitted. "There have been an unusually high number this past year. This morning's pretty open for me; I'll go through the files and pull any poison cases, and we can take a look at what we find. See you soon for lunch?"

I glanced at my watch. "That sounds terrific," I said. "Only not at the Blue Onion, please. I don't want to make anything harder on Quinn than I already have."

"We talked about Rosita's. Will that work?"

"That sounds perfect," I said. If I was lucky, I might run into Roger and his waitress friend, too. "Noon still good?"

"See you there," he said.

Chapter 26

I pulled up outside Rosita's about five minutes before noon, parking under the red-painted sign proclaiming that the restaurant served "Down-Home Mexican." The restaurant was right next to Hruska's Bakery and Gas Station, right on 71, and had a good mix of out-of-towners and locals. They were doing a brisk trade today; I had to park in the back.

As I walked up the Saltillo tile walk to the front door, I noticed the F-150 truck from the Kocureks' house parked three spots from the entrance. I glanced in the back out of curiosity, but the manure bag was gone. Was Roger dining with Flora? I wondered. Or stopping in to say hi to one of the pretty waitresses?

The smell of sizzling fajitas greeted me as I opened the door and stepped inside. A green, white, and red Mexican flag was draped on the wall behind the bar—a refreshing change from the ubiquitous Czech flags that dotted Buttercup. I scanned the tables, looking for Tobias, and was not surprised to see Roger in a booth near the end of the front bank of windows, smiling at an attractive young woman with short, dark hair.

"Table for one?"

I turned to see the waitress, who was holding a

menu and looking at me inquisitively. I didn't recognize her, and with relief, I realized she didn't seem to recognize me. It was getting hard to be constantly eyed with suspicion.

"Two, actually," I said. My eyes turned back to Roger. There was an empty table next to his. "Can we sit in that booth near the end?"

"Sure," she said, and I followed her down the aisle, seating myself so that my back was to Roger. I was worried he'd recognize me, but fortunately, he was too focused on the waitress standing by his booth to notice.

As I settled into my booth and opened the menu, I focused on the conversation occurring behind me.

"So, are you working this weekend?" he asked.

"Saturday night," she said. "Why? You going to bring your girlfriend?"

"She hates Mexican food," he said. "Takes after her mother that way."

"I still can't believe she's gone," the young waitress replied. "I thought she'd live forever."

"Me too," he said.

"So now you're going to be married to a rich lady," the young woman suggested.

"Looks like it." I could practically feel him puff up in the booth behind me.

"Lucky for you," the waitress said. "I hear someone stuck the old bat with a skewer." I could almost hear her shudder in delight. "Who do you think would do such a thing?"

"The cops think it's that woman who bought the Vogel place," he said.

"What do you think?"

"If I'd put my life savings into a piece of property only to have the woman who sold it to me turn around and turn it into an oil well, I'd want to kill her, too."

"So, she stuck her with a skewer? I heard they found a jar of her jam on the scene, too. Broken."

"I heard that rumor, too," he said. Before he could say anything else, I heard my name and looked up to see Tobias walking to the table, a big smile on his handsome face.

Roger and the waitress must have heard it, too, because as he approached, she hurried away, glancing over a shoulder at me with wide eyes. I sighed internally. If the hostess hadn't known who I was before, she certainly would now.

"Hey," I said as he slid into the booth across from me. Tobias wore jeans and a green plaid shirt, and smelled of laundry detergent and hay. Our knees brushed, and again I felt that tug.

"I hope you haven't been waiting too long," he said. "I had to field a call on my way out the door. Chuck's doing great, by the way; he'll be back to his old self again in no time."

"That's a relief. What was the call?"

"Nothing urgent," he said. "Mitzi Karp's orange

tabby is pregnant, and she just needed reassurance."

"How's the golden retriever who was hit by a truck, by the way?"

"Recovering nicely," he said. "He'll be good as new in no time." He slid a folder across the table to me. "You were right about the poisonings. There were two the year before last, one last year, and six this year."

"Really?"

"Yes," he said, pulling out a map of Buttercup. Several tracts were circled. "All of this year's are right on the edge of town."

"Where were the previous poisonings?" I asked.

"They were scattered," he said.

I grabbed the sheet of listings out of my bag and slid it across the table to him. "Any of these?"

He looked at the list and his eyebrows rose. "Yes," he said. "At least four of these had poisonings on them. All pesticides, all beef cattle—they must have grazed on some contaminated grass."

I was about to reply, then realized that Roger was still behind me and had probably heard every word we'd said. I had no idea if the Kocureks had anything to do with the dying cattle, but there was always a chance. I folded up the map, jerked my head toward Roger, and said, "Well, I guess these things come and go." Tobias looked puzzled, and I pulled a pencil out of my purse and scrawled on the back of the map "Roger Brubeck behind me."

He nodded in understanding and changed the subject. "How's Blossom doing? Let me know if she gets into trouble; sometimes these chemicals drift, and then cows eat contaminated grass."

"I hope that doesn't happen," I said. "The last thing I need is a dead heifer."

"Has she gotten out since we checked the fence?"

"Not that I know of. You did a great job fixing the fence."

"Give her time," he warned me. "That one is a free spirit."

I groaned. "I can't afford that many geraniums."

"At least she's a good milker," he reminded me. I laughed, and we spent the next few minutes perusing the menu. I opted for the chicken chipotle enchiladas—chipotle sauce had an afterburn that required pitchers of water, but I couldn't resist it—and closed up my menu.

"What are you having?" I asked.

"Chicken chipotle enchiladas," he said.

I laughed. "Me, too. That sauce is addictive."

"Too bad I've got appointments this afternoon, or I'd try to talk you into a swirl margarita."

"Next time," I said, feeling a pang of regret for the frozen strawberry-lime concoction that was Rosita's specialty.

We ordered a moment later and spent a pleasant

fifteen minutes discussing the cases Tobias was working on in his practice. I kept one ear out for further conversation behind me, but my presence seemed to have shut things down. Roger stood up just as his friend delivered our enchiladas.

"Good to see you, Roger," the waitress said to him with a flirtatious smile.

"Likewise, as always."

"I'll be looking for you," she said in a saucy voice that made Tobias's eyebrows rise.

When the two had drifted away, I picked up my fork and looked at Tobias. "So. Back to poisonings," I began.

He leaned toward me. "You think Roger is involved?"

"I don't know," I said, "but I have a hunch someone in the Kocurek household might be. When I found Nancy, I also found a label that I'd seen in the back of a pickup truck at the Kocureks' house. It said 'cow manure,' but it was obviously covering something else."

"Do you have it?"

"I left it—it was evidence—but I jotted down what was on it." I fished in my purse and read off what I'd found.

"Fifteen milligrams. That sounds like some sort of pharmaceutical."

"Why would you store it in a paper bag and put a fake label on it?"

"And why was it in Nancy's honey house?" he mused. "Still. It's not a lot to go on."

"Do you think whatever was in that bag might have something to do with the cattle deaths? Nancy was upset about pesticide usage at the Kocureks'; she lost a couple of hives. Maybe she went investigating and confronted someone with the evidence."

"Is that worth killing over, though? The death of some bees and maybe some cattle?"

"It does seem like a stretch," I said, feeling glum again.

"I wish I could figure out what was in that bag," he said. "I can't think of anything that has MIK in it, though." He thought about it. "The only pattern I can see is that all the affected properties seem to be right on the edge of town. Only two of them are connected, though. If you wanted to do a big development or something, it would be hard—everything is scattered."

A thought occurred to me. "Wait a moment. That anti-fracking ban the mayor got passed. Is that just Buttercup?"

Tobias nodded. "And a good thing, too. Fracking is awful for groundwater."

I glanced at the map. "But all of these properties are right outside of Buttercup."

"Don't you think it would be all over the grapevine if a fracking company was buying up land?"

"Who *is* buying it?" I asked. "Do you know?"

He shrugged. "I don't usually pay attention. Do you really think it's relevant to what happened to Nettie?"

I sighed. "No," I admitted. "But I'm desperate enough to hope anything could be relevant." I looked at the map again, toying with the corner. "What killed the cattle?"

"I sent tissue samples to the lab, but haven't heard back yet. Whatever it was, it worked like some sort of nerve toxin. The animals were all found dead, not far from the stock tank."

"Why the stock tank, I wonder?" I put down my fork. "Do you think the tanks were contaminated, maybe?"

"It's possible," he said. "I hadn't thought about that. I should go and get a sample of the water, too."

"It may be too late, but it's a good thought." I felt excitement rise in me. There was something weird going on, and I had an inkling that what happened to those cattle was connected, somehow, with what had happened to Nettie Kocurek. "It seems strange, you have to admit. Somebody's been vandalizing machinery, too; it's not just the cattle."

He blanched. "If this is all true, someone poisoned hundreds of cattle. They suffered terribly; pesticide poisoning is a pretty awful thing— like nerve gas. I waited to see if any might recover, but when it was sure, I had to put them down."

I shuddered. "It's hard to say for sure that it was intentional," I said, "but I think it's a pretty good guess."

"How do we find out who bought the properties?"

"I was planning on heading down to the county clerk's office to look up an old marriage certificate," I said. "I might look at land records while I'm down there."

Lunch had been delightful, and not just because of the enchiladas. Despite my rather dire circumstances, I felt a smile creep across my face as I drove back toward Buttercup, Tobias's truck on the road in front of me. I followed him to the clinic, where I gave Chuck, who struggled to his feet at the sight of me, a few head rubs and a treat. He wore a large splint on his right side, and a cone of shame, but was wagging furiously and licking my hands, probably in search of stray enchilada sauce.

"Settle down, buddy," I said, kissing him on top of his shaved head and nicking my nose on the plastic cone. "Relax and get better, so you can come home." I turned to Tobias. "He looks great," I said. "I can't thank you enough."

"I hope Quinn's doing okay," Tobias said. "I imagine she'll have some colorful bruises for a week or two."

"She's lucky that's all she's got," I said, shivering.

"Is she going to move back to the Blue Onion now that Jed's in custody?"

"We haven't talked about it. I hope she stays with me for a few days so I can take care of her, but we'll see."

"You're a good friend," he said.

"I try to be," I said, giving Chuck's head another rub.

Tobias gave me a smile. "He should be ready to go in a couple of days. I'll keep an eye on him and let you know."

Hopefully, I'd still be available to pick him up, I thought.

Chapter 27

The county clerk's office was in La Grange, which was about twenty minutes away from Buttercup. Although the sign above the double glass door read 2002, it looked much older from the outside. I found street parking, then headed inside, relishing the cool interior. It was late spring, but it was already heating up outside.

The woman behind the desk was about my age, with a pleasant smile and dimples. She and I appeared to be the only ones in the building. "How can I help you today?" she asked.

"I need help tracking down some deeds," I said, holding the copy of the real estate listings Faith Zapalac had given me. "Recent sales."

"That should be easy," she said. I handed her the page with the properties circled, and a few minutes later, she had assembled a list of all the purchasers.

"That's strange," I said. "They're all being bought by companies—but all different companies."

"I see what you mean," she said. "Lovelace Limited, Golden Acres Properties, Happy Endings. I've never heard of any of those."

"Me neither," I said. "I'll have to Google them when I get home." I was expecting one purchaser to have picked up all of the properties, but it looked like that thought was a dead end. Still— it was strange that not a single one of the properties on the borders of town had been bought by an individual. "Can you look up these sales inside town?" I asked.

She did. All the sales within the town limits were to actual human beings, not companies. Something fishy was going on; and unfortunately, Faith Zapalac wasn't likely to help me figure it out. I looked at the map of properties and compared it with the list Tobias had given me. Of all the properties bought by companies on the outskirts of town, every one of them had also had livestock illnesses that had made it tough for the owners to pay the bills.

Why was someone collecting properties on the border of Buttercup? And why were cattle on those properties turning up dead? And how could it possibly be connected to Nettie's death? When I got home, I was going to have to put my old reporter skills to work.

"Thanks for your help with this," I said, tucking the papers into the bag I'd brought with me and pulling out the lockbox. "I have one more question for you. Can you get me a copy of an old marriage certificate?"

"Do you know the year and the names?"

"I know the year," I said, pulling the certificate out of the box, "but the names got washed out. I found this up in my barn, along with a picture and an old bouquet, but I have no idea whose it is."

"Oooh," said the woman, whose name was Christa, according to her name tag. "I love mysteries. May I see it?"

I set the lockbox on the counter and handed her the certificate. She smoothed it carefully on the counter. "Definitely Fayette County," she said. "And we've got a date. That'll help. Let me see what I can find," she said, and disappeared into the back.

It was almost twenty minutes before Christa reappeared, beaming. "Here it is," she said, offering up a yellowed piece of paper.

"Wow," I said, looking at the record. "Nettie Kocurek's mother married Thomas Mueller?"

"Nettie Kocurek?" she asked. "The one that was killed out in Buttercup?"

"That's the one," I said, deciding not to let her know she was talking with the sheriff's primary suspect. "This guy didn't do too well, either. He was killed at a train station in Gruenwald the week after they were married. How old was Nettie when she died?"

Christa pulled up her death certificate. I did some math and came up with another question. "The widow married again—I'm guessing very soon afterward. Is there any way to track down her second marriage certificate? And a birth certificate?"

"Of course," she said. "It might take a while, but I'll bet we can find them. And now I want to know!"

It took almost forty minutes, but when she was done, I had copies of both Nettie Kocurek's birth certificate and Anna Baca's second marriage certificate in my hand.

"Huh," I said, looking at the date. "Nettie must have been premature."

"Or not," Christa suggested.

"That's what I'm thinking," I said. Even though Alvin Kocurek was listed as the father, the numbers just didn't add up.

"Was Anna with him when he died?" she asked.

"There's no mention of it in the papers," I said. "And I've never heard anything about them being married—it wasn't in the article on his death."

"A secret marriage, then." Christa pointed to the birth certificate. "And perhaps a love child."

"That would be ironic," I said. "From what I've heard, there wasn't a lot of love lost between the Czechs and the Germans in those days."

"I wonder what happened to the young man?" she asked.

"I don't know," I said, "but I suspect Anna Baca's father may have had something to do with it. I have no way to prove it, though."

"There may be," she said. "Does she have any family alive?"

"Only one person I know of," I said, "but she's

not too likely to talk to me." I looked at the certificate. "Why do you think she got married so quickly?"

"Maybe she knew she was pregnant," Christa suggested. "In those times, that could be a real scandal, especially since no one knew she was married. And I'm sure there was talk about the timing, anyway; Nettie was born seven months after her mother remarried."

"And people say there aren't any secrets in a small town," I said, shaking my head. "Can I get copies of these?"

"Sure," she said. "Let me know what you find out though, okay?"

"Absolutely," I said, grinning at her and trying to forget that Rooster was planning to arrest me.

I drove home as fast as I could without being pulled over by one of Fayette County's finest, slowing down as I entered downtown Buttercup. I cruised past the Blue Onion and the sheriff's office and was turning past Buttercup Properties when I noticed a familiar vehicle outside of the real estate office alongside Faith Zapalac's BUYBUTT-plated Cadillac. It was Roger Brubeck's F-150. I was wondering about this when my phone rang. It was Tobias.

"Hi," I said, picking up on the second ring.

"How are you?"

"Been better," I said. "Thanks for lunch,

though—it was the highlight of the week. That, and seeing Chuck in such good spirits."

"It was the highlight of mine, too," he said. "There's been another cattle problem—I wanted to let you know."

"Where?"

"The Stolzes' place, out on Skalicky road," he said. "Right on the outskirts of town."

"Just like the others," I said.

"I know. I'm headed over there now."

"By the way, I just stopped by the county clerk's office."

"What did you find out?"

"All of those properties that sold up? They were bought by different companies."

"Weird," he said. "Do you think it's related?"

"It may be," I said. "Is this a poisoning, too?"

"I don't know yet, but I'll report back," he said.

"Let me know as soon as you can," I said. "Before Rooster shows up with an arrest warrant for me."

There was a silence on the line. "Oh, Lucy . . ."

A knot formed in my throat. "Call me when you know, okay?"

"Of course," he said, and we hung up a moment later. I took a few deep breaths to steady myself as I turned down the dirt road to Dewberry Farm. Everything had seemed so perfect just a few weeks ago. And now, I stood to lose everything.

I pushed that thought from my mind as I hurried

inside to my computer and typed in the names of the companies. I came up with nothing but PO boxes—all in Houston, at the same zip code. No owner, no CEO—nothing. Nothing that I could find out, anyway . . . but I knew someone who could. I leaned back in my chair and reached for the phone, dialing a familiar number.

"*Houston Chronicle*, Ben Ford."

"Ben? It's Lucy Resnick." Ben was the business reporter for the news desk, and if anyone could find out who owned a company, it was him.

"Lucy? How are you?"

"Doing great, but I need some help." I told him the situation—omitting the part about my potential impending arrest—and asked if he could identify the owner.

"Absolutely," he said. "I just turned in today's story; I should have an answer for you in an hour."

"You're the best," I said. I gave him my new number and hung up, thankful for my friends.

I had typed "MIK 15 mg" into the computer, with no meaningful results, when the phone rang again. I hurried to pick it up, expecting it to be Ben—but it was Tobias.

"A hundred cattle down," he said.

I sucked in my breath. "Oh, no. Can you save them?"

"I'm trying. It's pretty bad, though."

"What is it?"

"Nerve toxin. But I can't figure out where it's coming from. It must have gotten into the feed, somehow."

"Huh." I had an inkling of who might be responsible.

The problem was, the person I had in mind couldn't have been the person who lost a lamb pin.

As soon as I hung up with Tobias, Ben called me back.

"I know who owns those companies."

"Who is it?"

"Frac-Tex," he said.

"They're buying up all the properties outside of town," I said.

"Looks like it."

"And somebody's sabotaging the farms to make them sell out." I was willing to bet Faith Zapalac was in on it, but it wasn't likely I'd get her to admit it.

"Why buy outside of town?" he asked.

"Because the council just passed a law against fracking in the city limits. So they buy up the property on the outskirts of town and drill horizontally, without breaking any laws."

"Except for the whole killing off livestock thing, of course."

"And destroying farm machinery," I added.

"Sounds like that could be a lawsuit."

"And a big story," I added.

306

I could practically hear him smiling on the other end of the line as I hung up a moment later, but I didn't share his glee. Despite solving the puzzle of the dead cattle, I wasn't any closer to saving my own skin. I might be closer to figuring out the cattle deaths, but I was still coming up empty on identifying Nettie's killer.

And I was running out of time.

Chapter 28

Fifteen minutes later, I was pulling up outside the *Zephyr* and praying that Mandy Vargas would still be there.

I knocked on the door, almost fainting with relief when Mandy opened it, looking confused.

"I was about to head home for the day," she said. "I heard about Quinn; is she okay?"

"Yes, and she probably doesn't want it in the papers."

"I'll have to put a small article in," she said, "but it doesn't have to be front-page stuff. Do you think she'll give me an interview?"

"I'll ask her," I said.

She gave me an appraising look. "But that's not why you're here, is it?"

"No. I know it's late, and I'm sorry to bother you, but do you have the photos from the Founders' Day Festival?"

"Of course," she said. "Why?"

"Because I think we might be able to identify the killer," I told her.

She blinked at me for a moment, then said. "Come on in."

Mandy pulled up the photo file on her laptop, and we both pulled up chairs. "What are we looking for?" she asked.

"Remember I told you about a small, gold lamb pin attached to a torn scrap of fabric at the scene of Nettie's death?" I said. "I think Nettie must have torn it off whoever killed her."

"Rooster never mentioned any pin."

"I bet," I said. "He probably didn't want to admit to a reporter that he hadn't investigated the crime scene."

"Sounds about right," she said.

"Anyway, Father Mikeska gave out the lamb pins last Christmas, to congregants who had performed special services for the church. I have a copy of the photo they took when they issued them, and I want to go through and see who was wearing one during the festival."

"And who might not be wearing one at the end of the day," she added.

"Exactly."

I took out the photo, and we combed through the file of Mandy's shots from the Founders' Day Festival. Four people had chosen to wear their lamb pins that day: Edna Orzak, Faith Zapalac, Bessie Mae Jurecka, and Flora Kocurek. Of all of them, Flora was the most likely suspect. We were more than halfway through the photos when I stopped on a group shot, jabbing a finger at the screen.

"Is that what I think it is?" I asked.

She zoomed in. "I think so," she said as we stared at the gleaming gold pin.

"But he's not on your list!" Mandy said.

"He's not in the photo, that's for sure. Did you take any pictures after Nettie died?" I asked.

"Yes," she said, moving quickly through the next shots until the jocular faces turned worried and long. "We'll slow down and look to see if the pin is still there."

We made it through about thirty photos before Mandy stopped. "He lost his sash," she said.

"No he didn't," I said, pointing to a bit of red sticking out of a pocket. "He took it off."

"Because the pin was torn off?"

"That's my guess," I said.

"But it still doesn't prove he did it," she said.

I told her what I had found out about the cattle deaths and the land sales, and her eyes grew wide. "He's involved in that?"

"I think so," I said.

"Nettie was totally against fracking," she said. "Not traditional oil drilling, of course, but she didn't want the town's water getting polluted, particularly with all this drought. She was a big supporter of the fracking ban."

"Was she?" I asked.

"Maybe she found out he was involved with the company—helping them get established. Maybe she threatened to tell Rooster."

"I wish there were some way to prove it," I said.

"And what about Nancy Shaw?"

I thought about it for a few moments. "It still fits." I told her my theory.

"All we're missing is proof," she said.

"That's why I'm going over there tonight," I told her.

"Are you sure that's a good idea?"

"No," I said, "but it's the only idea I have."

I was on my way home when Tobias called.

"I got word back from the lab on what happened at the Chovaneks' farm," he said.

"What was it?"

"Pesticide poisoning," he told me. "A really toxic one—a carbamate insecticide—but I can't figure out where it's coming from. John Chovanek must have come in contact with it, too; his wife found him lying in the field. He's on his way to the hospital."

"Poor guy . . . I hope he's okay. What was he doing when he came out to check on the cattle?"

"Replacing the salt lick," he said. We were both quiet for a moment, then, at the same time, said, "The salt lick."

"Can you get it tested?" I asked.

"I'll go and get it now," he said.

"Be careful."

"I'll wear gloves," he promised. "I'll let you know what I find."

"Stay safe," I warned him.

311

"You, too," he said, and I decided not to mention what I planned to do that evening.

"Are you sure you want to do this?" Quinn asked as I pulled a black hoodie on over a navy-blue T-shirt. She had come over to let me know they were charging Jed with breaking and entering and assault, and had stayed when I told her what my plan was. I figured someone should know.

"I need to see if I'm right," I said. "I can't send Rooster in if there's no evidence."

"How are you going to get in?"

"Martin Shaw is still in La Grange" I said. "I'll go through their fence."

"You know it's legal to shoot trespassers in Texas," she said.

"Thanks for the reminder."

She got up from the rocker she'd been sitting in, her voice still a little strange sounding due to the swelling in her cheek, which had turned an alarming shade of purple. "I should come with you."

"After last night? No way. Besides, I need somebody I can call if I get into trouble."

Quinn gave me a look.

"Not that I'm going to get into trouble."

"What kind of security measures do they have? They seem pretty serious about it; they've got that intercom and video feed at the front gate, remember?"

"I'll figure it out," I told her. "Just keep your cell phone handy, okay?"

I wasn't feeling quite so optimistic when I turned off at the Shaws' house about twenty minutes later. My heart clenched as I bumped down the long, dirt drive, and I found myself wondering how the bees were doing without their caretaker—and how Martin was holding up without his wife. I was glad he had family nearby.

I parked my truck behind the house and turned the engine off, listening to the sounds of the night. A few cattle lowed in the distance, and the first cicadas had started humming. Peaceful sounds under normal circumstances, but tonight, they put my nerves on edge.

It took a few moments to get myself together enough to get out of the truck. I double-checked to make sure my phone was charged, slipped my rubber rain boots on over my tennis shoes, and tucked a penlight into the back of my pocket before opening the door and stepping out into the night.

It was only fifty yards to the fence. Once I got there, I put on the rubber gloves—I'd researched how to get through electric fences—and cringed as I touched the two wires and prayed Google hadn't lied to me.

Either the fence wasn't on, or the Internet was right; the rubber kept me from getting shocked. I stepped through unscathed and pulled off my rain boots, setting them next to the fence post. Since my tennis shoes had rubber soles, the boots were probably overkill, but I figured it was better to be safe than sorry.

The compound was another few hundred yards away. I walked toward it, praying I would go unnoticed, and jumped when a cow shuffled toward me, mooing in surprise. I'm not sure who was more startled.

I paused to let my heart rate return to a reasonable level before moving forward again, still scanning the compound for signs of life. Lights burned in the brick ranch house, but there were no security lights on the outbuildings, and the barn windows were dark.

I slowed down as I got to the edge of the barn, clinging close to the wood exterior wall as I searched for a door. I wasn't sure where I would find the bag that had been in the F-150, but I knew it was no longer in the truck—at least it hadn't been when I was at Rosita's for lunch. I just hoped the bag hadn't been emptied and/or thrown away—or that if it had, it was still here some-where.

The main doors were held closed with a length of chain, but no padlock. I undid the chain and sidled into the barn, pulling the door closed behind me, and turned on the penlight.

There weren't any animals, but there was a lot

of junk. The little light skimmed over the hoods of two old cars—also Cadillacs, from the familiar hood ornaments—and piles and piles of rusted farm equipment that looked like it dated back from the last century. There was a broken butter churn, an ancient, derelict tractor, and even a yoke. The Kocureks didn't ever throw anything out, it seemed; it was an antiquer's dream come true.

The problem was, I had no idea where to look for the bag I'd seen in the back of the F-150. Or even if it was in here.

I poked around a heap of old feed bags in the front corner of the barn, but they were dusty and had obviously been here for a while. I was beginning to wonder if what I was looking for was in the barn at all, and after fifteen minutes of stirring up dust, I decided to look in the other buildings.

I slipped out of the barn, still watchful for any signs of movement, and crept up to the driveway. The barn was outside the fence that surrounded the Kocureks' compound; I leapt across the cattle guard into the fenced portion of the area, feeling too close to the house for comfort. Particularly since there was movement on the other side of the sheer curtains covering the big bay window. I'd have to be very careful.

First, I decided to recheck the back of the F-150. Unfortunately, the only thing in the truck bed was some dirt and a small pile of dead leaves, and a quick sweep of the cab with the penlight turned up nothing but an empty Big Gulp cup and an old newspaper. I headed next to the small outbuilding furthest from the house—it looked like it had once been a smokehouse. My guess was confirmed when I swung the door open; it still smelled like smoke, and the walls inside were black. I closed the door before flashing the penlight around, but other than a small pile of charcoal on the floor and a few withered onions hanging from a beam by dried stalks, there was nothing to be found.

I slipped out of the smokehouse and crept over to the next outbuilding, which was a modern metal shed not too far from where Nettie's Cadillac was parked. Unlike the barn, this door was padlocked shut, which meant there might be something the Kocureks wanted to hide behind the door. Unfortunately, it also meant I couldn't easily get in.

The lock was a combination lock, with a row of four numbers along the bottom. Three of the numbers were centered, but the fourth was between the 3 and the 4. I pushed it to the 3 and tried the lock; nothing happened. But when I pushed it to the 4, the lock clicked open like magic in my hand.

I was in.

Chapter 29

A strong chemical smell hit me, and as I closed the door behind me and turned on the penlight, I could see why. There were stacks of fertilizer bags along the back wall, and several drums of Roundup along the side, but no sign of the white bag I'd seen in the back of the truck. Peter Swenson would hate the way this ranch was run, I couldn't help thinking; nothing happened without the help of chemical manufacturers. I wasn't crazy about it, either—but an inventory of the Kocureks' fertilizer and weed-control choices wasn't what I was here for. I ran the penlight around the room twice, searching, and was just about to give up when I caught a glimpse of white behind the yellow fertilizer bags, up at the top of the stack.

I reached for it, but the bag was too heavy to pull down, so I slid one of the Roundup drums over and used it as a step stool.

My heart thrummed with excitement as I saw the label. Most of the lettering was faint—I could tell this was the bag the label had been ripped from—but it was still legible. *"TEMIK 15 mg"* it read . . . and underneath it, the words *"Aldicarb Pesticide,"* along with the word *"POISON"* in bright red.

As I stepped down from the drum, it tipped. I stood on one foot, suspended on the edge of the drum like a clumsy ballerina, before pitching into the metal door with a loud thunk, sending the penlight bouncing out onto the grass, where it landed with its beam aimed directly at one of the ranch house windows.

Terrific.

I scrabbled to my feet and launched myself at the penlight, praying that no one had heard my less-than-graceful exit from the shed—or seen the beam of the wayward penlight. I hobbled back to the shed as fast as I could—I'd hit my hip on the metal lip of the floor—and closed the doors, fitting the lock back on with trembling hands. I was just snapping the lock shut when the yard flooded with light, and a door creaked open behind me.

I turned, tensed to run, and found myself looking at the barrel end of a shotgun.

"This is private property," Roger Brubeck said in a menacing voice.

"I'm sorry," I said. "Um, Blossom—my heifer—got out, and I've been looking for her."

"In my shed?" he asked. "On a fenced property?"

"I must have gotten turned around," I said, shuffling to the side. The barrel of the gun, unfortunately, followed me.

"What are you really doing here?" he asked. There was a shadow behind him; Flora had come to the open door. He turned back to her for a second to tell her to go inside, but before I could do anything stupid, his eyes were back on me. I watched Flora; she went inside and closed the door, but when Roger turned back around, she opened it again, just a hair.

"Nothing. Sorry to bother you. I'm going to head home now," I said, and took a shaky step toward the cattle guard—and the section of fence I'd slipped through earlier.

"Maybe I should call the sheriff," he said in a voice that chilled my blood.

"Do you really want to do that?" I shot back, sounding braver than I felt. "I know about your deal with Frac-Tex."

The barrel wavered. "I don't know what you're talking about."

"No?" I asked. "You know, you sent a rancher to the hospital today. I know you put a toxic pesticide on the salt licks of properties Frac-Tex wanted to buy. I'm betting you tampered with the farm equipment, too. You even sugared one of the engines on this ranch, to throw anyone off your trail."

"You don't have any proof," he said.

"Oh, no? One of the labels from your pesticide bags was found near Nancy's body," I said. "She knew about the poisoning. And soon enough, the police will come knocking at your door." I took a small step, back toward the shed. "Why did you have to kill them, though? That's what I can't figure out. Poisoning cattle is a crime, but it's not enough to put you away for life. Did Nettie find out about your deal with Faith Zapalac and the fracking company?"

"Shut up," he said, advancing on me.

I backed up, wishing there were something I could put between Roger and me, and kept talking. "And Nancy," I said. "She knew what you were up to, too."

"Stupid woman, crazy about her bees. She was going to ruin everything," Roger said. "Poking around over here, eavesdropping, stealing things from my truck."

"Like fake labels on toxic pesticides?" I sucked a deep breath and risked another question. "How did she know you'd killed Nettie?"

That was the million dollar question; I still didn't know the answer. Fortunately, Roger provided one, and I found myself wishing I'd thought to run the recording app on my cell phone. "She figured it out," he told me, anger in his voice. "She was over here on the sly, poking through the back of my truck, and heard me talkin' to the real estate lady about takin' care of the ol' bat. I shoulda been more careful. But I will be from now on," he said. "I can promise you that."

"What about Nettie?" I remembered what Molly had told me about Alfie's cousin and the will.

"She found out about what you were up to with Faith Zapalac and the fracking company, and was going to change her will if Flora didn't sign the prenup, wasn't she?"

"I had Flora talked around, thinking the prenup was nonsense, but then that witch found out about the fracking deal and pulled the will business on me that day at the festival." He glanced back toward the house, but didn't register the slightly open door. "It didn't matter what she told Flora; if Flora's mama cut her off, there'd be no point in marrying her." He shook his head. "Years of taking her out to dinner and buying her flowers and listening to her complain about her overbearing mother, all for nothing."

"So you cut Nettie off before she cut Flora off."

He nodded. "That's the long and short of it. Lucky for me, you were a perfect suspect. Still are. And with you dead, the case will be closed."

I swallowed hard and played for time. "Smart of you to damage the Kocureks' equipment, too—take suspicion off of you."

"I ain't stupid," he said. "And I don't plan on goin' to jail. Lucky for you, you won't be goin', either. 'Cause I'm goin' to shoot a trespasser, and then I'm going to marry Flora Kocurek and her money, and then, when I'm done with her, I'm goin' to do whatever the hell I want."

"With that waitress you were talking to, down at Rosita's?"

321

"Maybe," he smirked. "Maybe not. A lot of young ladies like a well-off man. But you won't be around to know, will you?"

"I'm not the only one who knows you killed Nettie," I blurted. "You left your gold lamb pin at the scene—the one Nettie tore off of you when you stabbed her. I went down to the *Zephyr*; she's got pictures of you with it on, and then with the sash stuffed into your pocket."

"Well then," he said, "maybe I need to stop on by the newspaper office when I'm done here," he said. He clicked back the hammer of the shotgun.

And several things happened at once.

The gun blasted. The door of the house slammed open. I launched myself to the side, falling into a painful roll. And Flora stepped out of the house, a pistol in her hand, the end of it trained on her fiancé's back.

"Put down the gun, you double-crossing bastard, or I'll shoot till there's nothing left in this pistol." I never thought I'd be so happy for someone to discover her inner Nettie Kocurek, but boy, was I glad.

Roger raised his flabby arms. "Flora, sweetheart." His voice was shaky. "I can explain everything."

"Don't you go sweetheartin' me, you murdering, yellow-bellied snake. Get down on your stomach, where you belong, and toss that shotgun to where the Vogel girl can pick it up." She looked up at me. "You got a phone on you?"

I nodded as I picked up the discarded shotgun, laying it carefully out of reach.

"Call my cousin Rooster," she said, still training the gun on Roger. "Tell 'im we got some trash that's ready for pick-up."

Chapter 30

"So, it was Roger all along," Quinn said as we raised two jam jars filled with wine to toast my new non-suspect status later that night. When Flora told Rooster what she'd heard Roger say, he looked as if he'd swallowed something that wasn't sitting right. He didn't look at me all night—until I asked if he still wanted me to come down to the station. The answer, thankfully, was negative.

"Thank goodness Flora kept the door open and heard everything," I said as I relaxed back into the saggy couch. Quinn had used her nervous energy tidying the little farmhouse while I was at the Kocureks', and it felt warm and cozy. The only sign of Jed's recent intrusion was a small dent in the pie safe—and the absence of my chunky poodle begging for bits of the cheese and crackers Quinn had set out on the coffee table. I kept reaching to pet Chuck, and then remembering he was still at the vet clinic. I missed him.

"Thank goodness Flora had the presence of mind to lay hands on her pistol," Quinn added, shivering. "I know people think I should have one around, but I hate guns."

"Me too," I said. "But I'm glad Flora feels differently."

"Sounds like she channeled her mama for a few minutes there."

"Certainly the force of will was there, but the language was a bit more colorful."

"Did she really tell you to call Rooster to come and pick up some trash?"

I nodded. "I didn't know she had it in her."

"Me neither." Quinn took a sip of her wine. "Think she'll be okay?"

"I think so," I said. "I'm sure it's got to be a real letdown, though. She seemed to be crazy about him."

"First love," Quinn said, swirling the contents of her glass. "It will be hard. Maybe we can reach out to her a bit."

"That's a good idea," I said. "She's going to have to do some work to find herself; she's lost her mother and her fiancé in the same week."

"Maybe you can talk her out of drilling for oil on Dewberry Farm. You kept her from marrying a man who planned to murder her, after all. That's got to be worth something."

"I hope so," I said. "I'd hate to see Buttercup turned into an oil and gas hub."

"Speaking of oil and gas, what does this mean for the properties that were bought up by Frac-Tex? Will they be able to frack them?"

"I don't know. They'll probably be sued for property damage—maybe even fraud," I said. "There'll be huge penalties, I imagine. I'm guessing we won't need to worry about fracking just yet."

Quinn and I were silent for a few minutes, thinking, before she asked, "Why did Roger kill Nancy?"

"She'd overheard him telling Faith Zapalac that he'd done in Nettie," she said. "Plus, she knew he was using pesticides to contaminate salt licks."

"I heard about John Chovanek going into the hospital," Quinn said. "I hope he's okay."

"Does that mean Faith will be arrested?"

"I imagine so," I said. "Accessory after the fact. She's also been involved in that shady land deal with Frac-Tex, too. She's got a lot of explaining
to do."

"You've had a busy night," she said. "Solved two murders, saved yourself from jail, and freed a woman from marrying a black widower."

"Not bad for a night's work, I suppose," I said, reaching for a cracker. "But there's still one case we haven't solved."

"Oh, really?"

I pointed to the lockbox that was sitting on the counter. "We still don't know what happened to Thomas Mueller."

"You have an idea, though," she said.

"I do. And I think Flora may have another shock coming to her."

● ● ●

The sun was high in the sky and the fields of bluebonnets were rippling like waves in the breeze when I got in the truck the next morning, setting a fresh dewberry cobbler on the seat next to me, beside the lockbox. Blossom was in the pasture, sniffing around the bluebonnets for tasty morsels as I pulled out of the driveway and headed to the Kocureks' ranch.

This time, when I stopped at the end of the driveway, I didn't even have to speak into the intercom before the gate swung open. By the time I made it up to the cattle guard at the end of the driveway, Flora was standing at her front door, bony arms crossed tight over her chest, waiting for me. I grabbed the cobbler and hurried to the door.

Whatever fire had animated Flora the night before had gone out. She was ashen, and looked as if she hadn't slept at all. "Are you doing okay?" I asked.

She nodded in a way that was not at all convincing, and invited me in with the barest wave of a pale hand.

I ducked through the door and waited for her to come in, then followed her listless walk to the kitchen, where I set the cobbler on the gold laminate countertop. The lights were fluorescent rods, one of which was flickering, and it looked as if nothing in the kitchen, including the green-

and-gold-flecked linoleum flooring, had been touched since 1975.

"Coffee?" she asked.

"Sure," I said. "But I'll make it. You just sit down. Can I cut you a piece of cobbler?"

"I'm not hungry," she said, "but go ahead."

At least she hadn't thought I'd poisoned it.

I busied myself measuring Folgers into the yellowed Mr. Coffee, then sat down across from Flora.

"Thank you for saving my life last night," I said. "You were absolutely amazing."

She sighed. "Mama was right. Mama's always right."

"No she wasn't," I said. "Maybe Roger didn't turn out to be Prince Charming—maybe she was right about that."

"Not Prince Charming?" For a moment I saw a glimpse of the fire she'd displayed last night. "He was a murdering sonofabitch!"

"Okay," I said. "So your first love didn't turn out as well as you'd hoped. It happens to almost all of us. Was he your first love?" I asked.

She nodded.

"First loves almost always crater; it's part of the learning process. You're just getting started a little later than most of us," I said.

She looked up at me. "Really?"

"Really. And I ended up with quite a few duds. I almost married one."

"What happened?"

"He ran up the credit cards spending money on his girlfriend," I told her, still feeling the sting, even though it was years ago. Last I heard he was in Topeka selling used cars. And probably still living off one of his serial girlfriends.

"How did you find out about the girlfriend?"

"When she called him to say the credit card he'd given her was being rejected, and I picked up the phone," I told her. "I'm still a bit gun-shy, to be honest." I grinned at her, remembering how she'd leveled the pistol at her fiancé's head the night before. "Thankfully, you're not."

"That's pretty bad," she said, smoothing back a strand of brown hair, "but at least he wasn't planning on killing you."

"Not that I know of," I said. "Come to think of it, he was pretty lucky to get off without me killing him."

"So was Roger," she said.

"You were magnificent. 'Murdering, yellow-bellied snake . . .' He was shaking in his boots!"

A small smile crept across her pale face. "You think so?"

"I know so," I said. "You've got spunk. You might not have had a chance to let it out much yet, but it's there."

"Thanks," she said in a small voice. It was quiet for a moment, except for the gurgling of the coffeepot.

"The one thing I wonder," I said, "was where he got that Moravian lamb pin. I saw a picture of the people who were awarded pins, and Roger wasn't in it. I didn't even know he attended the Brethren Church."

"He went on Sundays because of me, and helped them fix the roof. Father Mikeska gave out the pins on Christmas, but he wasn't there because he had the flu," she said. "I brought his pin home for him."

"That explains it," I said, and got up to pour two cups of coffee.

Flora started up. "I can do that."

"I can take care of it," I told her.

"Are you sure?" When I assured her I'd be happy to do it, she said, "Milk's in the fridge, and sugar's on the counter." I doctored our cups and returned to the table, and we both sipped the rather bland brew. She put down her cup and looked at me. "I've made a decision about Dewberry Farm, by the way."

My stomach tightened, but I put my cup down slowly. "Yes?"

"I'm giving you the mineral rights," she said. "It wasn't fair, what my mama did."

"Really?"

"Really," she said, smiling.

"Thank you," I said, feeling giddy with relief. The thumper truck wouldn't be back again. Ever.

"It's only fair," she said. "And it's the least I can do, considering you saved me from marrying a murderer." Her smile tugged down a bit.

"Speaking of fair," I replied, not sure if this was the time, but not sure if it would ever be the time, "I've come across some information on your family—your grandmother, to be exact—and I think you should know about it."

"My grandmother?"

"Your mother's mother. I started researching when I found a lockbox up in my barn," I said. "Let me get it; it'll be easier if I show you."

I hurried out to the truck and returned quickly with the lockbox.

"What does this have to do with my grandmother?" she asked, puzzled.

I took a deep breath as I opened the box, removing the copies of the marriage certificates and the birth certificate I had put inside. "Your grandmother was married before she married Alvin Kocurek," I said, handing her the piece of paper recording Anna Baca's marriage to Thomas Mueller.

Flora blinked. "What do you mean?"

"She fell in love with Thomas Mueller," I said.

"But . . . but he's German! My great-grandfather never would have allowed that!"

"You're right," I said.

She shook her head. "This can't be right. I've never heard anything about it."

"He died about a week after marrying your grandmother. She married Alvin Kocurek about a month later." I handed her the second certificate.

"I didn't know that," she told me. "But what does that have to do with anything?"

"Here's your mother's birth certificate," I said. "Look at the dates."

Her brow furrowed in confusion. "Why?"

"Just look," I said, and she did. Then her eyes widened. "She was born only seven months after she married my grandfather." She looked up at me. "Do you mean . . . Mama was half German?"

"I think so," I said.

Flora looked at me, and then, a moment later, began to giggle. It was contagious; soon, the two of us were laughing so hard I was doubled over, wiping tears from my eyes. "I don't believe it," Flora gasped between giggles. "My mother didn't want me to marry a German . . . and she was half-German after all!"

And then she burst into tears again.

Chapter 31

When I'd gotten her calmed down, Flora asked the question I was wondering if she'd come around to. "So the guy who died must have been my grandfather," she said. "I wonder what happened to him?"

"He was murdered at a train station a few towns away from here," I said. "It was never solved."

She blanched. "That's terrible!"

"I know," I said. "I keep thinking there's got to be another side to this. Do you think there might be some of your grandmother's things stashed away somewhere? If so, maybe there's a clue to their relationship."

"There's a trunk that used to belong to her out in the barn," Flora said. "I've never opened it."

"Are you up for taking a look?"

"Sure," she said. "It's not like I've got wedding planning to do anymore."

Together, we hopped across the cattle guard and walked over to the hulking barn. As she opened the oversized doors, the light gleamed on the nearest Cadillac. "Are those all your mom's old cars?"

"She couldn't bear getting rid of them," Flora said, standing with her hands on her bony hips. "Now. If I could just remember where I saw it."

"What does it look like?"

"It's brown," she said. "Wood."

We dug through the barn for about twenty minutes before I spotted a likely suspect under a rusted push mower. "Is this it?" I asked. Flora waded through the stacks of junk toward me. "I think so," she said. Together we excavated it from beneath the mower and carried it to the front of the barn, sneezing from the dust we'd disturbed.

It wasn't locked, and yet another cloud of dust billowed up as we lifted the lid.

A crushed pink hat, yellowed with age, was the first thing we saw. Flora lifted it; under it was a tray filled with what appeared to be costume jewelry and little mementos. "Look," she said. "It's a ticket for *The Nutcracker* in Houston."

"What's the date?"

"Nineteen thirty-nine," she said. She picked up a cameo brooch. "I recognize this from a photo my mama had," she said. "This is Grandma Anna's trunk."

Grandma Anna had kept all kinds of things: ticket stubs, broken jewelry, handkerchiefs, and hats. It was amazing that all of it had been stuffed into a small trunk. We were nearing the bottom when Flora uncovered a small book bound in blue leather and a stack of yellowed letters tied with a faded red ribbon.

Flora looked at me. "What do you think?"

"Let's take a look and find out," I said. She

carefully untied the ribbon and opened the first letter. It was addressed to Anna, in a masculine hand.

"Bingo," I breathed. We skimmed the letters, hoping for a clue. We found one, toward the end of the stack. *I don't care how much money your daddy offers me*, Thomas wrote. *You're worth all the money in the world to me.*

"So romantic," Flora said, and I could sense the emotion in her voice. We looked through the rest of the letters; they ended abruptly, just before the date of the wedding.

"So we know Josef Baca wasn't too excited about the marriage. And that he did offer money to him." I thought about it. "They thought robbery might be the cause of the murder—Thomas' wallet was missing when they found him."

"Do you think he took the payoff and left town?"

"It doesn't make sense," I said. "They were already married."

"Unless he was planning on taking the money and then having her meet him somewhere?" Flora suggested.

"I don't know," I said, picking up the leather-bound book at the bottom of the trunk and handing it to Flora. The word "DIARY" was embossed in gold on the front. "Maybe the answer is in here."

She opened it up. The pages were filled with a

neat, schoolteacher-ish hand. "The entries are dated," Flora said.

"Can you find the time near the wedding?"

She flipped through the pages. "Right here," she said, and I sat down beside her to read the entry dated May 25, 1939: the date of the wedding.

We did it. Thomas borrowed a truck and met me in town, and we drove to the courthouse in La Grange. We're married! We'll take the late train to Dallas next Tuesday; Thomas heard about a job there, and that way we'll be far away from Daddy. I hope he changes his mind; I love him, and I will miss my family so much. But I can't live without Thomas.

"So they were leaving on the train," I said. "What's the next entry?"

There were a couple more talking about preparations for the journey, and a secret rendezvous in a barn loft, presumably at Dewberry Farm. She flipped through another few pages, then stopped, her finger at the top of a page dated June 1. "Here's one from the day he died."

Daddy suspects, she had written. *He must have heard something; he's forbidden me to leave the house. I'll have to sneak out a window after dark; I hope I won't be too late to make it to the 8:00 train. We should have left last week. I should have known we couldn't keep everything secret. Somebody must have told him he bought the tickets. I can't believe this is happening, and pray we will get away.*

The next entry was in an unruly script, jagged. No change in date.

He left without me. Daddy got home late, after midnight. He says he met him at the station at eight and paid him five thousand dollars to leave me alone, and then he got on the train without me. I am devastated. I can't believe he's gone; surely something happened, and he's taking the money to help us start our little family and will call for me to follow him. He wouldn't leave me like that—I know it. We're married now. I have money in my bottom drawer; as soon as I can leave the house, I'm going to the station and getting on the first train to Dallas. I'll find him there. I know I will.

There were smudges on the page where the ink had smeared. Tears, likely. And the next entry—loose, disjointed script, almost a scrawl.

Thomas is gone. My husband, the love of my life, is gone. He's dead. Daddy says someone must have stolen the money he gave him and killed him, but I don't believe him. His shotgun wasn't in the gun rack after he left to go to the station; I checked. I don't know how he did it, but he made him go to Gruenwald without me and then he shot him and left him dead. And I can't tell the police. They'd never believe me.

I have to get out of this house. I cannot live with the man who murdered my husband.

Flora looked up at me. "My great-grandfather was a murderer," she said.

"I hate to say it, but it sounds like it," I said.

"And he murdered my grandfather!" She closed the book and sighed. "And my grandfather was German, of all things. My whole life has been turned upside down. My mother, and then Roger, and now . . . this."

"Oh, Flora," I said, and reached out and gave her a hug. Her bony body shook with sobs, and we sat that way for a long time before she leaned away and dried her eyes. "Everything happens for a reason," she said. "I've got to believe that."

"Doesn't mean it's not going to be tough for a while," I said.

She looked down at the diary. "What do I do with this?"

"Whatever you like," I said. "Why don't you let it digest for a while, and then decide?"

"That's probably a good idea," she said.

"Hey," I said. "Why don't you put this stuff away and come over to my place for a bit? I'll cook you dinner—I owe you one, anyway."

"Are you sure?" she said. "After what my mother did to you?"

"Of course," I said. "You saved my life, remember?"

She smiled and agreed. "Thank you," she said. "I didn't want to be alone today."

"Go get anything you need," I said. "I'll close up the barn and you can follow me home in your car."

"Thanks," she said. "My mama was wrong about you, you know."

"Well, she had a legitimate beef with Grandma Vogel, from what I hear."

"That's past history," Flora said. "We're living in the now," she said, and smiled as she headed back to the house.

I had closed the barn doors and was heading to my car when my phone rang. Tobias.

"Hello?" I answered.

"You want the good news, or the bad?"

I groaned. "Start with the good."

"Chuck should be ready to go home tonight," he said. "And John Chovanek is out of the hospital and should heal completely. And I'm not sure whether it's good or not, but Rooster Kocurek just took Faith Zapalac in for questioning."

"Accessory after the fact?" I asked.

"That's the word on the street—plus the property damage and fraud."

"Well, I guess that's good news," I said. "Now tell me the bad."

"Blossom is in the town square again."

"No," I breathed.

"Yup. And she just ate half the tomato plants in front of the Red and White."

It took two hours for Tobias and Flora and me to corral Blossom and get her back to the house. Tobias had had to go back to the clinic, but Quinn came over in the afternoon with a big chocolate cake. I'd made turkey sandwiches and iced tea, and we'd spent lunch getting to know Flora, who was shy but had a surprisingly tart tongue that made both of us laugh, reminiscing over lost loves and processing the events of the last few days. Now that Nettie and Roger were gone, I suspected Flora was going to feel adrift for a while. I hoped Quinn and I could help her find herself again. As the afternoon waned, we ate not just the turkey sandwiches, but the entire cake, polishing it off with a bottle of sweet Riesling Flora had brought. "Chocolate therapy," Quinn had announced as she ate the last slice, getting frosting all over her chin.

They left late that evening, leaving me alone in my grandmother's farmhouse. The house and land were safe; no oil derricks would go up in my broccoli patch, and Dewberry Creek would flow untainted by fracking chemicals. I could feel my grandmother's presence tonight more than ever; her lavender scent seemed to follow me from room to room as I tidied the house. I touched the rolling pin in the kitchen, now safely in its crock, and thought about how it had rolled to me the other night when Jed was attacking

Quinn—and the newspaper that had floated down from the hayloft on a nonexistent breeze. Had my grand-mother suspected the truth about Thomas's death? She must have known him; he worked for my grandparents for a while, and surely she knew that he was sweet on Anna Baca. Had she wanted us to clear up the mystery of what had happened to poor Thomas? And had she dropped that branch on Rooster's car when he came to harass me—and made the thumper truck stall the day they were planning on starting the exploration process?

I'd have to ask Teena Marburger about it, I thought—then froze. "A wolf in sheep's clothing," she'd said back at the Founders' Day Festival— back before any of this had even happened. Flora had told me today that Roger's middle name was Wolfgang—and he'd been wearing a golden lamb pin when he killed Nettie Kocurek. Goose bumps rose on my arms as Chuck and I headed up the stairs to my bedroom, where I was met with another waft of lavender.

I smiled and sent my grandmother a little prayer of thanks as I slipped off my slippers and crawled into bed. Chuck nestled in beside me, and I fell asleep listening to the sound of crickets and the wind in the leaves, feeling like I'd finally come home.

Grandma Vogel's Cottage Cheese

1 gallon milk
¾ cup white vinegar
1½ teaspoons kosher salt

Pour the milk into a large saucepan, and place over medium heat until it reaches 120 degrees F. Remove the milk from the heat, and gently pour in the vinegar, stirring slowly for 1 to 2 minutes until the curd separates from the whey. Cover the mixture, and allow it to sit at room temperature for 30 minutes.

Line a colander with a tea towel, then pour the mixture into the lined colander, and allow it to sit and drain for 5 minutes. Gather up the edges of the cloth, and rinse the curds under cold water for 3 to 5 minutes until they are completely cooled, squeezing and moving the mixture as you rinse. Once the curds are cool, squeeze them until they are as dry as possible, and transfer them to a mixing bowl. Add the salt and stir to combine, breaking up the curd into bite-size pieces as you go. Eat or refrigerate immediately.

Fresh Strawberry Custard Pie

3 cups sliced strawberries
1 cup white sugar
4 tablespoons butter, divided
1 egg
5 tablespoons flour, divided
1 uncooked pie shell
2 tablespoons brown sugar

In a mixer, combine 1 cup of sugar, the egg, 2 tablespoons of butter, and 2 tablespoons of flour until smooth. Fold strawberries into the batter, and pour into an uncooked pie shell.

In a second bowl, mix brown sugar, remaining 3 tablespoons of flour, and remaining 2 tablespoons of butter. Mix with a fork, and sprinkle over the unbaked pie. Bake at 375 degrees F for 50 minutes or until set (cover the crust with strips of foil if it browns too quickly).

Serve warm or cold, with whipped cream if desired.

Killer Dewberry Jam

Note: If you can't get Texas dewberries, black-berries work well, too!

1 pound dewberries or blackberries
½ cup water
2 tablespoons lemon juice
¼ large cooking apple, grated
1 pound granulated sugar
1 vanilla pod

Sterilize four 8-ounce jam jars, and put a small plate in the freezer, then wash the dewberries (or blackberries), and put into a heavy-bottomed pan with the water and lemon juice; add grated apple into the pan. Bring mixture to a boil over a medium heat, and simmer for 5 minutes.

Add the sugar, stirring gradually until all the crystals have dissolved, then scrape the seeds from the vanilla pod into the jam and stir. Increase the heat and boil until a candy thermometer consistently reads 220 degrees F.

To test the jam to see if it's set, drop a little jam onto the frozen plate; when jam has set, the liquid will be gel, not liquid, when touched with a finger. If jam is still liquid, continue to boil for a few more minutes, then test again.

When set, pour the jam into sterilized jars, leaving a little bit of space at the top of the jar, and screw lids onto the jars while the jam is still hot. As they cool, the jar tops should "pop," indicating the seal is good. Leave jam jars untouched for at least 24 hours to help the jam set.

(You can put the scraped vanilla bean in a mason jar with a cup of sugar to make vanilla sugar!)

Quinn's Famous Glazed Maple Twists

Dough:
2¾–3 cups all-purpose flour, divided
¾ cup milk
¼ cup butter
3 tablespoons sugar
½ teaspoon salt
1 tablespoon yeast
1 teaspoon maple extract
1 egg

Streusel:
¼ cup melted butter
½ cup white sugar
⅓ cup chopped walnuts
1 teaspoon cinnamon
1 teaspoon maple extract

Glaze:
1 cup powdered sugar
2 tablespoons melted butter
1–2 tablespoons milk
½ teaspoon maple extract
½ teaspoon vanilla extract

Heat milk and butter until very warm. Blend in a stand mixer with 1 cup of flour, and the sugar, salt, yeast, egg, and maple extract. Beat on low for 2 minutes, then add the rest of the flour, ½ cup at a time (you may not need all 3 cups). Knead into a soft dough until smooth and elastic, about five minutes. Cover bowl with plastic wrap, and let it rise for 45 minutes, or until it has doubled in size. While dough is rising, combine streusel ingredi-ents and set aside.

After the dough has risen, divide it into three pieces and roll each piece into a 12" circle. Place the first circle on a buttered 14" pizza pan (or large cookie sheet) covered with parchment paper. Top the first circle with ⅓ of the streusel mixture, and spread it in a thin layer; repeat with second and third pieces.

Find a glass that is 2" across, and center it on each circle (press down a little to make a mark). Using scissors, cut from the outer edge into the cup mark, making 16 wedges.

Gently lift and twist each wedge 5 times, tucking in the ends so that they stay twisted, and arrange on the pan.

Lightly cover the dough with plastic wrap, and let it rise for about 45 minutes to an hour. Bake in a 375 degree F oven for 20 to 25 minutes. While twists are baking, whisk together glaze ingredients. Remove twists from oven, and let rest for 5 minutes, then drizzle glaze over twists.

Mason Jar Beeswax Candles

1½ pounds filtered beeswax
1 cup coconut oil
40 inches of cotton wick
Wick clip or clear tape
8 six-ounce candle jars
Double boiler
Candy thermometer
8 popsicle sticks, pencils, or pens

Cut a length of wick that is about 2 inches longer than the height of your jar. Tie the wick around a pencil, and position the wick over the center of the jar. Use a wick clip to keep the wick on the bottom of the jar, or simply tape it down with clear tape. Turn the stove to low, and melt the wax in a double boiler. When the beeswax is liquefied, add coconut oil and stir until everything is melted and combined, and heat to 165 degrees F. Pour a thin layer of beeswax in the bottom of your jar, making sure some of it covers the end of the wick. Push the tip of the wick into place with your finger or the end of a pen or popsicle stick, then pull on the wick so that it hardens in an upright position (this will take 60 seconds or less). When the wick has set, pour the rest of the hot wax into the jar, leaving ½ to ¾" of space at the top of the jar, and check the position of the wick to make sure it is centered. Continue with remaining jars.

Allow the candles to harden for 24 hours, then trim the wicks to about ¼ inch, and allow it to set for another 24 hours before using. Light the candle at the base of the wick so that some of the wax is drawn up into the wick.

(Tip: for longer-lasting candles, burn until wax melts all the way to the edge of the jar before extinguishing the flame.)

Acknowledgments

First, I owe a great deal of thanks to Maryann and Clovis Heimsath for opening their hearts and home to me . . . and for introducing me not only to the coast of Maine, but to their beautiful corner of Texas. I am also grateful to Writers Who Write for their camaraderie and support through the writing of this book, particularly Jason Brenizer (writing buddy and plot doctor extraordinaire), Mary Chipley, and Nano "Boye" Nagle. Thanks to beta readers: Olivia Leigh Blacke, Samantha Mann, Norma Klanderman, Mary Mulconrey, Melissa Balsam, and J. Jaye Getman, for their thoughtful and thorough reading of the manuscript (not to mention excellent suggestions). Thank you to Skyler White for her wise counsel, and thanks also to Dr. Kaori Sakamoto and Dr. E. Murl Bailey, Jr. for their help with veterinary particulars. And of course, oodles of gratitude to Anh Schluep, Kjersti Egerdahl, Alan Turkus, Tiffany Pokorny, Jacque Ben-Zekry, and the rest of the fabulous Amazon publishing team for all of the amazing things you do!

And, as always, thanks to my family, Eric, Abby, and Ian, for putting up with me. I love you!

About the Author

Karen MacInerney is the author of numerous popular mystery novels, including the Agatha Award–nominated series The Gray Whale Inn Mysteries and the trilogy Tales of an Urban Werewolf, which was nominated for a P.E.A.R.L. award by her readers. When she's not working on her novels, she teaches writing workshops in Austin, Texas, where she lives with her husband and two children.

Center Point Large Print
600 Brooks Road / PO Box 1
Thorndike, ME 04986-0001 USA

(207) 568-3717

US & Canada:
1 800 929-9108
www.centerpointlargeprint.com